Photo © Christa Holka

JAMES FOX

Boy Vs Reality is James Fox's second book. James lives and works in London. His debut *The Boy in the Suit* was shortlisted for the Waterstones Children's Book Prize and the Branford Boase Award, and on publication was highlighted as a best new children's book in the *Times*, the *Guardian*, the *Daily Telegraph* and the *Observer*.

ALSO BY **JAMES FOX**

"A really lovely book, so tender and truthful"
Jacqueline Wilson, bestselling author
of *The Story of Tracy Beaker*

"A tender, moving story, beautifully capturing
life in all its light and shade"
Hannah Gold, author of Waterstones Children's
Book Prize winner *The Last Bear*

"It's a beautiful, heartfelt gem of a book –
I loved it" Tom Vaughan, author of *Hercules*

"This story is full to the brim with heart" Helen Rutter,
author of *The Boy Who Made Everyone Laugh*

JAMES FOX

■SCHOLASTIC

Published in the UK by Scholastic, 2026
Scholastic, Bosworth Avenue, Warwick, CV34 6UQ
Scholastic Ireland, 89E Lagan Road, Dublin Industrial
Estate, Glasnevin, Dublin, D11 HP5F

SCHOLASTIC and associated logos are trademarks and/or
registered trademarks of Scholastic Inc.

Text © James Fox, 2026
Illustrations by Tika and Tata Bobokhidze © Scholastic, 2026
Author photo © Christa Holka

The moral rights of the author and photographer have been asserted by them.

ISBN 978 0702 33311 8

A CIP catalogue record for this book is available from the British Library.

All rights reserved.
This book is sold subject to the condition that it shall not, by way of trade or
otherwise, be lent, hired out or otherwise circulated in any form of binding
or cover other than that in which it is published. No part of this publication
may be reproduced, stored in a retrieval system, or transmitted in any form
or by any other means (electronic, mechanical, photocopying, recording or
otherwise), or used to train any artificial intelligence technologies without prior
written permission of Scholastic Limited. Subject to EU law, Scholastic Limited
expressly reserves this work from the text and data-mining exception.

Printed in the UK.
Paper made from wood grown in sustainable forests and other controlled sources.

10 9 8 7 6 5 4 3 2 1

This is a work of fiction. Any resemblance to actual
people, events or locales is entirely coincidental.

Scholastic does not have any control over and does not assume any
responsibility for any third-party websites or other platforms, or their content.

www.scholastic.co.uk

For safety or quality concerns:
UK: www.scholastic.co.uk/productinformation
EU: www.scholastic.ie/productinformation

For the sticky-minded.

And for Tom.

PROLOGUE

"*Action!* ... Hi, I'm Geoff Lacey, and welcome to another *Meet the Laceys* daily vlog. Today, we'll be showing you our grocery haul, plus Colin's exciting trip to the vet's. Spoiler alert: he's fine. But first, a word from today's sponsor." Dad pauses. "That's your cue, Annabel."

Mum takes her position by the kitchen counter.

"Are you tired of scrubbing grass stains and mud from your kids' football kits? I know I am. That's why Dazzle White laundry pods are the perfect, convenient detergent for on-the-go mums like me. They contain active ingredients that cut through stubborn stains like child's play."

"That's your cue, Ethan," whispers Dad.

I have the starring role. I trudge into the kitchen

in Mason's old football kit. Dad spent ages artfully caking mud into the fabric, dragging it through puddles in the garden. Then he smeared mud in my hair and on my face to make it look like I'd just been playing a match. I can feel the germs multiplying on my skin. I don't even *like* football.

"*Muuum*," I say, reciting the lines. "My kit got all muddy, but I need it for tomorrow's tournament. Coach says it has to be *pristine*."

My older brother, Mason, appears beside me. "Mum, my PE kit's covered in grass stains. Can you wash it for sports day tomorrow?"

Then Dad appears in his hiking gear. He's also covered in mud and stains. The joke is that he's even messier than Mason and me, even though he's a grown-up.

"Annabel…" He looks down at his mud-caked clothes. "It happened again!"

"Oh no!" Mum groans. Then she cracks up.

"Cut!" Dad yells, then runs over to the camera. "I'll edit that bit out."

"Sorry, sorry," Mum says. "These lines are so cheesy. I can't take it seriously."

"Well, it's what the brand wants," replies Dad. "Let's just get it over with, then we can all get on with our day."

I can't wait for this to be done, so I can get the mud off my skin. I want to have a long hot shower and scrub myself three times over.

"Action!" shouts Dad.

"*Oh no!* Or … that's what I *would* have said before I found Dazzle White laundry pods." Mum holds up a box of Dazzle White to the camera. "To all you mums out there, try Dazzle White today and use the code LACEY25 at the checkout for twenty-five per cent off your first purchase!"

"Thanks, Mum," I say. "Now I won't be on the substitute bench tomorrow!"

"Thanks, Mum," Mason says. "Now I won't get detention!"

"Very good," Dad mutters from behind the camera. "Now for the final bit. Three, two one…"

"*And now we can wear our sports kits with confidence!*" Mason and I say in unison, exactly like we've been practising all morning.

We high-five. The sting vibrates in my palm. We beam into the camera, smiling like how Dad taught us. We show all our teeth, because the camera makes smiles look smaller, and the followers need to see them. Everyone needs to see exactly how happy we are. That's the whole point.

THE TRUTH ABOUT
MEET THE LACEYS

EthanExplains ✓
@EthanExplains
0 subscribers
2 views, posted 9 minutes ago

Hi, guys, and welcome to my channel.

That's right – my very own channel that no one can post from, except me. The first thing you should know is that I'm here to tell the truth about everything. Even if the truth makes me look stupid, which it probably will.

My name's Ethan Lacey and I've just turned ten, making me a Year Five.

I want to give a shout-out to Omar and Arlo – the

Blue Pencil Case Crew, or the BPCC for short. We've been best friends since the first day of Reception. Crazy how time flies, isn't it?

Back then we were in Mr Rowley's class. We got put together because it was supposed to be boy–girl–boy–girl, but there weren't enough girls in the class, so we were sat boy–boy–boy. We all had exactly the same blue pencil case – that's why we became the Blue Pencil Case Crew.

Omar and Arlo don't care about *Meet the Laceys*. They just treat me like a regular kid, which I suppose I am, mostly.

My least favourite things are germs, being filmed and my irritating older brother, Mason. Miss Isaacs taught us about understatements recently and I think "irritating" might be one of those. Mason's *infuriating* in every way possible. More on *him* later.

Oh, I almost forgot Viral Buzz, my *least* favourite thing of all. It's this horrible online forum that people use specifically to hate on influencers, especially us. There's even a hashtag for them: #LaceyHaters. Mum says I'm not allowed on Viral Buzz, but sometimes I sneak a look.

This guy here is Fidget. He's a plushie monster with a squeezy stress-ball filling. Mum got him for me last year after I'd been feeling ... weird. Fidget makes me feel much better. Other than Omar and Arlo, Fidget's my best friend. And I don't care if he's not *technically real*. He's real to me. Isn't that right? See, he's nodding.

"Sure thing, big man!"

It might be me doing Fidget's voice. I can't confirm or deny that.

And yes, Fidget's meant to be a bit ugly. I like his funny shape and odd button eyes. He's a monster, only he's a *kind* one, and he's actually an "Anxiety Monster" – that's his species. Fidget comes everywhere with me. I squeeze him whenever I get worried, or whenever I want to punch Mason.

Mason's always had an evil streak, but it's got worse since he went to St Hot Dog's School for Boys. OK, the proper name is St Mark's, but everybody says their brown-and-yellow uniform makes them look like hot dogs.

The best thing about Fidget is his zippy mouth. He's evolved to eat worries and secrets. His care leaflet said they're Fidget's primary food source. All you have to do is write the worry down on a scrap of paper, then feed it to Fidget. *Nom, nom, nom* ... and the worry goes into his tummy, safely stowed for ever.

Luckily, there's a never-ending supply of worries

and secrets in my brain. It's win-win. They keep Fidget fed, and I feel better. Before I got Fidget, my worries went round and round my head in a loop. *Sticky thoughts*, that's what Mum calls them. They're thoughts that are impossible to get rid of, like PVA glue on your hands.

Sticky thoughts can be anything: germs, diseases, even random things like, *What would happen if I went to the front of the class and poured Miss Isaacs' cup of tea over her head?* I'd definitely get suspended. Best not to do that, I think.

So that's settled, then.

But oh no – *then* I think there's something wrong with me for imagining that in the first place. Maybe I'm a bad kid? The most evil in the whole town, even. Then I imagine doing it again, just to check I don't *actually* want to. Then I think about it again, and again, and … surprise, again. That's how a thought becomes sticky. It stays there for ever until I fall out with my brain.

Now, though, my worries don't stick around as long. I know feeding my worries to an Anxiety Monster is a *bit* babyish, but I don't care. So there.

Anyway, if you recognize me, it's probably from *Meet the Laceys* – the YouTube channel all about my family. My family is kind of famous. *Meet the Laceys* is Mum and Dad's full-time job. They're *influencers*. There are loads of videos on our channel. Go and look if you don't believe me. Open up a new tab – I'll wait right here.

They've posted holiday vlogs, unboxing hauls, the cinnamon challenge, the mannequin challenge. You name it, *Meet the Laceys* has done it and probably gone viral. You might remember the time we filled a paddling pool with slime in the back garden. That got four million views and the *Daily News* wrote an article about it. I admit it *was* cool swimming in the slime, but it was gross picking it out of my hair. And it did attract quite a lot of ants. Too many ants. I had a sticky thought about ant infestations afterwards.

The *Daily News* writes about us all the time. They pay Mum and Dad to do special adverts for their website. They write headlines like "The Fabric Softener Annabel Lacey Can't Get Enough Of" and add a fake quote like "I can't stop smelling it!" from Mum. Next thing, every supermarket's sold out of Spring Breeze fabric softener and people are fist-fighting over the limited-edition bottle with our picture on the front.

There's loads of stuff we've been paid to advertise. It started with nappies, with my face on the packaging, then wet wipes once I was out of nappies. Then it was baby food, then an app for baby-led weaning, whatever that means. That was just the baby years. We've done holidays, toys, Lumpy's Soft Play Centre, washing-up liquid and candy-flavoured toothpaste.

I think Mum and Dad are addicted to it. First, they only got comments and likes, then it was free stuff, *then* came the money. Before long, it was so much money that Mum and Dad could quit their jobs – and they started filming *everything*. We upload a video every day without fail. Dad says that "everything is content".

But the channel has taken over. I don't even class us as a proper family any more. We're actors playing a role for Mum and Dad's cameras. As soon as those cameras switch off, it's arguments, lies and everyone stomping off to different rooms in an almighty storm cloud of a huff.

It wasn't always like this. Me and Mum used to do Just the Two of Us Day every Saturday. Me and Mason were like two peas in a pod. He taught me how to play *Werewolf Files X*, even though I had to have it on baby mode, which removed all the jump scares.

Now those days are gone. Instead of Just the Two of Us Day, I have Just the One of Me Day on my own because Mum is always out filming or at some influencer event.

Mason's gone off me too. He'd rather eat a bucket of mouldy yogurt than play *Werewolf Files X* with me. And Dad? Well, Dad is Dad, content-obsessed, always filming. That's why I'm posting this video, to tell the truth. I want to make everything better again, like how it used to be.

To all the *Meet the Laceys* fans, this video might sting a bit, like an injection. It hurts you before it makes you better.

Our videos look so happy and smiley, with the cutesy jingly background music, but not everything you see online is real. For the last few weeks, everything posted on *Meet the Laceys* has been nothing but lies, lies and more lies. I'm here to shut it down. So buckle up tight, because this is going to be the most explosive, twisty-turny, mega-viral, mind-blowing, universe-shifting story time ever.

Well, maybe not *that* explosive. There are no explosions, sorry.

Where to start? I always have trouble starting stories. I think it all began at the party.

1

I hate unexpected visitors.

"SURPRISE!"

I stumbled backwards, bumping my head on the door frame as I entered the kitchen. The bag of groceries in my hands slipped, sending a grapefruit rolling across the floor. Faces – loads of faces – stared at me with dinner-plate eyes and beaming grins that quickly drooped to disappointment. What were all these people doing in our kitchen?

I blinked the stars from my eyes, my mouth opening and closing like a goldfish's. Silver helium-filled balloons were strung across the wall, spelling out *1 MILLION FOLLOWERS*. A huge buffet had been spread across the kitchen table. Bottles of champagne were cooling in a bucket of ice.

"False alarm," Mason grunted. "It's not her. Ethan's in the way … as usual."

"Get out of the shot, Ethan," Dad hissed, peering round his video camera. A red light flashed beside the lens, showing it was recording. "Don't ruin the surprise!"

Someone tugged me aside and forced me to crouch beside the dog bowls in the corner of the room. My foot knocked one of them. Spitty dog water lapped over the rim and began to creep along the floor towards me. I tried not to think of the germs.

"What surprise?" I asked, rubbing the sore spot on my head. "What's going on?"

"Our followers, obviously," Mason said. "We hit a cool millie on the channel this morning, not that *you* would have noticed. So we're throwing Mum a surprise party. Are you with us now?"

"Who's Cool Milly?"

"It means *a million followers*." Mason rolled his eyes like he always did.

I nodded, taking it in. "How was *I* supposed to know?"

"Well, you could pull your weight with the

channel for a start, then you might have noticed the follower count creeping up. But we didn't tell you because you'd have ruined the surprise with your massive mouth."

"Shhhhh," somebody hissed, slicing through our argument. "I don't want to miss the money shot!"

That was Mum's best friend, Oonagh – *Oonagh's Perfect Life*, as she was known online. She was filming with a fancy-looking camera on a stick that swivelled from left to right effortlessly, the lens gliding across our faces. A fluffy mini microphone was clipped to the strap of her handbag.

"That's better," Oonagh said. "Play happy families while we get the footage."

Happy families. Yeah, right. That's what we pretended to be, but it was only for the cameras.

"You nearly ruined everything." That was Luna, Oonagh's daughter, who was crouched beside me. "Like you always do." Her voice was annoyingly sing-song, even when she was being mean (which was all the time).

"Shut up, Luna," I muttered.

"Say that again and I'll tell your mum on you. *And* mine."

"*Good*." I scowled, despite the thought of it

making my stomach twist. I hated getting into trouble. No one ever believed my side of things. Plus, Mum always sided with Oonagh and Luna, no matter what I did.

"How's your little friend, Fidget?" sneered Luna. "Eaten lots of your secrets lately?"

I felt for Fidget in my pocket. Fidget was secure. I did my best to ignore Luna's snide remark.

Silence spread through the room like a shadow. Mason and Dad kept grinning and winking at each other in anticipation. Even Colin, our Border collie, was sitting upright, the tip of his tail twitching with excitement. The moment stretched and stretched until it started to get boring.

Where *was* Mum? It never usually took this long to bring the shopping in from the car. We'd only bought a few bags of groceries and some loo roll, which I obviously refused to carry in case people thought it was for me. My thighs were starting to go numb from crouching, and Luna's smug breath tickled the side of my neck.

"Any second now," Dad said.

He was filming his POV (point of view) for his side channel, *Dad on the Rocks*. His channel's mostly about camping, hiking and van renovations for his so-called

#VanLife. Sometimes he uploaded clips of family stuff too, like my Year Three nativity play when I forgot I was on stage and picked my nose. Or the day Mason opened his incredible SATs results on camera, but I'd accidentally dropped a glass of blackcurrant squash all over Colin in the background and it dyed his white bits purple. It was about letting his followers see the *real* Dad, apparently, but too often it was the real *me* in the background.

"What's all this about?" Grandad piped up.

He was at the table, wearing his favourite maroon cardigan with the patches sewn on. Grandad was *forgetful* – that's why he had to move to Sycamore Village, which wasn't a village and didn't have any sycamores; it was a care home. I'd asked whether Grandad could live with us, but Mum and Dad didn't want him in the way of the channel.

"Is it Annabel's birthday?" asked Grandad. "I didn't think it was her birthday until… Oh, *drat*."

"*Shhhhh*," everyone except me hissed.

"For God's sake, Grandad. I told you – Mum hit a millie!" Mason moaned, as if repeating himself for the fiftieth time that day.

"Oh dear." Grandad's face crumpled like an old receipt. "Well, that doesn't sound good at all."

"Ugh, I literally can't right now," Mason said.

"Don't be mean to Grandad, Mason!" I said. "He can't help it, you know!"

"Why did we even invite him?" Mason's voice went high-pitched when he was angry. "He asks the same questions again and again the whole time!"

My fist tightened into a cricket ball, aka the hardest ball known to man. The urge to wallop Mason had never risen so quickly. Lately, I'd wanted to punch him a lot. My parents and I had our own theories on what was going on with Mason. Mum said it was too much time spent splatting zombies on *Zombie Freakout 4*. Dad blamed it on puberty (gross) and said Mason was "becoming a man" (even grosser).

I had a sneaking suspicion it was to do with the videos he watched online. Mason used to watch fun stuff, like #UltimateFails. Innocent clips of silly mistakes. But recently he started watching extreme pranks that went way too far. He's obsessed with this American guy called CheeseBlizzard who pulls the most brutal stunts on his family. Famously, he filled his little sister's mattress with rancid cottage cheese. He then filmed with hidden cameras as she gleefully hopped into bed, only to emerge dripping in creamy, smelly curds. It was in her hair and everything. I hated CheeseBlizzard, but Mason thought he was an absolute hero.

"Drop it, Mason," Dad snarled from behind the camera. "Show Grandad some respect."

Mason's cheeks flushed. "Sorry, Dad…"

My fist loosened. I couldn't start a fight now, especially not in front of so many people and their cameras. That, and Dad was glaring at me, shaking his head slowly. I grabbed Fidget and squeezed his leg until it bulged between my fingers.

"Cor, she's taking her sweet time, isn't she?" Oonagh said, shifting her weight from one heeled shoe to another. "I'm going to have to put a new memory card in the camera in a minute."

"Ethan," Dad said, nodding towards the kitchen door. "Go and see where Mum is, will you?"

"But what if she's coming in right now?" Mason whined, his voice three notes higher than before. "It'll ruin the whole surprise!"

"Ethan, just go and coax her in. We can't hide all day. It'll be a nightmare to edit out this dead air."

Dad was *always* going on about *dead air* and editing. Cutting, sticking and changing our real life like a scrapbook so it fitted neatly into the perfect fifteen-minute vlog. I swore he would edit me out of real life if he had the chance.

"What are you doing, idiot? Go and get Mum!" Mason snapped.

"Fine." I heaved myself up, my sleeping legs prickling back to life as I headed out of the kitchen.

There was no sign of Mum in the hallway. No casually tossed shoes or car keys on the side. In the living room, the TV was playing to no one. I opened the front door and tiptoed out on to the driveway. My damp socks absorbed even more water from the moss between the paving.

Mum was sitting in the car with the engine still running. She was staring at her phone with a blank expression on her face. I tapped on the window.

Startled, Mum fumbled her phone, dropping it into the footwell. She glanced up at me, plastering on the same exaggerated smile she used in her videos to seem perfectly upbeat and happy. The skin around her eyes was really pink, like she was upset about something.

"Wind down the window!" I said, gesturing. Once she had, I asked, "Aren't you coming in? Mason needs a massive poo, but the toilet roll's out here."

I'll admit, I wasn't sure where that came from.

Mum exhaled heavily. "They're all inside, aren't they?"

"Who?" I tried to fake confusion. "What do you mean?"

Mum smiled. "You're a rubbish liar. See, Oonagh's car is right there."

I followed Mum's gaze. Oonagh's gleaming red convertible was parked directly opposite our house, complete with the 00NAGH number plate and the "Powered by Family and Laughter" sticker on the back bumper. I'd recognize that car anywhere.

I held my hands out in innocence. "I didn't say *anything*."

Mum chuckled. "I know, I know. Don't worry – I figured it out on my own. I saw the balloons hidden in the airing cupboard this morning. A million followers, eh? That's an awful lot of people knowing who we are. Bit strange, if you think about it."

I tried to imagine a million people gathered in one place, but I couldn't. I didn't know how many school assemblies or football pitches or concerts it would take to fit a million human beings.

"Well done, Mum. You should be really proud of yourself."

"Thanks." She nodded. "I am, I think." Then she

looked down, and her blonde hair closed like curtains around her face.

This felt weird. Mum was always going on about wanting to hit a million followers. It was her biggest wish and, now that it had come true, it was like she was sad about it.

"Is everything OK, Mum? You don't seem that ... happy."

"I am." She nodded again. She looked like she was about to cry. "It's overwhelming, that's all. I thought it would feel different. Anyway, shall we go in?"

"Definitely. Oonagh will run out of memory on her camera if we wait too much longer."

Mum tutted and smiled, even though it was exactly the sort of thing she would worry about too. "Come on, then. I suppose this is prime content, right? It'll make great footage for the weekly catch-up vlog."

Mum climbed out of the car and walked towards the front door. As I turned to follow, I spotted my axolotl toy under the passenger seat. I'd been looking for it for days, inside coat pockets and down the backs of the sofas.

"Gimme a sec, Mum," I called after her. "I left something in the car."

I climbed in and leaned over to retrieve the axolotl,

which was now covered in fluff and carpet dust. That's when I saw Mum's phone. She had left it behind. I reached down into the driver's footwell to grab it.

"You forgot your—"

Mum was busy taking deep breaths by the door. I didn't mean to look at her phone, honestly. Or maybe I did a bit. On the screen was a message from Dad.

> Let's just get through the weekend, then we can tell Mason and Ethan X

2

*I'm worried about that weird
message on Mum's phone.*

What are they going to tell us?

"SURPRISE!"

To be fair, Mum was proper convincing. She planted both hands over her mouth and squealed in fake shock, before running over to Dad and Mason for hugs, totally trembling and overwhelmed.

"What on earth is all this?" she screamed, delighted and merry. Her face was flushed with joy. "For me? Seriously?"

Then she turned to me. "Did *you* know about this, Ethan?"

I shrugged. Wow, she really was good at pretending. I hadn't told her what I'd seen on her phone. I'd simply locked the screen and handed it back to her.

Music started playing – that song that goes "*Celebrate good times*", which old people always play – and someone let off a load of streamers that wriggled through the air like a swarm of multicoloured airborne worms. Like Mum and Dad always said, this was going to make *great* content.

"What's—" Mum kept stuttering, then pointing at different people around the room, gasping. "What on *earth*? You're here too? Oh my, I haven't seen you in ages!"

I grinned from ear to ear, even though I knew Mum was pretending. All Mum had ever wanted was for the channel to be popular, and now her dreams had come true. But I had a sticky thought that wouldn't unstick – something was wrong. That weird message from Dad sat heavy at the bottom of my stomach like I'd swallowed a stone.

Let's just get through the weekend, then we can tell Mason and Ethan.

The message scrolled on a loop in my mind. What were they going to tell us? Was it good news or bad? Maybe we were getting another dog. Or the African pygmy hedgehog I'd been asking for. Or had they signed another deal for us to advertise sweets or sensitive fabric softener that was "*perfect for the little ones' fragile skin*"? Everyone at school ripped me for that one. I'd already been called *sensitive* before the campaign, and that clip of me saying "No more itchy-scratchy rashes!" straight into camera really didn't help matters.

It was more likely to be something bad. Maybe Mum was dying. Or Dad was dying. Or Colin was dying. My eyes prickled. I felt my heartbeat speed up and I started squeezing Fidget again.

I watched as Mum hugged and kissed Grandad, then greeted one of Dad's mates with kisses on each cheek. Someone popped a bottle of fizzy wine, sending the cork flying across the room.

"Don't forget to fizz it up a bit!" Oonagh said, still filming. "Oh no, stop! Actually, let's do it over here in the natural light," she said. "This kitchen *can* look a bit dark and dingy on camera, can't it?"

"Exactly," Luna said, nodding. "It's all about the right lighting, isn't it, Mum?"

"That's why we went for the south-facing extension, sweetheart."

I gritted my teeth as I watched Luna observing us

through her mum's viewfinder. A yellow snot bubble in her left nostril inflated, popped, then formed again with each smug breath. It would feel so good to tell Luna she needed to blow her nose on camera, right in front of Oonagh. But she'd only make my life hell. After all, she was in my class at school, so she had plenty of opportunities for revenge.

Oonagh and Luna made me feel opposite feelings all at once. On one hand, they had always been around. Technically, I'd known Luna since I was a baby in Mum's stomach, because Mum and Oonagh had been pregnant at the same time. I was born three weeks before Luna, and she'd been in my life ever since.

On the other hand, Oonagh and Luna left a funny feeling in my head, like a rain cloud coming or the start of a sticky thought. They had a special trick of saying nice things with a hint of meanness that was hard to detect, like salt in a cup of tea.

Oonagh pointed her camera at me, so I pretended to inspect the balloons bobbing in the air: *1 MILLION FOLLOWERS*. Mum cared about each and every one of them. She said it at the end of every video, like a reminder. *"Thank you for being here. We truly care about each and every one of you. You're like family."*

Mum's followers definitely cared about her too.

That's why people sent her gifts, and companies sent us free stuff to do unboxing. Bath bombs, make-up kits, dog toys, wax melts, sunset lamps, dog costumes for Colin: we'd unboxed it all, tearing through the cardboard packaging until our hands got sore.

"What do you think?" Mum would ask.

"It's amazing!" we would say. "We absolutely love it!" Even if it was the most boring piece of useless junk I'd ever seen, it's part of the agreement. Companies send us stuff and we post a video saying it's amazing. Then the companies sell more stuff, and we get paid money, which Mum and Dad say doesn't grow on trees. It's a win-win situation, if you think about it.

We've done so many brand deals that I've lost count. We've done Mother's Day gifts, moisturizer, mattresses – and that's just the M's. Oh, and who could forget the shoelace collaboration Lacey Laces (because "@MeetTheLaceys love our shoelaces!")? You can imagine how boring that video turned out, but people watched, and Mason and I each got some money to put in our Junior Saver Accounts.

Mum got loads of comments and messages. Mostly they were positive, saying how much they loved Mum's blonde hair or make-up, or our pristine house. People left comments like *"Drop the skincare routine, stat!"*

and "*Omg LOVE that dress, where's it from?*" and it made Mum feel really good about herself. There were plenty of comments saying how "perfect" Mason and I were. I didn't particularly like being called perfect, because I'm not. Mason definitely isn't.

Sometimes the comments were mean, but Mum and Dad told us to ignore them. "Don't let the praise go to your head," Mum would say, tapping the top of her hair. "And don't let the hate go to your heart." Then she would tap ... you guessed it, her heart. Even so, I always caught her reading hate comments when she thought I wasn't looking.

It's hard to ignore mean comments. Once someone commented that I was too short for my age and I got a new sticky thought about my height. I spent ages doing stretches from an online tutorial called "Grow Four Inches in Four Weeks!" Shock of the century: it didn't work.

Not long after that, another person commented that I was freakishly tall and should be checked for a growth hormone disorder. Then I got a sticky thought about *that* and googled growth disorders so much that I probably could've qualified as a doctor.

We all got mean comments now and then. Dad for his cringe dancing and flatline jokes. Mason for the bulbous spots that sometimes show up on his nose ("*When did Rudolph move in?*"). Mum for being too cheery, or for the lines on her forehead, or the hairs that stick out after she bleaches her hair.

You can't win. Mum says that's why you shouldn't listen to anyone on the internet. Except her and Dad, I assume.

Mum and Dad quite liked the idea of Mason and I starting our own channels. Mason loved the idea. He wanted his own cameras and lighting and editing software, so he could go *viral*. As for me, I wanted to do something useful with my life.

"How's it going, Ethan?" Dad appeared in front of me, watching me through his camera's viewfinder rather than with his own eyes. "You look a bit pale. Have you had too much from the buffet?"

"I'm fine!" I lied, giving two thumbs up and my usual camera-ready smile. "I absolutely love it!"

"Are you proud of Mummy for hitting a million followers on her channel?"

"I'm so proud – I knew she'd do it! Oh, you have food or something on your shirt, by the way…"

Dad sighed and tilted the camera down at the floor. "For goodness' sake, I'll have to edit that. Could you not have waited two minutes to tell me?"

I waited while he scraped at the crusty green stain with his fingernail. I think it was guacamole. Dad was dressed head to toe in mountaineering clothes, even though he wasn't hiking; he was just standing in the kitchen eating chips and dips.

"OK, ready to go again?" Dad aimed the camera back at me. "Remember, speak nice and slowly so I can edit out any of your unexpected ... observations."

"Fine." I clapped my hands to give Dad a point to match the audio with the video, a bit like those black-and-white clapper boards in movies. Action.

"Ethan! Are you proud of Mummy for hitting a million on her channel?" Dad asked again.

"I'm super proud. Well done, Mum – we knew you could do it!" Then I blew loads of kisses into the camera and grinned so widely my jaw ached.

"Bravo!" Dad gave a thumbs up. "That's what I was looking for. Right, I just need a couple of shots of you and Mason spontaneously chilling out, and you're off the clock!"

Ten minutes later, with Colin in tow, I took the stairs two at a time up to my bedroom. I couldn't wait to watch #UltimateFails online. Like every genre, there were classics: old people climbing into boats, people crossing rivers on slippery logs, overenthusiastic trampolining. Those aside, I loved that there were always new fails, new drinks getting dropped and stains getting made, new mess-ups that made me laugh until my stomach ached.

"Ultimate Fails" were a million miles from the content we made. There's no way Mum would post a video of herself falling into a muddy river. No way Dad would find it funny if he dropped a bag of oranges on the floor and they all rolled away.

Anything less than perfect was edited out and binned as if it never happened in the first place. It was like we were living in a really boring film. Definitely *not* a comedy.

Curled up in my beanbag, I selected "Ultimate Fail Compilation 2026" from the menu on my TV. Colin cuddled up to me as the first fail began to play. The noise of the party faded into the background.

3

The next morning, Mum woke me up the usual way, by opening the curtains and saying, "Rise and shine, porcupine." Then she placed a glass of blackcurrant squash beside my bed.

Mum had woken me up the same way since I was tiny. Well, except for the time she went away on a shampoo company's brand trip for three whole days. That had meant Dad was on wake-up duty, which wasn't the same. He didn't wake me up gently, and definitely didn't say the porcupine thing. He just yanked the curtains open and started going on about early worms catching the bird or something while I lay there, dazed. Who wants to think about worms first thing in the morning?

"Morning, Mum," I croaked. "Did you enjoy the party?"

Mum turned off my TV, which was still auto-playing from last night.

"You disappeared!" Mum said. "I was so wrapped up in the fun that I didn't realize you'd taken yourself off to bed."

"I didn't want to bother you," I said, stretching. "It was your special night."

"*Our* special night," she said. "But that's very considerate of you." Mum opened the window to let some fresh air in. "What a nice surprise. Everyone I knew in one place, all celebrating little old me. I couldn't believe my eyes!"

I frowned. "But I thought you said you knew everyone was—"

"What?"

"When you were outside. You said you knew everyone was—"

"Oh, shush." Mum waved my words away. "I *was* surprised, even though I knew something was happening. You know what I mean."

I didn't. I went all funny inside from thinking about Mum sitting in the car crying, and that strange text on her phone. I felt the grip of a sticky thought gluing itself inside my head.

"Can we have a Just the Two of Us Day today?" I asked.

Mum grimaced. "We're filming a vlog at H2O, remember?"

My stomach dropped a floor. H2O, the giant indoor water park that had opened in town. As influencers, we had the privilege of being invited to a special open day. Besides us, there would only be a few other families. No entry fee, no queues, no problem. Oh, and we got paid too. Mum and Dad leaped at the chance, even though I had worries about drowning and hygiene.

It had taken forever to build H2O. The site had been rubble and drilling and diggers for years. Eventually, though, a huge glass building was unveiled, complete with five pools and water slides that snaked through the walls in every direction like a knotted ball of string. The advert said, "H2O boasts the UK's biggest wave pool, complete with tsunami mode. Not to mention the UK's steepest waterslide: AquaDeath. Do you dare ride it?"

I didn't like the sound of tsunami mode or AquaDeath much. I would have preferred a nice warm bath with a #gifted bath bomb, thanks. I hated swimming pools. They were rife with skin-crawling sticky thoughts: verrucas, germs, wet plasters floating in the water. I saw a video that said over a hundred per cent of people freely admit to peeing in the pool. Can you believe that?

Mason was buzzing about the trip, obviously. In between moaning about every part of life, he'd managed to moan about H2O not being ready yet. When the opening was announced, he banged on about how he would "own" AquaDeath and go into "Absolute Beast Mode" in the wave pool.

"I'm feeling a bit sick," I said to Mum feebly. "I don't think I should go."

"It'll be clean, you know. It's brand new." How was it that Mum could always read my mind? "It'll be fun. Luna will be there! You can go on the Lazy River together while Oonagh and I kick back with a smoothie."

"Why can't *I* kick back with a smoothie?" I groaned.

Mum started rummaging through my chest of drawers.

"You know why, Ethan. We need to film you kids having fun!" She sighed. "I never can find your swim shorts. I could swear you hide them on purpose."

"No comment."

*

"Tripod?" said Dad.

"Check," said Mum.

"Extra memory cards?"

"Check."

"Waterproof camera cases?"

It was always the same routine whenever we went out filming. Dad called out every possible piece of equipment we owned, while Mum rifled through the boot of the car.

As professional influencers, the day was a write-off if we forgot the camera or the battery for the camera or the extra memory card. Once, I'd been in charge of packing the boot before we filmed our "Day at the Zoo" vlog. I accidentally forgot all the camera batteries and Dad got super annoyed. He said the whole day was pointless and only spoke in one-syllable grunts like "yep" and "cool". Even the lemurs didn't cheer him up. Ever since, we'd done the checklist.

"Swimming costumes?" said Dad.

"Definite check. Even the ones that were sneakily hidden in the laundry basket, *Ethan*. Geoff, yours have a hole in the backside, remember? You might want to check if they sell trunks there."

"Hmm," Dad grumbled as he fumbled for the car keys. "Did you pack the kids?"

"Check!" Mum got into the front seat and started filming us. "Are you excited, boys?"

Mason popped the buds from his ears, adding an eye-roll for good measure. "What?"

"I said, are you excited?"

"You bet I am." Mason clocked the camera was on and rubbed his hands together with glee. "This is going to be so epic. I can't wait to tell the lads at school that I was one of the first-ever people to survive AquaDeath."

"What about you, Ethan?" said Mum. "Think you'll give AquaDeath a go?"

I shrugged. "I'll have to see how steep it is."

An evil grin spread across Mason's face. "Steep isn't the word, Loser Little Bro. Or should I say LLB for short. It's beyond steep. Rumour has it, it's actually *steeper than vertical*."

My stomach twisted as I pictured a slide so high that the pool below was a tiny drip of water. I groaned and shook my head involuntarily.

"Oh, leave him alone, Mason," said Mum, as Dad started the engine. "Of course, it's not *steeper than vertical*. Always exaggerating."

Mason smirked and put his earbuds back in.

"I'm just a bit nervous, that's all," I said weakly.

"Well, try to keep it in your head," Dad said. "We're supposed to be showing everyone how much fun we're having, OK? Not how scared we are of the water slides."

"Got it," I said, breathing deeply.

The car rolled out of the driveway and I squeezed Fidget in my pocket the whole way there.

4

I stood by the pool, shivering in my trunks. I curled my toes upward from the tiled floor, thinking about the germs and verrucas and stray hairs waiting to get stuck to my skin.

Five other influencer families were with us, listening while a lifeguard explained the safety rules. He told us not to run, not to dive-bomb into the water, not to go down the slides in pairs. All these precautions gave me sticky thoughts. What if I ran by accident? Would I slip and knock all my teeth out, filling the pool with so much blood the whole thing turned bright red? Sharks would appear, and— *Stop it, Ethan.*

I went to squeeze Fidget in my pocket, but he wasn't there. He was trapped, all alone in the changing-room locker. Apparently, Anxiety Monsters weren't allowed in the pool, which is discrimination, if you ask me.

The lifeguard clapped his hands. "Does anyone know the most important rule of all?"

Silence.

"Not to wee in the pool?" I croaked. "Because of ... contamination?"

Laughter echoed around the water park. Mum put her hand on my shoulder, which I think was her way of saying, *That's enough*, without actually saying it.

"That should go without saying, fella," the lifeguard replied, chuckling. "The most important rule is to have FUN!"

"Oh, and get plenty of content," a manager in a suit chipped in. "We're talking action shots, slide reviews, slow-motion splashcams. You're the influencers – you know what you're doing!"

Everyone clapped, then broke off into families. Everyone except Oonagh and Luna, who followed us and started hogging Mum, leaving me standing there with no one to talk to.

"Everybody wave!" instructed Dad.

He stood in front of us, holding his camera in a selfie pose and pointing at our faces. Mum was right: there was a hole in his trunks, and the mesh lining was poking through. We all waved at the camera.

"OK, everybody say, 'Hi, we're the Laceys and we're at H2O water park!'"

"*Hi, we're the Laceys and we're at H2O water park!*" we repeated obediently, with grins so wide they showed every tooth in our mouths.

"I, for one, cannot wait to own AquaDeath!" announced Mason, approaching the camera and blocking everyone else out of view. He'd been doing that a lot lately. It was a signature CheeseBlizzard move.

"Unlike my kid brother here," Mason went on. "He's too scared. Aren't you, Ethan?"

Dad stopped filming and said, "You know what... Maybe that's our angle for the video. Ethan's too scared to go on the slides, but then we show him facing his fears and *destroying* AquaDeath. What do you think?"

Everybody started nodding – they *loved* that idea. Mum rubbed my shoulder as if I'd already agreed.

"That would be so inspirational!" Oonagh said. "I'm welling up just thinking about it. There's a reason you Laceys are so huge in the family-influencing space right now!"

"I'm getting so emotional too, Mum!" Luna fanned her eyes, even though they were bone dry. "It's the perfect hook. Very *hooky*, I would say."

"*Very hooky, I would say,*" I mimicked under my breath.

We padded around the main pool, while Dad filmed the surroundings. Kids were diving and messing about, making huge splashes lap over the edges. I tried to avoid the water touching my toes.

"How's school going, Ethan?" Oonagh walked beside me, tying her blonde hair into a ponytail. "You're sitting next to Luna, right?"

"Yeah," I said, but that hadn't been my choice. Miss Isaacs had put me and Luna on the same table. "We chat sometimes."

Oonagh nodded. "That's great. Your buddies are on the table too, I heard. Arthur and Omari?"

"Arlo and Omar," I said.

"That's it. I heard Omar got chosen for Gifted and Talented," Oonagh said, sounding impressed. She paused, then said, "Luna's excited about the residential trip. Are you looking forward to it too?"

"Um, it's for the Gifted and Talented kids only." I swallowed a mouthful of chlorine-smelling air. "Omar's really good at maths. Better than me."

"Ah … perhaps you just need to apply yourself," Oonagh said lightly. "I hear you *do* spend quite a lot of time chatting to Arthur."

"Arlo," I said, blushing. "Who said that, anyway?"

"Oh, no one." Oonagh fake-smiled at me. "But I think it's important not to distract anyone else on your table. It can be hard to pay attention when other people are chatting about video games."

I glanced over my shoulder and narrowed my eyes at Luna. She was a few steps behind us, pretending not to listen, but her smug smile gave her away. I wanted to push her into the pool, but obviously I couldn't.

"I don't talk that much," I said to Oonagh, thinking about how Luna chatted non-stop with Daisy, who was also on our table. "I'm probably the quietest one there!"

"I'm sure you are," said Oonagh, giving me another fake smile. "It's just something to think about. Wow – check out that slide, kids!"

We all stopped and gazed up at a colossal green slide that cascaded from the ceiling of H2O. It was so high I had to tilt my head right back to see the top. A network of flimsy-looking staircases snaked up to it.

"What do you make of that, Ethan?" Dad held the camera up close to my face. "You seem a bit pale there, buddy. Just don't overthink it, OK?"

"Don't be sick in the brand-new pool," Mason sneered. "Can you imagine? They'd have to shut the whole place down. Get cleaners in hazmat suits to fish out your puke."

"Mason, don't be gross," Mum said. "Always lowering the tone."

"Sorry, Mum." Mason looked down at his bare feet. "You don't have to do it if you don't want to, Ethan."

Dad tilted the camera down. "Well, he kind of does. That's the whole point of the video…"

I swallowed. "Can't we start with the smaller slides first?"

5

The worst thing about the water slides was the inevitable moment when stinging chlorinated water rushed up my nose as I crashed into the pool at the end. It made the inside of my head feel spicy, and the backs of my eyes feel dry.

It was my fifth time on a slide called Splashventure because Dad wanted plenty of action shots. He waited at the bottom, camera poised to catch each epic splashdown. He yelled, "Wave!" as I rocketed past, and I'd have about 0.347 seconds to look cool before I began to flail around in the water like a clumsy fish.

"Ethan, buddy. You need to wipe your..." Dad gestured vaguely at my face as I made my way to the edge of Splashventure's pool.

I ran my arm across my nose, and a stretchy snake

of snot and spit followed, clinging to my skin like alien goo.

"Ugh!" Luna screamed, and leaped back as if I was contagious. "Ethan's got snot *everywhere*! Mum, look!"

"Oh, wow." Oonagh raised one eyebrow. "Hold your nose next time, Ethan. It prevents ... whatever *this* is."

"Bro." Mason appeared next to me, adopting his on-camera persona. "Ethan's literally recreating the viral slime challenge over here! Follow along for Ethan's home-made slime recipe, am I right? No ingredients needed, a hundred per cent organic!"

"Go away, Mason!" I shouted.

Dad was no use. In fact, I'm pretty sure I saw him *zooming in*.

"One for your wedding day, I reckon!" he roared, laughter booming. "This has *viral* written all over it! *Literally!*"

I cowered away, trying to get the snot-snake off me. But the more I touched it, the more it stretched and stuck, and soon it clung between my arms and webbed between my fingers. My family's screams of laughter rang out, drawing the attention of everyone in the pool.

I wanted to sink into the water and start a new life down there.

"All right, all right. That's enough, folks." Mum finally arrived, armed with a tissue. She leaned down to me and removed the snot-cobweb in one swift move. Then she chucked it into a bin, out of sight for ever. "There we go. Good as new! Shall we do another slide?"

"That was wild," Mason said, tears streaming from his eyes. "That was *absolutely* wild. Literally, did you see the *amount* of it—"

"That's enough," said Mum. "You've been in some mucky states yourself, Mason. Does the term *poonami* ring any bells? I can get the pictures up on my phone if you like. It was like an explosion at a chocolate factory."

Mason's face fell. "Sorry, Ethan," he droned, before swimming away.

"I want to go home, Mum." Tears and chlorine made a painful mixture in my eyes.

Mum sighed. "We can't – I'm sorry. We're here to do a job, remember? We don't get to just go home."

"It's not fair!" I dashed my hand into the water.

"I know. But it's how we make a living," Mum said gently. "Try to have a good time … for the sake of the channel?"

I shook my head.

"For me?" she added.

"Fine."

I looked at my now snot-free arm. It was clean, but I felt dirty. The snot particles were probably still there, invisible to the naked eye. What if the particles got into the water and started a global pandemic killer snot-disease that would change life as we knew it, maybe ending all humanity?

Mason leaped up from below the water's surface and splashed me, dislodging the sticky thought. "Don't stress, brother. It's *snot* that big a deal!"

As the others laughed at Mason's stupid pun, I got out of the water and stomped to the next slide. I wished Omar and Arlo were with us. Omar would have pretended not to have seen the snot, because he was polite like that. Arlo would have told some exaggerated snot story, like about how a whole litre of snot had once erupted from his nose, making my own incident seem minuscule in comparison.

I tackled the other slides quickly, without doing the cool waves and thumbs ups that Dad demanded from behind his camera. Meanwhile, Mason and Luna did every trick in the book: backwards slides, face-first slides, even little flips before they crashed into the pool. Mum and Oonagh giggled and screamed as they took the two-lane slide, hand in hand.

"That's what mum besties do," Oonagh said into the camera as she resurfaced (annoyingly snot-free). Mum and Oonagh hugged, apparently not even caring about the germs. "We conquer everything together!"

"Mum power!" Mum did a peace sign into the lens, before cracking up.

Mason swam up to me and attempted to drag me under by my shorts. I wriggled free, spluttering, mouth filled with pool water.

"Ready for AquaDeath, Snot Monster?" Mason jeered. "Or are you going to stay down here and make more slime?" He flicked his wet fringe from his eyes. "It's steeper than vertical, remember."

I splashed Mason. "Leave me alone."

He flapped his elbows and clucked. "It's OK if you're too much of a chicken. I guess I'll be the star of the video, after all."

I peered up at AquaDeath. Water streamed down its smooth surface like Niagara Falls. The loud crashing of the water, the cliff-edge drop. I swallowed, sensing Dad filming in the edge of my vision.

"Fine." I waded to the steps at the edge. "I'll do it."

*

"I'll pass," Mum called up to us from the level below. She had never been good with heights. "Yep, it's definitely not for me."

"Am I glad you said that?" Oonagh agreed. "That's enough mum power for one day. I'm thinking it's cappuccino and gossip time – what do you reckon?"

I watched Mum nod in agreement with Oonagh, then they went off to the cafe with Luna in tow.

Mason, Dad and I were on the fourth flight of stairs. Halfway up. The pool below looked as small as a postage stamp. My legs had been shaking since the second set of steps.

"What do you reckon, Ethan?" Dad cut in, peering through the camera. "Braving the big-boy slide with me and Mason?"

"Obviously he won't," Mason said. "Why don't you go and have a nice sit-down with the ladies?"

"I'm doing it," I said through chattering teeth.

So we pressed on. Step by slippery step. At the top, Dad asked the lifeguard to film the three of us standing at the entrance to the slide. The water sloshed and foamed like white-water rapids.

"So here we are, you guys," Mason said into the lens. "We're at the top of H2O's AquaDeath. Rumour has it this slide is potentially *lethal*, so stay tuned to see if we survive!"

"Cut." Dad turned to Mason. "You can't say that, Mason. The H20 people would *not* be happy one bit."

Mason rolled his eyes then said his piece again, this time ending with: "Personally, I'm looking forward to diving in and seeing what happens!"

"Nice," said Dad. "You're not scared of the drop?"

"Nah." Mason shrugged. "I'm quite an extreme person – this is nothing for me. My delicate brother, on the other hand…"

"I'm fine," I snapped.

"Ethan, uncross your arms," Dad said under his breath. "Open body language when we're on camera."

"It's cold," I said. "And I don't want to."

"OK, so Ethan's a bit up in his feelings," Dad said to the camera. "But can he overcome his debilitating fear of heights and show AquaDeath who's boss? Go ahead and leave a comment below. Do you think he'll bottle it?"

"He'll bottle it, for sure," Mason muttered. "Although, fair play if you do it, Ethan. It would be sick."

"The moment of truth." Dad stepped away and took the camera. "You're up, Ethan!"

"All right, young man," the lifeguard began. "There are only three rules: go feet first, keep your arms crossed, and don't breathe in the water. Got it?"

"I'll try." I shivered, edging towards the water in millimetre steps.

"You've got this, Ethan!" Dad cheered. "Want to give me a thumbs up?"

I raised my thumb weakly.

"You've got this, little bro!" Mason chimed in. "Just try not to have another snot explosion!"

At the mouth of the slide, the lifeguard told me to lie back, cross my arms and wait. Once I was ready, he would pull the lever and release me to certain death. I tensed my body, scrunched my eyes tight and tried not to breathe.

"On three!" The lifeguard grinned. "*Three, two, one!*"

Nothing. I opened my eyes a crack.

"Hold on a sec," the lifeguard said. He frowned into his control panel. "*Error message.* Looks like something's wrong with the…"

I glanced from the lifeguard to Dad, then from Dad to Mason. "Something's wrong with the *what*?"

"Something's wrong with the … *TRICKED YA!*"

The lifeguard yanked the lever, grinning like a maniac as the floor opened under my feet.

The last thing I heard was Mason's howling laughter as I was sucked into blackness, spinning and rolling in every direction, water crashing and covering me. The taste of chlorine flooded my mouth as I screamed. My stomach leaped towards my mouth, the same feeling as when you miss a step and think you're falling. Only this time I *was* falling. This was it. The *death* bit of AquaDeath. The steeper-than-vertical, free-falling-into-oblivion part.

I scrunched my eyes and thought of nothing as I fell.

Crash!

My body plunged into the water. My ears and nose filled with chlorine. I let out what little breath I had been holding. I opened my eyes. Everything was blue. Bubbles rose towards the light. I began to kick, kick, kick.

I heard cheers as I broke the surface, gasping for air. Mum was cheering at the side of the pool. So were Oonagh and Luna. Dad and Mason were cheering from the top, just two tiny stick people in trunks waving their arms.

I sputtered, and watery spit flew from my mouth.

"I did it!" I shouted, half sinking again. "Shove it, Mason. I did it!"

6

I was exhausted after the trip to H2O. At home I showered twice and lured Colin to hang out in my room. I had plenty of worries to feed Fidget. Everything about the pool, the germs, the snotnado incident got scribbled down and stuffed into his mouth before I'd even had my dinner.

What if I get a verruca?

What if there was bacteria in the swimming pool?

What if my snot infects the whole town and causes the collapse of civilization?

After dinner, I drifted off to the sound of Colin's snores and Dad editing the day's footage in his office room next door. He kept replaying Mason's snot commentary and chuckling. *"Follow along for Ethan's home-made slime recipe, am I right? No ingredients needed, a hundred per cent organic!"*

Mason's *so* funny. Not.

The next morning, Mum didn't wake me up, which was weird. No *"Rise and shine, porcupine"* and no gently parted curtains. Certainly no fresh glass of squash. Beneath my duvet, I knew I had woken up in Worry World. I could tell because there was this weird fizzy feeling in my arms and legs. Everything felt wrong.

Instantly I remembered that message I'd seen on Mum's phone: *Let's just get through the weekend, then we can tell Mason and Ethan.* Something sank like an anchor in my tummy. Tell us what? I threw back the duvet and climbed out of bed, certain that today was the day life would turn upside down.

It was Sunday, which was usually editing day in the Lacey household. That meant Mum and Dad would be glued to their laptops, while me and Mason made our own fun. Well, we used to…

Before Mason changed, we would watch cartoons together, or he'd teach me video games. If it was sunny, we played outside and fed biscuit crumbs to the ants, or went on the climbing frame in the garden. Mason had taught me how to spin upside down and hang there so long that I thought my head would explode from the pressure.

Now, Mason's gone off cartoons and climbing frames. He's certainly not interested in feeding crumbs to the ants. All he ever does is fester in his musty room, playing video games that are too scary for me to join in. Or worse: he's watching CheeseBlizzard pranks or mean street-interviews, cackling with evil laughter at the stupid stunts.

That morning felt different. There were no sounds of machine guns or blood-curdling zombie screams blaring from Mason's computer. In fact, it was silent.

Downstairs was silent too. The silver *1 MILLION FOLLOWERS* balloons had lost their helium and gone baggy. There was no typing or clicking from Mum and Dad's laptops. No snippets of footage playing on a loop as they edited out our *um*s and *er*s.

"Hello?" My voice echoed around the empty house. "Mum? Dad?"

Nothing.

"Colin?" I shouted. "Come here, boy!"

But no claws came clattering towards me, eager for treats or to play fetch with his gross spit-drenched tennis ball.

"Mason?" I tried, knowing he wouldn't reply even if he could hear me. "Annoying, stinky, obnoxious Mason? Are you here? No? Good."

I gave Fidget a squeeze. Something wasn't right.

I stood in the kitchen, still and lifeless like a robot that hadn't been activated yet. Perhaps they'd forgotten me. It was like that old *Home Alone* film we'd watched last Christmas. The family had flown off to Paris for a holiday, leaving their son behind by mistake to ward off two creepy burglars all by himself. Mum and Dad hadn't mentioned a trip to Paris, had they?

My heart jittered. "Calm down, Ethan," I said. "*Home Alone* isn't real."

It was more likely that Mum and Dad had finally realized how independent and grown-up I was, and had decided to leave me at home for the day while they went out to film content.

"Yeah, exactly," I said, replying to my own brain. "They saw how brave and capable I was on AquaDeath yesterday and left me here to relax."

But those words didn't ring true. Sure, Omar

and Arlo said their parents left them home alone sometimes – only for a few minutes or so, while they went to get groceries. But Arlo was brave. Omar was sensible. I, Ethan, was neither.

I crept through the house, opening the door to the garage. No sign of Dad: no radio playing or sounds of his muttering as he tinkered with the van. Dad's #VanLife van was mostly dismantled into rusty parts, surrounded by spanners and tools. We all knew he'd never finish renovating it, let alone drive it to Cornwall like he always talked about.

Next, I headed into Mum's filming room. It smelled like a headache in there: perfume, make-up, scented candles, all the products companies sent her that ended up piled in the corner for ever. Also deserted. No Mum typing or editing or filming fingernail ASMR with her special mic.

A strange sensation trickled from my head to my toes. This was a dream come true – and a nightmare. I took a deep breath and squeezed Fidget. The whole house to myself. If I looked at it with a Positive Mental Attitude (PMA) like Miss Isaacs always said, this might even be fun.

"It'll be all right, won't it, Fidget?"

"Sure thing, big man. You should make the most of it!" Fidget replied. "Imagine telling Omar and Arlo everything you got up to!"

Consider me convinced. I ran to the kitchen cupboards and took out two types of chocolate cereal, mixing them in a bowl and drowning them in a huge lake of milk. Then I made myself a huge glass of blackcurrant squash – loads stronger than I was allowed. The house was my oyster, or whatever the saying was.

"Alexa," I called into the empty room. "Play party music at volume ten!"

"*OK*," the robotic voice replied. "*Playing party music at volume ten.*"

That annoying "Celebration" song from the party blared through the speakers in the ceiling.

"Alexa," I sighed. "Not *cringe* party music. Play something cool."

A new beat flooded the house and pulsed through my body. I began nodding along, tapping my foot to the rhythm. I felt like a teenager in a Hollywood film. Freedom surged through me as endless possibilities entered my mind. Cheese on toast, uninterrupted TV. If I could find Dad's wallet, maybe I could even order my own takeaway. I would hide the boxes in the bin before everyone got home – I wasn't stupid.

"This sure beats another day of filming, right, Fidget? Poor Mason. He's probably being forced to hike up yet another mountain for *Dad on the Rocks* or film a pointless day-in-the-life for *Meet the Laceys*."

"That's right, big man," Fidget replied. "This day will be commemorated for ever more. I hereby pronounce it: National Ethan Day!"

I liked the sound of National Ethan Day. Maybe every kid in the country would get a day off school to do *whatever* they wanted, all in honour of me! No rules, no limits. I danced into the living room and turned on the TV. How could I choose what to watch with all this *freedom*? I settled on a grown-up show with swearing and rude jokes I didn't understand, because who was going to stop me? I stretched out on the sofa and drained my super-strength squash. Both feet on the coffee table like royalty.

"Aahhh!" I let out a burp so loud I would have been grounded if Mum had heard. But Mum *didn't* hear. Nobody did. I was *free*.

"Fidget, it's time for a takeaway!" I announced after a while. "Now where *does* Dad keep his wallet?"

At that moment, an ear-splitting siren interrupted

the show, and the music blaring in the kitchen stopped abruptly. The TV screen flickered before going bright red. Text appeared on the screen.

A robotic voice blared out: "THIS IS AN EMERGENCY BROADCAST ISSUED AT THE REQUEST OF THE GOVERNMENT OF THE UNITED KINGDOM. THIS IS NOT A TEST."

My heartbeat paused.

"Mum!" I called. Why was I on my feet? "Dad? Something's wrong with the TV!"

"ANYBODY RECEIVING THIS ALERT SHOULD PAY CLOSE ATTENTION. THE INFORMATION CONTAINED IN THIS MESSAGE IS VITAL FOR YOUR SURVIVAL."

Shaking, I grabbed the remote control and jammed the buttons so hard my fingernails turned white. Nothing was working. The channel wouldn't change. The TV wouldn't even turn off.

"PLEASE LISTEN CLOSELY," the robotic voice droned. "THE UNITED KINGDOM IS EXPERIENCING AN ALIEN INVASION. A NUMBER OF UNIDENTIFIED SPACECRAFT HAVE LANDED IN LOCATIONS ACROSS THE COUNTRY. CITIZENS ARE ADVISED TO STAY INDOORS."

"Aliens?"

I ran to the window and peered at the sky. No flying saucers here.

"FOR YOUR OWN SAFETY, DO NOT APPROACH THE LANDING SITES. DO NOT INTERACT WITH ALIEN BEINGS."

The driveway was empty. Neither Mum's nor Dad's car was there. My pulse quickened.? What if the aliens had captured them or crushed them with their ship?

My stomach plummeted. *Grandad*. What about Grandad? He'd be so confused, stuck in Sycamore Village, his TV blaring nonsense at him.

"THIS IS A NATIONAL STATE OF EMERGENCY. DO NOT LEAVE YOUR HOMES. DO NOT ATTEMPT TO USE PHONE LINES. THESE SHOULD BE KEPT OPEN IN CASE OF EMERGENCY."

A gloopy sob slipped from my mouth, which I tried to stifle with both hands. I didn't want to be home alone any more. I wanted Mum and Dad. I even wanted Mason. Guilt rose in me like a flood. I had been too happy that they'd left me here. Now they'd all been abducted by alien beings and would never come back.

And Colin. Little Colin, with his black and white fur and his horrible meaty breath. I would miss that breath so much. I hoped the aliens would play fetch with him. If they didn't eat him first.

Tears spilled from my eyes, streams of snot snaked from my nostrils. I couldn't get enough air into my lungs.

"ALIEN SPECIES MAY BE AGGRESSIVE. DO NOT ENGAGE. ENSURE ALL WINDOWS AND DOORS ARE LOCKED IN CASE OF DEADLY RADIATION."

I crumpled to the carpet, stuffing my fingers into my ears to block out that creepy siren. Maybe if I waited, tucked in a ball, everything would be back to normal when I opened my eyes.

Suddenly the siren stopped and the TV made a muffled *pop* as the screen went black. This was it. The aliens had found me. I opened my eyelids a crack, half expecting to find green aliens towering over me. Instead, I saw a familiar pair of trainers, just in front of my nose.

"It's only a prank, Snot Monster," said Mason, smirking. "I can't believe you *actually* fell for it!"

"What?"

"It's a prank – look!"

Mason showed me his phone, which had the same red warning screen that was on the TV. It was a video titled "Alien Invasion TV Prank", which he had cast to the TV.

A drum pounded in my mind as the words registered. I got to my feet and wiped my snotty nose with the back of my arm.

"Oh."

"I can't *believe* it worked," he jeered. "Oh, man. Did you not see the cameras?"

Mason pointed to a small camera tucked into the corner of the room and then another one beneath the TV. Small black devices with shiny lenses. They seemed obvious now.

"*Alexa*," he said in a high-pitched voice. "*Play party music!*" He burst out laughing.

My face pulsed with embarrassment and rage.

"Where are Mum and Dad?" I asked, barely keeping the tremble from my voice.

"Chill out, Ethan. Christ."

"*Chill out?*" I squared up to Mason's face so our noses nearly touched. "I thought you were goners!"

"Everyone's fine. No need to crash out, LLB."

Mason stepped away, then crouched down in front of the camera under the TV and started talking to it in his internet voice. Cheerful, animated, annoying.

"What's up, you guys? You're watching your boy, MasonMayhem, and *what* a first video for my channel. As you can see, my kid brother totally fell for my alien invasion prank – hook, line and sinker. Let's hope he doesn't get abducted, am I right?"

"What are you doing?"

He stopped, then sighed, irritated. "It's for my new channel. Yep, I'm finally following in Mum and Dad's footsteps. I'm gonna be a star content creator. And you're gonna be the subject of my debut prank video, Snot Monster."

"You can't do that, Mason!"

'Uh … *yes*, I can." He turned back to the camera. "Anyway, I'm here with my baby bro, now that he's finally calmed down. We're gonna get the word from the horse's mouth. So, Ethan, tell me: what did you think the aliens would look like? Little green men or arachnid vibes?"

I started to vibrate like a kettle reaching boiling point. I needed to squeeze something hard. I needed Fidget, but I'd dropped him in the panic. My jaw clenched so hard I was in danger of crumbling my teeth to dust.

"That's enough, Mason!" Mum appeared in the

living-room doorway. "Don't wind him up too much. Ethan, I'm sorry, love – I didn't realize it was going to be so scary. We were in the loft, watching."

"How is that fair?" Mason's voice went high. "How was I supposed to know he'd get so—"

Whack.

My fist popped him right on the nose. Mason fell to his knees, clasping his face. Tears came instantly. It felt strangely good watching him flail.

I hadn't done that in ages.

7

I hate Mason's guts.

Monday's breakfast was silent yet somehow noisier than usual. Thanks to Mason's swollen nose, he was mouth-breathing as he ate his cornflakes. He sounded like a donkey chomping on hay. Every chew and snuffle went through me.

I kept dropping my spoon, thanks to the bruised fingers on my right hand, sending milk and cereal splatting across the table. It had been a surprisingly good hit, even if I did hurt myself too.

Mum was sitting with us, but she might as well have been in Australia. Her eyes were all puffy, like she hadn't been to sleep. She kept stirring her bran flakes round and round, barely eating any. Not that I blamed her. Bran flakes are liars. They sneak up on you pretending they're chocolate flavoured, then ambush you with the taste of pure cardboard. I'd be miserable too if I had those for breakfast.

'Something the matter, love?' Dad said. "No appetite today?"

Mum yawned. "I think I'm still tired from H2O."

She pushed her bowl away, then opened her phone and began scrolling through comments on the latest *Meet the Laceys* video. "The video's doing well. So many nice comments about Ethan beating AquaDeath!"

I scowled at the table. I didn't want to know.

More silence passed.

"What a delightful family breakfast," Dad said sarcastically. "Have you two forgiven each other or are we still best of enemies?"

"I don't need to be forgiven," I grunted. "Mason deserved to get hit and I'd do it again."

"*Ethan*," Mum and Dad scolded in unison.

"I'd like to see you try," Mason replied nasally. "One mention of aliens and you'll be on the floor crying like a *wee wittle baby*."

"*Mason*." Both Mum and Dad had a warning look in their eyes.

I glared at my brother. "Post that video and you'll soon find out."

Mum slammed her mug on the table. Coffee slopped over the brim and under the coaster. "Stop it, *now*. Both of you. We had such a nice time at the water park, and now you've fallen out over nothing."

"It's not *nothing*," I retorted. "It isn't fair that he gets to post that video of me!"

"I *will* be posting it," Mason said. "So let's go. Do you want to take this outside?"

I stood quickly, my chair screeching against the floor.

"RIGHT." Dad marched around the table and sat me back down in my seat. "Nobody's taking anything outside, got it?"

"Sorry, Dad," Mason said.

Dad turned to me. "Mason can post his video—"

"He can't!" I yelled.

"Let me *speak*. Mason can post his prank video, OK. *But* he'll edit out the part where you get ... upset. How does that sound? He'll take out anything you don't want included—"

"I don't want *any of it* included!"

Dad sighed. "Well, that's ridiculous. He spent a lot of time and frankly *our* money setting up that prank, and it'll be great for his channel. You'll look back and laugh in a few hours."

"What channel?" I muttered. "It's only got three followers and two of them are you and Mum."

"Ethan," Mum said. "Don't be spiteful."

"All great channels start somewhere," Dad said wisely. "I remember all too well the days of posting consistently on *Dad on the Rocks* before I had one single follower. No likes, no comments. I was uploading into the void. But look at me now – six hundred thousand and counting, and your mum's on a million!"

Mum nodded, smiling as if the whole argument had been neatly packed away, never to be discussed again.

"It won't be long until you'll be starting a channel of your own, Ethan," said Dad. "And when you do, we'll be behind you every step of the way."

I snorted. "Fat chance of that happening. I want to do something *useful* with my life, not post pointless unboxing videos and pranks." That last bit got me a sideways glance from Mum.

"Cheers to MasonMayhem, the next big thing." Dad raised his mug into the air.

"Will he keep the part where I punched his lights out and he started *crying*?" I chimed in.

Mum and Dad sighed, looking exhausted. Mason's face clouded with rage.

I walked to school grumbling and dragging my shoes along the pavement. Now that Mason got the bus to St Hot Dog's, I got to walk with Omar and Arlo. I preferred it that way. It was tons better than walking with Mason and his annoying friends, guffawing at his stupid jokes.

At least Omar and Arlo were funny. Omar cracked me up with his super smartness and Arlo with his stories that were taller than the skyscraper office block in town. Every school-day morning we mucked about and took wrong turns, which was fine as long as we made it to class by nine o'clock, which we usually did.

If we ever arrived late, we'd let Arlo do the talking. That was his talent: lying on the spot. He'd dazzle Miss Isaacs with some made-up story about the postman slipping on a BLT sandwich and, next thing I knew, us being late would be forgotten.

That morning, however, leftover anger from Mason's prank raged through me. I squeezed Fidget harder and harder with each step. Even though I'd punched Mason hard, the feeling hadn't gone; it was stuck inside me. Reliving the moment the TV had blared that announcement, my face turned red and hot.

An alien invasion, of all things. Stupid, gullible me. My life would be over when the video went live. Everyone would call me Alien Boy and I'd become a meme. My face would be shared and re-shared by strangers spanning the globe. It wouldn't be the first time either.

Sometimes it felt like the internet was specifically designed to embarrass me. Mum and Dad had been posting about me since before I was even born, so almost everything I'd ever done in my life had been caught on camera and posted for the world to see.

Top Five Embarrassing Videos of Me

1. Me being born. That's right, Mum and Dad filmed the entire thing, even Mum's waters breaking on the garden patio. This video included close-up shots of newborn me, all purple and coated in gloop from Mum's tummy.
2. Me being potty-trained. Including Mum explaining in great detail about how it took

me longer than Mason to get the hang of things. Especially "number twos".

3. The nose-picking nativity-play incident. I thought I was hidden behind a pillar. I didn't realize everyone could see. It would have been nice if Dad hadn't zoomed in though. I can still picture the camera shaking as he wheezed with laughter.

4. The time Mum let me play with her phone and I accidentally called 999, causing three fire engines to rush to our house, complete with sirens. They didn't arrest me in the end – I was only three. Luckily, Dad got the whole thing on camera, because the fire brigade turned up right in the middle of the weekly vlog.

5. The travel-sickness incident. Picture me in the back of the car, covered in my own chunky puke. Then picture Mason covered in it too. Projectile, Mum called it. Actually, you don't need to picture it; you can see it all online. Dad had to wash us off with a hose when we got back. Apparently, that car never smelled the same again.

I had to admit that not all the *Meet the Laceys* videos were bad. Good memories were captured on film too, like the Thorpe Park vlogs, that viral clip of Grandad using the dance machine at the arcade, Mason and me meeting Goofy at Disneyland. Even my first-ever steps were recorded, me in a nappy waddling towards Mum's open arms. Sometimes it was nice to go back and look. It was *everyone else* watching that made me feel weird.

The free stuff didn't hurt either. How could I complain about free games consoles, free dinners out, shopping sprees in toy shops? How could I say no to film premieres and theme-park tickets?

Mum constantly reminded us that not everyone was so lucky and we shouldn't take it for granted. I used to think I was the luckiest boy in the world.

But it wasn't like that any more, was it? Stupid Mason ruining everything.

Omar and Arlo lived on the same street as each other, so they always arrived at our meeting spot – the conker tree on the corner of Seabrooke Street – together. I swallowed down my anger as I approached them. They didn't need to know what had happened. Not yet, at least. It wouldn't be long until they found out how pathetic I was ... as soon as Mason uploaded that video.

8

Our mums might have been best friends, but it didn't mean me and Luna were too. In fact, Luna was my least favourite person in school.

Miss Isaacs thought we were best friends though, which is how I knew that she followed *Meet the Laceys* online. Mum and Oonagh were always filming us together, making out like Luna and I were inseparable outside school. We'd been forced to go to soft play, zoos – we even made our own slime together. And Miss Isaacs had obviously seen it all, so she'd put us on the same table on the first day of term.

"Good weekend, you two?" Miss Isaacs would ask, welcoming us into the classroom before the register. Then she'd add something like: "That Jacuzzi bath-bomb challenge looked mighty fun!"

I would cringe. Had she also seen footage of me asleep and dribbling in the back of the car or trying not to throw up after Mason kept ramming me on the fairground dodgems? I didn't get to watch Miss Isaacs outside of class, so why should she get to watch me at home?

Luna didn't mind one bit. Even though she didn't have her own channel yet, she already called herself an influencer. Her gang's favourite game was What's in My Bag? Thrilling, I know. The group would take turns to go through their school bag in detail, telling super-long stories about every pencil or key ring or water bottle inside – where they got it, how much it cost, always rating it out of ten.

With Luna around all the time, I couldn't get away with anything. She was always threatening to tell her mum everything I said, and if she told her mum, then my mum would find out too.

In English that afternoon, we learned about antonyms and it got me thinking how Luna was the antonym of me. Luna's hair was pristine; mine was wonky and slept on. Luna's pencil case was fresh and new; mine was covered in ink splotches and patches where I'd picked off the plastic. Luna loved being online, but I felt allergic to it. Being watched made me go itchy. Not my skin, but something inside me, deep in my brain.

> I don't like Luna, but I can't say anything because our mums are best friends.

9

I'm worried Grandad is going to forget who I am.

Mondays were Grandad Day, so I always visited him straight after school for a roast dinner. I'll be honest, Sycamore Village's roast wasn't winning any awards. The canteen staff were nice, but that didn't stop the chicken being dry as a kitchen sponge and the gravy thick and lumpy like porridge. But Grandad loved it, and that was what mattered.

Roast dinners aside, Grandad loved visitors. It brightened him up, brought something into his eyes that sometimes went away. He usually phoned Mum after I'd left, telling her how lovely the visit had been, how it was the highlight of his week.

I loved Grandad. He was kind and gentle. He never told me off. Most importantly, he was the only person in my family who didn't film everything. Grandad didn't have time for all that. He didn't even have a camera.

In a way, Grandad couldn't cling on to the past because of his memory problems. He could only do things *now*. There was no second take. No editing out, no clever cuts to make things perfect. Life happened, then it drifted away. But I reckoned that for everything he forgot, he remembered twice as many interesting things from the olden days.

Sure, he couldn't remember his grandchildren's names or the people who worked at Sycamore Village. But he could name all the flowers in the garden and every bird that pecked on the bird feeder. Nuthatches, starlings, sparrows, that kind of thing.

He could remember the dates of every battle in the First and Second World Wars. He could tell you who the prime minister was in any given year. But he couldn't remember anyone's birthdays, including his own. Last month, my card said *Happy 8th Birthday*, even though I was ten. I didn't mind. It's the thought that counts, right?

Grandad's favourite thing to do was sit by the lounge window with his binoculars, watching the birds. He used to sit outside on the bench, but he started to feel the cold, even on sunny days. He preferred it inside, where the radiator was on full blast and the TV chatted away in the corner.

I wasn't going to miss out on Grandad Day just because of Mum and Dad's secret message and Mason's evil prank. I'd feel guilty if I didn't go. Once, I forgot to go and I spent all night imagining Grandad staring at the door, his wrinkled eyes full of tears, waiting for me to turn up. Anyway, why would I want to go home? Where the air was thick with bad moods and expectations. No thanks.

Sycamore Village was round the corner from Edison Grove Primary, so I was allowed to walk there on my own. Grandad moaned about living so close to a school. Apparently, we caused such a racket at playtime that he could barely hear his wildlife shows. That's why he had the TV in his bedroom on volume 71. It was *definitely not* to do with his hearing.

On the doorstep, I pressed the doorbell and waited while it played its melody. It was the same tune as Sunday church bells: that *BONG-bong bong-bong … BONG-bong bong-bong* one.

The sound of the TV in the lounge boomed through the walls. Some show about canals or something.

"*Britain's waterways,*" the muffled voice said, "*represent one of the biggest engineering something something this country has ever something something…*"

A figure appeared and approached the door. I saw dyed purple hair and a light-blue tabard. Sylvia was easy to recognize, even through frosted glass. Sylvia was Grandad's favourite of the Sycamore Village staff. My favourite too. On the day Grandad moved in, she made it all feel OK and not sad. She showered us with sugary teas and told us how Grandad would "love it here". I'd liked her ever since.

"Hello, superstar!" Sylvia said. She called me superstar because of the whole influencer thing. "How's celebrity life treating you? Been to any fancy premieres lately?"

"Stop it, Sylv," I said, blushing. "I'm not a celebrity."

"Oooh, I don't know," she said. "My daughter was watching you last night, visiting that new water park. You're a celebrity to me!"

Sylvia winked and I went all embarrassed. If she'd seen the H2O video, she'd seen the snotnado.

"How's Grandad today?" I asked.

"He's fine. He'll be delighted to see you. No brother today? We haven't seen him in a while."

I don't have *a brother*, I thought.

I looked at my feet. "He's too busy now he's at St Hot Dog's – I mean, St Mark's. He's got clubs after school. Karate and stuff."

"Oh, shame," Sylvia said, turning back into the hallway. "But karate must take precedence sometimes. Come on in."

I didn't ask what *take precedence* meant. All I knew was Mason hadn't visited since he started Year Seven – in other words, ages ago. The main reason was, according to Mason: "He doesn't even have superfast Wi-Fi!" (said in an almost-crying shriek while slamming his bedroom door at Richter Scale Five).

Mason was obsessed with Wi-Fi. Last year, we had a power cut and our internet went down for six hours. Mason couldn't handle it. He started sobbing when Dad suggested *reading a book*. The mention of *going out to play* nearly triggered a nuclear event. Not that Mum and Dad were much better. They kept opening their laptops, scrolling absent-mindedly, before slamming them shut in a huff.

"You remember the way, don't you?" Sylvia asked now. "Second floor, right to the end of the corridor. Room 227."

"Got it. Thanks, Sylv."

Grandad had been at Sycamore Village for two

years now. I could have found Room 227 even while dizzy and with my eyes closed.

I passed the lounge and took the stairs two at a time. Sycamore Village had a unique smell. A combination of roast dinners, cups of tea, antiseptic and dust. That, combined with the subtropical heating, was quite a combination. I tried not to stare at the residents as I walked past, the ones who nobody visited, with tissue-paper skin and trembling hands.

"Mason's at karate again, eh?" Grandad nodded, standing by his door.

Then he chopped his hand through the air towards me, not fast enough to scare me. I flinched, just to be polite.

"He said to tell you sorry he can't come," I said. "He says hello."

"He must nearly be a black belt by now. I'll bet he's kicking and chopping his way to the top of the class. I must go and watch him at the bojo, one of these days."

The only things Mason was kicking or chopping were digital zombies in *Zombie Freakout 4*.

"It's called a dojo, Grandad. Mason would love that," I said. "He's getting really good."

If lying was a crime, lying to Grandad felt extra illegal. But this was only a Little White Lie. That's what Mum called the things we told Grandad to "smooth things over", like icing covering a split in a birthday cake. Grandad was Mum's dad, so she was allowed to tell him lies. That's what she said anyway.

Apart from the super-slow Wi-Fi, Mason wasn't patient enough with Grandad. Mason rolled his eyes when Grandad repeated something once, twice, seventeen times. He'd sigh, shift around in his seat. He'd glare at the clock, as though willing time to move faster so he could go back online.

I preferred visiting without Mason. It meant that Grandad and I could talk properly, without Mason texting his school friends or staring at his phone while Grandad was speaking to him.

"Can I come in, Grandad?" We were still standing by his door.

"Yes, what a splendid idea!" Grandad's face sprang into a smile. "A visitor!" he announced into his empty room.

He hobbled into his flat, turning to check on me every few steps.

"It's not much." He stretched both arms in display. "But it suits me down to the ground, especially with me being on my own. I've got the bedroom through there. Kitchenette round the corner, not that I use it. Never been much of a cook."

"I've been here before, Grandad," I said. "Loads of times. I know my way around!"

Grandad tutted at himself. "Of course you do. Bathroom's there for tinkles and all that business. You have to hold the flush down; the water pressure isn't ideal. Are you keen on biscuits?"

"I love biscuits, Grandad. But we'd better save some room for our roast, don't forget!"

"Of course, the roast. I shall ask if they have that wonderful cranberry jelly they once served."

He said this every week. They had never *not* served cranberry jelly at Sycamore Village. There would be an uproar.

"Did I ask about biscuits?" he said.

"Biscuits would be great."

While Grandad searched for the least broken biscuits in the tin, I busied myself looking at the photos in the living room. Grandad's walls were lined with photographs, even proper old ones from when he was a kid and the world was black and white. Then Grandad got older and the world came into colour, but even those photos looked old. The people wore flared trousers and big permed hair. They stood next to vintage cars, which apparently were just *normal* cars back then. Weird.

One picture showed Granny when she was young. She was smiling, talking on an old-fashioned phone. She wore lipstick and had long painted nails. She was very pretty, like someone from an old movie. The phone had fascinated me since I was little. It had a round dial on the front, a handle and a curly wire that she twizzled round her fingers. Little did she know phones wouldn't have wires one day, that they'd be filled with videos and photos and games and you could even *pay for stuff* on them.

The photos on Grandad's walls were supposed to help him remember who everyone was, but they stopped working after a while. He would stare at the photos, face wrinkled with confusion. Even looking at photos of himself as a young man, he frowned as if that person was a distant cousin, someone he barely knew.

Eventually Mum had come over with a label machine and stuck everybody's names to the bottom of the frames. The labels worked well, as long as Grandad could find his glasses. Most of the time he couldn't, even when they were hanging around his neck on a string.

Get this: the wildest thing in Grandad's place was the machine next to his bed. Every morning at 6 a.m., it poured a cup of tea all by itself, with milk, sugar and everything. It came out piping hot and it actually tasted all right. The tea-robot was the one futuristic item Grandad owned, and it turns out it originates from the Good Old Days. I wished they made a similar machine for squash. I've googled it, but nope.

Grandad returned with an assortment of biscuits arranged on a saucer. Chocolate bourbons, malted milks, rich tea. Banging combo, if I do say so myself.

"I used to have a bigger house," said Grandad, "back when Marie was here. There was a garden with an oak tree. Sun room, grand piano, you name it."

Grandad's eyes went shiny like two glass marbles and his voice went dry. His voice always went dry when he talked about Granny.

"Of course, she isn't with us any more. This place is ample for one though. It suits me *down to the ground*."

"It does, Grandad," I said, nodding. "It suits you down to the ground, doesn't it?"

"Precisely. It suits me down to the ground." He nodded sharply. "Forgive me, but what did you say your name was again? It's Ellis, isn't it? Evan? Edward?"

"Ethan, Grandad."

"Ethan, Ethan, Ethan. I knew it was Ethan, I *really* did, but it gets cloudy. So many names to keep track of. It's like rummaging for a jumper in the back of the wardrobe. Sometimes the one you pick out isn't quite the one you wanted, but you try it on anyway. Often it fits."

"That's all right, Grandad," I said, stuffing a bourbon in my mouth. "I'm Annabel's son, remember?"

"Ah, my daughter, Annabel!" Grandad's face lit up with the memory. "She's done rather well for herself. Did you know she's on the television nowadays? She's becoming well known – a *star*, you could say." His knobbly hands stretched out and then dropped to his lap.

"I know, Grandad! You like watching her on TV, don't you?"

The staff at Sycamore Village streamed *Meet the Laceys* on the smart TV for him. Grandad thought YouTube was the same as regular TV, like where they show the news and *Strictly Come Dancing* and antiques shows. He thought we had a film crew following us around, not just Dad with his camera and mini microphone, manufacturing the perfect shot of me and Mason high-fiving like the *best brother-chums ever.*

"Very much so." He nodded. "I'm rather proud. You must meet her next time she's here. She likes those biscuits too."

I thought about explaining again, but I didn't. I didn't want to make him sad.

"I'd like that, Grandad. You came to her party to celebrate a million followers the other day, remember?"

"Ah, yes. It was a fabulous do, wasn't it? All that razzmatazz. Utterly joyous. I *adored* the oysters. My wife, Marie, always adored oysters."

"They were amazing, weren't they? Really yummy." But I wasn't sure there were oysters at all. "Speaking of yummy, how about dinner?"

"A wonderful idea. If I'm not mistaken, they offer a rather scrumptious roast dinner on Mondays. There's this excellent cranberry jelly."

"Well remembered, Grandad."

Carefully, we made our way to the canteen, me walking at the slowest possible pace while Grandad did his best to keep up. It wasn't that he couldn't walk – more that he forgot the way and stopped often to check which direction he had come from.

"It's this way," I'd say, beckoning him down the corridor.

"Ah, quite right," he'd say, nodding. "Quite right."

10

I shuffled home from Sycamore Village slowly, beyond stuffed with roast dinner. I was in no rush. After all, I had somewhere I didn't want to be. On Monday nights we filmed Meal-Prep Mondays, even though I always ate at Sycamore Village first.

I hated Meal-Prep Monday with a passion. Unfortunately our followers loved it and always wanted more. Our channel had a Meal-Prep Monday playlist, showcasing over one hundred of the most miserable Mondays of my life.

It went like this: every Monday I had to stand in the kitchen chopping smelly onions and garlic while Mum and Dad spoke endless nonsense to camera. Mason and I were expected to chime in and say positive stuff like "Wow, sure smells amazing!" and grin from ear to ear, even if the food was burning and producing noxious smoke in the oven.

"You can't smell the burning through the camera!" Dad would say, usually while wafting smoke out of the window with a tea towel.

Mum said Meal-Prep Monday was all about being relatable and showing the world the "real us" and how we were "just like everyone else". I didn't think *everyone else* spent their whole lives on camera, but I didn't say anything.

Opening the front door, I wondered what today's recipe would be. Usually it was something bizarre like tuna lasagne or savoury bacon cheesecake. Mum told us it was best to cook unusual food that would keep viewers hooked. I suspected there was a reason why nobody had heard of shepherd's pie pizza or toad-in-the-stir-fry.

Sure enough, Mum and Mason were waiting in the kitchen, wrapped in pristine aprons with *Meet the Laceys* logos on the front. Three cameras on tripods stood around the kitchen, ready to capture every angle.

"Finally," Mason grunted. "Felt like joining us, did you?"

"Shut up," I snapped. Seeing Mason made my eyelid start twitching. "Made it to four followers yet?"

"I haven't posted your little freak-out yet, loser," Mason spat. "When I do, *MasonMayhem* will go stratospheric and your life is *kaput*."

"Come on, Ethan." Dad appeared, hurrying me to take off my coat and backpack. "We need to record while there's still natural light."

Dad was obsessed with natural light. He was constantly figuring out when there would be most of it, what angle it would be coming from and when it would disappear.

"Ethan, jumper," said Mum.

I put my arms up and she took off my school jumper. I wasn't allowed to wear my uniform on camera.

"Arms out," she ordered, as she dragged an apron over my head, then set about tying it around my waist in a double knot. It was too tight.

"Grandad OK?" asked Mum, ushering me behind the kitchen counter. Four red onions, a few garlic cloves and a knife were waiting for me on a chopping board.

"No time for small talk," Dad said tersely before I could reply to Mum. "Are we ready to hit record?"

He dashed between the cameras, turning them on, then he quickly skipped back behind the counter.

"Good evening, guys," Dad said cheerfully.

"Welcome back to Meal-Prep Mondays with *Meet the Laceys*, where we prepare budget-friendly meals and update you on the family news. If you're not following already, why not smash that 'subscribe' button below? So … what are we making today, boys?"

I looked at Dad blankly. "I don't know. You haven't told me yet."

Dad sighed. "For goodness' sake, Ethan. Let's try that again, shall we?" He took a moment to pause and asked again, "So, what are we making today, boys?"

"Barbecue hot-dog spaghetti!" Mason said, giving two thumbs up to the camera. "And don't forget to follow *MasonMayhem* for the sickest, most mind-blowing viral pranks you've ever seen!"

"That's right." Dad chuckled. "My boy's channel, *MasonMayhem*, is officially heading to launch and *you* – yes, *you* – can be among the first followers. Check out the notes below!"

"But more on that later," Mum said cheerfully. "First, let's get chopping those vital ingredients. Ethan will be in charge of the onions and garlic, and MasonMayhem will be slicing the hot dogs!"

An hour later, we gathered around a steaming plate of barbecue hot-dog spaghetti for the final shot.

"Time for the taste test!" Mum announced.

In unison, everyone dug their fork in and twirled it so the spaghetti looped around the prongs. I took a mouthful and chewed. I swallowed hard, trying not to gag. Some foods really shouldn't exist.

"What's the verdict?" said Dad, grinning.

"Tastes amazing," I said, giving a weak thumbs up.

"It's sick," Mason said, his words muffled through half-chewed food. "In a good way."

At that, Mum and Dad did this weird fake laugh.

"Looks like another family meal-prep hit," said Dad. "They can *barely* stop eating it!"

"And, as always, the recipe can be found on our socials," Mum added. "We hope you enjoyed spending time with us. Do subscribe if you haven't already and we'll see you tomorrow for more Lacey family content!"

"And don't forget to follow me on *MasonMayhem*, the internet's sickest new channel!" Mason said quickly, before Dad yelled, "Cut!"

"Right." Mum undid her apron and set about scraping the barbecue hot-dog spaghetti into the bin. "What are we thinking for dinner, then? Takeaway? There's a new Sichuan place—"

"I want burgers!" Mason announced.

"Something quick," Dad said, switching the

cameras off and dismantling the tripods. "I need to start editing this footage to upload before ten tonight."

I walked out of the room. My feet ached and I couldn't bear being near Mason for one second longer. All I wanted was to see Colin, who had been whining outside the kitchen door for the last twenty minutes, desperate for a chunk of hot dog.

"Somewhere to be, Ethan?" Dad said.

"I wish."

Barbecue hot-dog spaghetti tastes like puke.

11

I felt no better on Tuesday. Tuesdays meant double science, and I really had to concentrate to know what's going on. But my mind was overstuffed with barbecue hot-dog pasta, alien invasion pranks and dreading Mason's next move. Today's lesson was about photosynthesis, so Miss Isaacs showed us close-up diagrams of leaves and cells on the smartboard until my eyes clouded over.

"Ethan!" Miss Isaacs called on me. "How have plants adapted to ensure high rates of photosynthesis?"

She stared at me expectantly. Everyone did.

"Um…" I felt like I'd fallen into ice water. "Large surface area?" That was my go-to answer for science. It was almost always right, even if it wasn't *technically* what Miss Isaacs wanted.

Miss Isaacs shrugged. "Correct, but a lucky guess, I suspect. Do stay with us, Ethan."

I nodded, my face throbbing as heat rose to my cheeks.

"The old 'surface area' technique," Omar said on the walk home. "A classic. But you might want to consider listening. I think Miss Isaacs is wising up."

"Leave the boy alone," Arlo said. "It's no big deal to zone out in class. I do it all the time. In Year Two I fell asleep in RE – next thing I knew, I woke up in the dark. All the lights were off and everyone had gone home, even the cleaners. The police were flying helicopters over town searching for me and everything."

"No, they weren't," Omar said, stopping dead. "That literally *never* happened."

"Yeah, I know. Would've been class if it had though," Arlo said with a wink. "Are you all right, Ethan? You seem spaced out."

"Just tired," I said. "Busy time with the channel. Did the usual filming last night: barbecue hot-dog spaghetti."

Omar grimaced. "Tell your parents that sleep is crucial at this stage in a child's development," he said. "Maybe then they'll let you off Meal-Prep Mondays."

"Nah, the sleep thing's not true," Arlo said, shaking his head. "That's what grown-ups *want* us to think. I don't have a set bedtime and I'm fine. Sometimes I stay up for three, four days straight, powering through life."

"Rubbish. I can see your bedroom from my window!" Omar laughed. "Your light goes off at half eight sharp with a kiss on the forehead from Mummy, like the rest of us."

Arlo sighed. "Fine, you got me. Is it a crime to like being nice and cosy?"

We laughed until we got to Seabrooke Street. I walked the rest of the way alone, a weird feeling growing in my head. Jealousy, I think. Their lives seemed so *normal*.

Entering the house, I knew something was wrong, because the dining table was laid with a fancy tablecloth, nice china plates and neatly folded napkins. There were even a few candles flickering on the table. It was a bit much for a Tuesday if you ask me.

"Mum?" I called. "What's all this for?"

She appeared from the kitchen, holding a big bowl of salad.

"Oh, nothing much," Mum replied, setting the

bowl down on the table. "I felt like doing dinner properly for once. No cameras, no arguing. It'll be nice, won't it?"

She went over to the mirror and started putting on lipstick.

"Why?" I asked.

Mason burst through the front door before she could answer. He kicked his trainers in opposite directions and dumped his bag on the welcome mat with a thump.

"We're in here, Mason!" Mum shouted. "How was school?"

"Pretty lit," Mason said. "Double PE, then drama, so a total doss TBH. Why's it all dark in here? What's with the candles? It's giving Halloween vibes."

Mason flicked a wall switch, plunging us into bright white light.

"Turn that off, will you?" Mum ran over and hit the switch. "I'm trying to create an *ambiance*."

"Whatever," Mason said as he turned away. "I'll be eating in my room anyway. There's a livestreamed *Werewolf Files X* league that I want to watch."

"Oh, no, you won't be," Mum snapped. "You'll be having a civilized family dinner with the rest of us. No phones, no arguing, no werewolves, got it?" Then she muttered something that sounded a lot like, *Might be the last time*, but I wasn't sure.

"But, *Mum*!" Mason whined. "I'm going to miss it!"

"It'll do you good not to be staring at a screen for an hour," Mum said as she laid knives and forks beside the plates.

I scrunched my face up. *What?* We never had dinner without phones. Mum and Dad were the worst culprits, replying to comments or texting about their next sponsored collaboration. Worst was when they answered calls from our manager, Cindy, who always popped up with requests at the most random times. Like when me and Mum planned a Just the Two of Us Day and Cindy ruined it with some skincare unboxing that took over the whole weekend.

"But what about my channel?" griped Mason, getting even whinier. "I need to monitor the comments and followers!"

"What followers?" I mumbled.

"The world won't combust if you're not online for an hour, Mason," Mum said firmly.

Mason's hands curled into fists. "Where's Dad? He'll back me up!"

Mum rolled her eyes. "I'd like to see him try. He's upstairs getting ready."

"Ready for *what*?" I said. "It's only dinner – what's the big deal? Why are you being weird?"

"I'm not being weird." Mum walked into the kitchen and returned with the posh glasses we weren't allowed to use. "I want everything to be just right, OK? Have you washed your hands?"

I checked my palms. There was grime in the creases, and flecks of paint on my fingernails from art.

"No," I said, feeling the thought growing sticky in my head. There would be germs. Millions and millions of germs.

Mum raised her eyebrows at me. "Well, go on, then. Dinner's nearly ready!"

I washed my hands seven times with Mum's expensive geranium-scented handwash, because seven is the luckiest number. Obviously I had to touch the door handle on the way out of the bathroom, which probably had a *few* germs on it, but I tried not to think about that and headed downstairs.

Dad soon appeared, clean-shaven and smelling of cologne. His shirt was buttoned to the top and crisp from the iron. Strange.

Together, he and Mum brought in plates from the kitchen. Steak and baby potatoes for Mum, Dad and

Mason. Chicken tenders and chips for me, because steak is chewy and gross.

"Well, this is lovely, isn't it?" Mum said, her voice sounding breathy and odd.

Dad cleared his throat and held up his glass of wine awkwardly. "Cheers."

We ate to the sound of knives and forks scraping on plates. Dad kept opening his mouth to say something, then clamping it shut and looking at Mum. She would stare back, eyes wide, then return to aggressively cutting her steak.

"Guys…" Mason shattered the silence. "What's going on? You're low-key bugging me out with all this … formality. Are we in trouble? Because if we are, I literally was not involved and it was mainly Ethan's idea anyway."

"*My idea?* I don't even know what he's on about! *Are* we in trouble?" My heart started to drum. "Because I am *trying* not to get so wound up. Fidget has really been helping. I know I haven't been perfect lately—"

Mason smirked. "That Fidget thing is so embarrassing, bro."

"He is not!" I gave Fidget a squeeze in my pocket, to show him I had his back.

"*Boys.*" Mum glared at us both.

"He started it," Mason grumbled.

"I did *not*."

"Seriously," Dad said. "That's *enough*."

"Sorry," Mason muttered, slicing into a potato.

I gritted my teeth and scowled. I wished Fidget was a voodoo doll of Mason so he would feel every clench and twist in real life.

Dad sighed. "You're not in trouble. I do wish you would *try* to get on a bit better though. You used to be thick as thieves, but now you're always at each other's throats."

"He's just an annoying LLB – Loser Little Bro."

"*Mason*," Mum said.

'He's a butt-face!" I snapped back. "He's been a butt-face ever since he went to high school!"

Mason smirked. "Whatever."

"Listen, we've got something we need to tell you." Mum said, looking to Dad. They sort of nodded to each other. "And we don't know how you're going to take it."

Dad swallowed, his Adam's apple sliding beneath his collar for ages while he chose his words. "What we're about to say might be hard to hear. You're going to have questions and that's perfectly normal."

"Oh my days." Mason dropped his fork. "Please

don't say you're having another baby. That's sick, and not in a good way. I'm literally not getting involved. No nappies, nothing. That's a *you* problem."

Mum laughed and shook her head. So did Dad. It wasn't a proper laugh though. Not a happy one.

"There's no danger of that, Mason," she said. "So you can put any fears of nappy-changing to bed."

I slumped back in my chair. It would've been nice to have a brother or sister around. A replacement for Mason. A fresh start, like starting a brand-new exercise book at school when your old one's full of mistakes and falling apart at the staples.

Mason exhaled. "Thank God. Well, that's the worst-case scenario out of the way."

"What is it, then?" I asked.

"Well, the thing is…" Dad sighed, staring down at the tablecloth. "Your mum and I, we've decided to get a divorce."

The silence rang in my ears, like someone had smashed a gong. The message on Mum's phone… It had been about this.

"What?" Mason's mouth fell open, then turned into a disbelieving smile. He looked from Mum to Dad to me. "You're not serious."

"I'm afraid so," Dad replied. "As I said, it's perfectly

normal to have questions or difficult feelings about this. We're happy to talk."

Mason burst out laughing. "Ha ha, very funny. Is this another prank?"

Mum shook her head. "It's not a prank, Mason—"

"No way. I'm not falling for that! Where are the cameras?" Mason got up and started searching the mantlepiece, peering behind the framed family portraits and YouTube subscriber plaques.

"Mason. Come and sit back down," Mum said.

My heart started pounding uncontrollably. I felt hot, like I'd opened the oven and stuck my head inside. I didn't want them to get divorced. Arlo's mum and dad got divorced four years ago. His dad takes him for bowling and pizza every other weekend, and apparently it's totally awkward. Arlo doesn't even like pizza, but he doesn't have the heart to tell his dad because he smiles so much watching Arlo eat slice after slice, while saying Arlo's a growing lad. His mum has a new boyfriend who farts all the time and makes them go camping. Arlo hates camping; he's allergic to grass.

"Seriously." Mason was still searching the room. "Where are the cameras? This is kind of a harsh prank, but I respect it, I won't lie."

"Stop it, Mason," I croaked.

'SHUT! UP!" Mason shouted. "You're so gullible, Ethan. It's a prank! It's *obviously* a prank!"

Mum started crying. Sharp little inhales like she couldn't catch her breath. She covered her eyes as tears fell, gathering her creamy-coloured make-up and dragging it down her cheeks. Dad's neck bloomed with blotchy red patches. Dad never cried, so that was how all his feelings came out, through the skin on his neck.

"Mason," Dad said. "Sit down."

"I have to say, this is going to do absolute numbers online, you guys," Mason said. "Call it 'You Won't Believe How These Kids React to Divorce Prank", something like that."

"I SAID, SIT DOWN," Dad shouted. His voice echoed around the room.

Mason sat, dumbstruck, his mouth hanging open. His face reddened as if he'd been slapped.

"So you're serious?" I asked quietly.

"We're serious," Dad said.

"But why?" I said. My voice came out squeaky. "Is it my fault? Is it because I keep punching Mason? Because I'll stop. We'll get along, won't we, Mason?"

Mason nodded blankly. "Yeah, we'll stop fighting, literally *now*."

"It's not that. You two are perfect," Dad said. "Even

if you are at each other's throats all the time. It's nothing to do with you two. Neither of you has done anything to cause this."

"We—" Mum's voice cracked. "We've just decided that ... we..." Her voice was gloopy, as if her throat was closing up. "We've realized that..."

"We've realized that we're not in love any longer," Dad cut in. "Nothing bad has happened, but we've drifted apart." Dad placed his hand on top of Mum's, then took it away again. "We've been together eighteen years and we don't regret a second of it."

"Especially not you two." Mum sniffed. "And that's never going to change. Is it, Geoff?"

"No," Dad replied, his voice as dry as sand. "No, it won't."

"Yes, it will." Mason's eyes had filled with tears. "Everything's going to change."

"Well, I suppose some things will change," said Mum. "But we hope not as much as you're thinking."

Mason turned away, shoulders juddering as he cried. "You don't know that. It's going to ruin everything! Why can't you sort it out? You always tell us not to quit, but you're quitting just like *that*!"

Everyone kept on talking, but their voices became muffled. I stared at the table as I pictured my life splitting in two. Two houses. Two bedrooms. Two different walks to school. Would that mean I couldn't walk to school with Arlo and Omar any more? How would we remember which days to meet at the conker tree?

My plate went in and out of focus.

"But what about the channel?" said Mason. "What about *Meet the Laceys*?"

Dad and Mum exchanged a glance, before quickly looking away again.

"Here's the thing," Dad said, the muscle in his jaw clenching and unclenching as if chewing on a thought. "We've come up with a plan."

12

The plan, it turned out, was *to lie*. About everything. Even though lying is illegal. Well, it should be anyway.

I sat there while my parents spoke to us, my forehead stuck in a permanent frown, my heartbeat hammering. Dad said the most important thing was that "our followers were none the wiser" and that we would keep making family content for *Meet the Laceys* "as if nothing was wrong".

"If you think about it, it'll probably make things a bit smoother for all of us," Dad said, eyes darting between me and Mason. "Think of it as easing ourselves into our new normal. We'll still get to spend plenty of quality time together. We can do activities, cooking videos, all the usual vlogs and hauls."

Mum sniffed, then nodded enthusiastically.

"But isn't that ... lying?" I said, finally daring to speak but definitely not brave enough to meet anyone's eyes. "Isn't it *wrong* to lie?"

"Well, I wouldn't call it *lying* as such," Dad said. "Think of it as a professional strategy for the sake of our livelihood. And we *do* deserve to keep some matters private, don't you think?"

"Only when it suits you," I grumbled.

Dad sighed.

Then I asked, "Why can't you delete the channel?"

"We are categorically *not* deleting the channel, Ethan." Dad's nostrils flared. "That's completely off the cards and you know it."

"Or at least stop making videos for a bit!" I huffed.

"It doesn't work like that, Ethan." Mum sighed. "It's our job, remember. We don't do it for fun – not any more. We need to pay for things – bills, this house, your clothes, the nice food we eat, Grandad's care at Sycamore Village. It all costs money. We can't stop making content. We have to keep it coming. Something fresh, week in, week out."

"Plus, the fans would be bereft," Dad said. "Don't forget, they're a part of our family too. We tell them at the end of every video, don't we?"

I rolled my eyes, remembering Mum's famous

sign-off: *Thank you for being here. We truly care about each and every one of you like family.*

"But I thought *we* were a family," Mason said.

"You know what I mean," Dad said.

"What your dad means is we *are* a family," Mum said. "We always will be. But it's simpler if we act as though nothing has changed."

"We have over a million people who care about us. We can't let them down after all these years together." Dad did this wheezy laugh, as if the idea was *so* ridiculous.

"*Together?*" I snarled. "We don't know them! They watch us every day like freaks!"

"Don't say that, Ethan. They're not *freaks*." Dad shook his head. "They're *fans*. They're *followers*. We owe them everything. Literally everything."

"Mason, tell them it's stupid." I turned to my brother, thinking he might back me up.

He was holding his knife and fork, cutting the same piece of steak over and over again into smaller and smaller chunks. Tears clung to his eyelashes.

"Earth to Mason!" I slammed my hand on the table. "Can you hear us?"

"Are you moving out, Dad?" Mason said, sounding dazed.

Mum and Dad looked at each other weirdly again, their expressions a question mark.

"We're figuring it out," Dad said. "I'm taking the spare room for now and, if we need more space, I can sleep in the van. I've been meaning to get out on the road anyway. Try out the whole van-life thing. It'll be great for content."

Mum made a tiny noise in her throat. A quick raise of her eyebrows said more. There was no way anyone was sleeping in the van.

"You're not actually going to sleep in that mouldy old van?" I said.

I shivered at the thought of it. Last winter, we took the van out for its one and only journey and it was so cold my breath had come out in plumes like a steam train. Dad had to wear gloves to hold the steering wheel. There was a layer of ice on the *inside* of the windscreen.

"I'm *working* on the mould situation," Dad said, offended. "Eventually I'll look at getting a flat nearby. A little one-bed bachelor pad, something like that."

"Oh, Christ." Mum massaged the top of her nose with her fingers. "You can get a nice beanbag. Table football, the lot."

"Well, that's the reality, Annabel," Dad said. "We're going to have to face it."

"Why should you move out?" Mason spat. "Why doesn't Mum move out and live in a flat?"

"Mum's the bigger earner. Plus, she needs the house to film," Dad said. "It's *Meet the Laceys* that brings the bucks in. *Dad on the Rocks* is pocket money for now."

"Well, why don't we split the house in two, paint a line down the middle?" suggested Mason. "I saw it on a film! Mum gets one side. You get the other. Then nobody has to leave."

Dad gave him a hard stare. "Let's leave the ideas to the grown-ups. We need to know that you're on board with the plan to keep things quiet. You do want our support with *MasonMayhem*, don't you?"

"What's *MasonMayhem* got to do with it?" he asked.

"Well," said Dad, "we can't help you build a following if we no longer have the channel, can we? What do you say we make a sort of deal? You support us; we support you."

A beat of silence.

"Fine." Mason sniffed. "I'll do it."

Dad turned to me. "Ethan?"

"Fine," I rasped, squeezing Fidget's squishy arm again and again. "I'll do it."

*

I don't want things to change.

I hate that stupid van.

I'm worried the divorce is all my fault.

13

Keeping secrets wasn't my strong suit. That's why nobody had told me about Mum's surprise party. I couldn't help blabbing, telling people what I'd got them for their birthday or Secret Santa before they'd had a chance to guess, let alone open the wrapping paper.

This secret wasn't like a present though. This was on a whole new level – one that would tear my family apart and make my parents lose everything. I practised keeping my tongue between my teeth to trap the slippery words inside. It was like keeping a marble inside my mouth: one wrong move and it would go *plop* on to the floor and roll away from me while the whole world looked on.

I couldn't believe Mum and Dad were getting

divorced. *Divorce*. The word sounded bad, like something people were only allowed to whisper. It reminded me of other bad words like *detention* and *devious* and *division*. I suppose that was it: a division of Mum and Dad.

Mum ÷ Dad = who knows what for me and Mason

Or maybe it was a subtraction. We were losing out, after all. I ran it round and round in my head until it made my neck go red.

I never saw it coming. I thought Mum and Dad loved each other and that was that: done, sorted. Nobody told me people were allowed to stop loving each other. Where did the love go?

I put my hand into my pocket. Fidget, as always, was there. I ran my finger over the stitching on his arm. I counted his claws: one, two, three on each hand. It's something Dad taught me, to help me cope better when my thoughts got sticky. Count something until the feeling simmers down: *one, two, three, four…*

Arlo and Omar were having a heated debate about conkers when they arrived at our meeting spot on Wednesday morning.

"You have to bake *and* vinegar them," Arlo said. He

was using his hands a lot so I could tell they had been discussing this for a while.

Arlo was saying, "It's some sort of reaction that hardens them. I've made conkers that have competed at an international level. I'll show you if you don't believe me!"

"Sorry, but you're wrong," Omar said. "It's all about clear nail polish. It creates a hard barrier, which—"

"Why would I own clear nail polish?" Arlo cut in. "More importantly, why do *you* own clear nail polish?"

"It's my mum's, *obviously*." Omar rolled his eyes. "When have you ever seen me with my nails painted? I'd never be allowed, for a start."

"I don't know," Arlo huffed. "Maybe you like to dress up all pretty in secret."

"Maybe I do," Omar said, posing with his nails by his face before cracking up. "Anyway … just put the nail polish on, let it dry, and those bad boys will be like rocks on string. As soon as the conkers start falling, I'll prove it and smash yours into atoms."

They both looked up at the tree. Green spiky shells hung down from the branches.

"Any day now," Arlo said, shaking the trunk, "these conkers will be ours. *All ours!* I'm going to collect them all."

"Fine," Omar said. "You're on. Winner takes it all."

"All of what?" I asked.

"I don't know." Omar shrugged. "I've just heard people say it. Anyway, what's your favoured conker-hardening hack, Ethan?"

"Not sure," I said. "I didn't realize it was such a big deal."

"It wasn't," replied Omar, "until Arlo became so adamant on using the wrong technique."

"It's not *wrong* – it's from *the internet*. Ever heard of it?" Arlo said.

Arlo and Omar were always like this. They argued constantly, but only about stupid stuff, batting words back and forth like a shuttlecock. They called it banter.

"He's still in a funk," Arlo said, looking at me. "You seem *weird*."

"No!" I said. "I'm fine! Never been better! Honestly!"

"He's glitching again," Omar said, eyeing me like a strange machine that was on the blink. "Earth to Ethan? Are you installing updates?"

"Yeah." I sighed and sneakily squeezed Fidget's leg inside my pocket. "Rubbish night's sleep again, that's all."

"We'll put you on charge when we get to school." Arlo mimed plugging a charging cable into my back.

"Thanks." I grinned at my best friends. "Just kick me if Miss Isaacs asks me another question."

Mum and Dad had spent hours the night before going on about how secret the divorce had to be if we were going to pull this off. All the while, their steaks got colder and colder, and Mason got moodier.

Nobody, they repeated, *nobody* could find out, otherwise the whole plan would go bust in our faces and *Meet the Laceys* would be over, *kaput*, and they would have to get office jobs again.

Dad especially did *not* want another office job; he'd made that *very* clear. He'd droned on and on about how he dreaded the thought of water-cooler chat and spreadsheets and deadlines and cheap instant coffee in the staff kitchen. He used to sell something called accounting software to other companies who didn't even need accounting software. He was bored out of his mind apparently, staring into space at his desk, occasionally treating himself to a game of Minesweeper.

I remember Dad working in the spare room, talking in a cheerful weatherman voice on business calls. He spoke about *pipelines* and *bottlenecks* so much that I thought he was a plumber, but apparently they're business words. Afterwards, he'd be all red with sweat patches under his armpits.

After a while, the calls sounded less cheerful and Dad stopped doing his weatherman voice. Listening through the door, I heard words like *losses*, *deficits*, *scale-backs*, *restructuring*. One day, Dad emerged looking pale and said he was redundant. Mum and Dad whispered loads that night.

There was talk of new jobs, but eventually Dad said enough was enough and joined Mum with *Meet the Laceys*. Filming, editing, coming up with ideas. Then there were so many ideas that we started filming every day. Every scuffed knee, birthday cake, sore throat and egg-and-spoon race happened in front of a camera. With videos came views, then came followers. Then free stuff, then adverts, then contracts for us all to advertise washing-up liquid, crisps, organic microwave meals.

I remember Dad's massive smile when he first realized we made more money from *Meet the Laceys* than he did selling accountancy software. He stuffed all his work clothes into the bin outside like a ceremony. It's online, if you want to watch it. The episode's called "We're Officially Full-Time Vloggers!" – uploaded on 13 June 2022.

Dad always said that filming and sharing our family memories was the best job he'd ever had and, without that, he didn't have a purpose. That's why the divorce was a massive secret, and we were going to be full-time liars as well as full-time vloggers.

We each had an extensive list of people we weren't supposed to tell. Miss Isaacs was at the top of mine, like an angel perched on top of a very stressful Christmas tree. Mum and Dad knew she watched our videos, so it was important she was none the wiser. Dad rehearsed it with me like a play in drama class:

MISS ISAACS (played by Dad): Ethan, you seem
   a bit off recently. A bit down in the dumps.
   Is everything OK at home? Is there anything
   you'd like to talk about?
ME (played by me): No, thank you, Miss Isaacs.
   [Innocent smile.]

Luna was next, even though there was no chance of me ever telling *her* a secret. Mum said Luna would definitely tell Oonagh, and Oonagh would tell everyone on planet Earth. That was weird because I thought Mum and Oonagh were best friends. Mum said it was complicated, but everyone likes to gossip now and then.

Omar and Arlo couldn't know either, even though they weren't interested in the channel. Dad said it was too risky to tell them, then said something about loose lips sinking ships.

Part of me wished I *could* sink the ship, but my family would never forgive me. Especially Dad, back in the home office in a too-tight shirt with sweat patches and twenty calls a day.

I couldn't tell. I mustn't.

When we got to the cloakroom, Arlo nudged me as I was taking off my coat. I hadn't said much on the walk to school.

"Is it Mason?" Arlo asked. "Is he winding you up again? Because if he is, we should do something."

"Yeah," I said, releasing two lungs' worth of air in a big sigh. "He's into pranking now. He got me bad with that stupid alien invasion prank that's going around."

"Brutal," said Omar. "The one where a warning comes up on the telly saying it's from the prime minister and all that?"

I looked at the floor, embarrassed. I didn't want to tell anyone about it. Not my over-the-top reaction, the uncontrollable shaking, the tears that flooded my eyes... The punch that came out ten times harder than planned and left me with a bruised hand.

"He thinks he's so big and clever because he's in Year Eight," Arlo said, "but he's no bigger or scarier than he was in Year Six. The only difference is that he has to wear a hot-dog uniform now."

I snorted and let out a laugh. But secretly I hoped that St Mark's would change their uniform to something less revolting by the time I made it to Year Seven, or we'd soon be eating our words.

"Mason's nothing but a dweeb inside a bully costume, you know," Omar chipped in.

"Yeah. He can't actually hurt you. Not with two tough guys like Omar and me around." Arlo flexed some arm muscles that didn't seem to exist.

A smile spread to my cheeks. Omar and Arlo always cheered me up. I wished I could tell them about Mum and Dad. I bit my tongue instead.

"Mason's starting his own channel," I said. "He wants to be a big YouTuber like Mum and Dad."

"You're joking." Omar rolled his eyes. "That's the last thing we need: more content from the Lacey household. No offence."

"None taken." I shook my head. "I actually agree."

"What's the name of Mason's channel?" asked Arlo.

"I can't say. It's too cringe."

"No, go on!" Arlo said, eyes wide with excitement. "You can't dangle that in front of us!"

"He's right." Omar nodded. "Technically it's illegal to withhold key information from your two best friends. BPCC rules. The Blue Pencil Case Crew won't hesitate to come at you with the full force of the law."

"Fine." I grimaced. "It's called *MasonMayhem*. All one word."

Arlo and Omar gawped at me and then at each other. Silence spread between us, then they both collapsed into laughter. Proper laughter that folded them at the stomach like a piece of paper and kept rumbling on ages after the joke ended.

"*MasonMayhem*," Omar wheezed, once he had finally caught his breath.

"That," Arlo said, "is hilarious."

My friends really are awesome.

14

At home that night, Mason shut himself away in his bedroom like always. Pressing my ear against his door, I thought it was worryingly quiet. For once, he wasn't playing *Zombie Freakout 4*. There were no blood-curdling screams, gunshots or frantic clacking sounds from his special gaming keyboard.

But what I heard was more troubling. The tinny sound of my recorded voice playing through Mason's computer. *"Mum! Dad? Something's wrong with the TV!"* Followed by Mason's sly chuckling as he looped the sound again and again, cropping and adjusting it on his editing software.

I burst into the room, shouldering the door open like I'd seen action guys do on TV. It kind of hurt, actually. The air inside his room was thick and stale, like he hadn't cracked a window open in six months.

"Wow, Mason." I pinched my nose with my fingers. "It literally stinks in here."

"No, it doesn't, and get out of my room!" Mason snapped, minimizing the editing window on his computer – but he hadn't been quick enough.

I glimpsed the image of myself shaking and stumbling around the living room as the TV blared the fake government message. Heat gathered in my throat.

"What are you doing?" I tried to make myself sound as scary as possible, but Mason just smirked.

"What do *you* think I'm doing, tough guy?"

"It's the prank," I said, glaring at him and trying to keep my voice steady.

"You bet," he said tauntingly. "It'll be ready to go live by bedtime. *MasonMayhem* is kicking off with a colossal bang."

"You can't," I said through gritted teeth. I slid one hand into my pocket and began squidging Fidget's head in rapid pulsing motions.

That didn't escape Mason's notice. "Your toy can't help you now, little bro."

"He's *not* a toy," I said. "He's an Anxiety Monster

– and I wouldn't even need him if it wasn't for you and your stupid channel."

Mason sneered. "You've had your little toy for ages. Don't act like my future online stardom is the reason you're so sensitive."

I squeezed Fidget so hard that one of his eyes popped off.

"I am *not* sensitive," I snarled. "If you don't stop this, I'll tell Mum!"

"Tell her… Go on," Mason said, and I wanted to slap the smirk off his face. "But I think Mum and Dad have got bigger things to think about, don't you?"

My eyelid began to flicker. He was right; I couldn't bother Mum and Dad, not after yesterday's announcement. Their bad mood was seeping through the walls like a bad smell.

Mason went back to his computer.

"Will you leave the bit in where I nearly punched your nose off?" I said.

Mason winked, then arched his fingers like an evil villain. "The power of editing, my friend. The power of editing."

"I am *not* your friend."

With that, I stormed out and slammed the door behind me, breaking the Guinness World Record for the Loudest Ever Door Slam. It sent shudders through the bones of the house. Everyone would be scared of me now.

If only I hadn't been snivelling so much, that might have been true.

I sat on my beanbag in my room and breathed so fast that sparks appeared in my eyes. Why did Mason have to be my brother? Why did our parents let him do whatever he wanted? Whoever decided which family I got born into really dropped the ball.

In my head, I had my Other Family that I sometimes went to visit. They were like us, only normal. There was no *Meet the Laceys*, no social media. My Other Family didn't have a camera, and nobody recognized us in town. Other Mum and Dad had so much time for me, and Other Mason was my best friend. Other Grandad had a perfect memory and knew exactly what was going on, without having to be reminded. Other Ethan was worry-free and didn't have an Anxiety Monster. The only person who was the same was Other Colin, and he wasn't a person; he was a dog.

I found the superglue from my drawer and stuck Fidget's fallen-off eye back into place. I felt sorry for

Fidget. He took a beating most days and it wasn't his fault. Plus, he barely got any thanks for it.

"There you go, Fidget. Looking better than ever. I'll try not to squeeze so hard next time."

"Cheers, big man," he said. "That's what I'm here for. I'm absolutely starvin' Marvin today. Have you got any yummy secrets and worries for me to nibble on?"

"You bet, Fidget. Let me get some paper."

I went over to my school bag and rummaged for my maths jotter. Maths was my worst lesson, so I didn't care about ripping pages out from the back, even though it made the pages fall out of the front too.

I tore the pages into strips, then began writing down everything that came into my head with my blunt pencil. Fidget was going to have the biggest meal of his life.

I <u>HATE</u> my brother Mason. I wish he would disappear.

MasonMayhem is a stupid name for a channel.

Why did I have to fall for that stupid prank?

Everyone's going to see me crying on the internet.

Everyone's going to call me Alien Boy.

Omar and Arlo won't like me any more.

Miss Isaacs will see the video and think I'm a baby and put me back in Reception.

Mum and Dad don't even care about me.

I want a new family.

I want my family to stay the same.

15

The next morning, there it was, waiting for me on a tablet that Mason had propped against my bedroom door. The video – "Insane Alien Invasion Prank Owns Little Brother!!!!!" – was paused at 0:01 seconds, ready to play.

I felt my heartbeat in the tips of my fingers. Mason's video was online and, despite the fact it was only uploaded last night it already had three hundred and nine views. That was the power of *Meet the Laceys*. Everything we did got attention, whether we wanted it or not. I knew Mason would already be so smug that his giant inflated head would never fit through the front door.

I pressed "play". A flashy animated intro started playing on the screen, accompanied by crunchy guitar music. "*MasonMayhem*," said an American voice that sounded a lot like Mason doing bad acting, "*where the mayhem begins.*"

"What's up, you guys!" Mason said, appearing on screen wearing a backwards baseball cap. He didn't normally wear a cap. "It's your boy, MasonMayhem, here. Congratulations, because you've just discovered the sickest channel on the internet."

A stock sound of applause and cheering played while he blew kisses and bowed to his imaginary audience.

The way he spoke made my fists clench. *It's your boy, MasonMayhem.* Why was he talking like that? Acting like some super-cool American dude, when actually he was a greasy Year Eight who usually smelled like the damp lost property cupboard at school.

"First things first," he went on, "you know what you need to do. If you wanna keep up to date with all the sickest new content from me, MasonMayhem, you need to smash that 'like' button as hard as you can. You're gonna do it with me on three, OK? One, two, *three!*"

Mason punched his hand over the lens so quickly I flinched. A huge explosion filled the screen. "Sick, I can already see those likes *pouring* in. Now, any guesses what I'm gonna make you do to that 'subscribe' button down there in the corner?"

I skipped forward by ten seconds, then another. Mason's image jerked like a sped-up robot.

"So, if you think you recognize me, yeah, you do. I'm Mason Lacey, aka the cool one from *Meet the Laceys*. Just about everyone I know thinks I've got the sickest sense of humour, am I right, St Mark's lads? So I figured it was time that I got a channel of my own."

"Nobody thinks you have the sickest sense of humour," I muttered to myself as a loud fanfare blared and the *MasonMayhem* logo flashed on screen.

"So, as you all know, we've got two brothers in *Meet the Laceys*. There's me, the legendary Mason. Then there's Ethan, aka LLB, Loser Little Bro." Mason creased at his own joke. I wished I could punch him through the screen.

"I'm joshing, I'm joshing. He's not a loser – he's just ten years old." The view cut to a different angle and Mason whispered as if telling a secret to a friend. *"And being ten is kinda rubbish, if you ask me...* No offence to the ten-year-old community – I'm just saying it how it is."

"But you were ten three years ago!" I roared at the tablet.

"OK, OK..." Mason went on, still laughing. "I'm probably being harsh – you guys know I love my bro, really. But he's definitely on the *sensitive* side, am I right?"

I couldn't take any more. I stormed over to Mason's bedroom door and pounded it with my fist.

"I am *NOT* sensitive, Mason!" I yelled.

Mum shouted from downstairs: "Ethan, what's going on up there?"

"N-nothing! I'm just talking to Mason!" I called back, my voice too shrill to be believable, but I didn't want to tell her about Mason's annoying video. Mum had enough going on with her and Dad.

"Well, tell him to get ready for school," she replied. "And don't forget your PE kit. It's folded up by the dryer."

"OK!"

In the meantime, Mason's video continued playing in my hand.

"So ... my sensitive little bro is kind of a fearful guy, and his main fear has always been aliens. Back when I used to play *Alien Surrender*, he always wanted to watch, but would literally burst out crying the second the aliens came off the spaceship! I was like, *Bro, that's LITERALLY the point of the game.*"

"That was years ago!" I shouted at his bedroom door.

Nowadays, I barely had time to worry about aliens when there were *real* things like germs, maths, the PE changing rooms and dust mites to contend with.

"Anyway, that got me wondering… What if I tried the viral alien invasion prank on little Ethan? Well, keep watching to find out – it's worth it. You'll wanna share this with *everyone*!"

"Mason!" I screamed. "Come out here now!"

"What's up, bro?"

I turned to my right. Mason was standing in the bathroom door, surrounded by a thick fog of deodorant. The odour dried the roof of my mouth.

"You need to take it down!"

"It's too late," he said with a grin. He checked his phone. "Three hundred and forty-seven views. That's another twenty since I've been in the shower."

"You're going to regret this, Mason!"

Without thinking, I launched the tablet right at him. It hurtled down the landing, spinning through the air. Mason caught it with one swift movement, just before it smashed against the wall.

Mason smirked and padded into his bedroom. "We'll see, LLB. We'll see."

16

I stomped to school in the rain without waiting for Omar and Arlo. I knew they'd be wondering where I was when they reached the conker tree on Seabrooke Street, but I couldn't face them. I had a feeling that I'd burst into tears the moment anyone asked how I was. And not easy-to-hide tears, but snot-nosed-hiccup tears that can't be stopped once they get started. My stomps rattled through my leg bones.

For the first time ever, I thought about skipping school. Why not catch a bus to another town or roam the aisles of a supermarket until home time came around? Anything but face anyone who might have seen Mason's video. But I didn't have bus money, and the supermarket people would wonder why I was lingering for hours without buying anything. The police would be called and I'd get sent to prison. Then Mason would make a video about *that*.

"Stop it," I said, scolding my sticky thoughts. "Just *stop it*."

Automatically, I'd walked to school. The crossing patrol lady smiled at me as she halted the cars. Had she seen the video? Was that a normal smile, or an "I've seen you online" smile? It was sometimes hard to tell.

Then I was walking through the gate, across the playground, into the cloakroom and hanging my coat on my hook. So much for a day of adventure.

In maths, our first lesson, I kept my eyes trained on my worksheet, even though the words and numbers were scrambling into a mess of scratches and scribbles on the page. My pencil trembled in my hand. *Write something*, I told myself. But my sticky thoughts wouldn't let me concentrate. I kept peering around me. Had anyone seen the video? Had Luna seen it?

"What time do you call this, boys?" said Miss Isaacs, breaking the silence.

I looked up to see Arlo and Omar standing at the door, dripping wet with rain.

"Sorry, Miss," said Arlo breathlessly. "We were waiting for Ethan. He didn't show up at our meeting spot. He's probably sick or something."

Miss Isaacs pointed at me, bemused. "Ethan arrived bright and early this morning. Maybe you two should take a leaf out of his book and work on your punctuality."

Arlo looked at me, like, *What?!* Omar's mouth was just a circle.

Sorry, I mouthed, before looking away.

They said nothing as they took their seats at our table. I didn't need to ask if they were annoyed – I could feel it like an icy breeze. I pretended to focus on my worksheet.

$11 \times 7 = \underline{}$
$11 \times 8 = \underline{}$
$11 \times 9 = \underline{}$

"The eleven times table is literally the easiest one." Luna peered down the length of her nose at my empty answers. "It's, like, eleven, twenty-two, thirty-three, forty-four. If you can't do the eleven times table, you probably shouldn't even be in Year Five."

"I *can* do the eleven times table," I said through a

jaw clenched hard enough to split an apple. "I just don't feel like it at the moment."

"Anyway, you'll never progress to the twelve times table," Luna sneered, "or even the *thirteen* times table with that sort of attitude. Look at my sheet."

Sure enough, Luna's worksheet was complete, with no crossing out or eraser marks. The answers were written in perfectly neat, joined-up writing, even the numbers.

"You're not supposed to join up numbers, you know," I commented.

"I'm not taking handwriting advice from a boy who doesn't have his pen licence. The pencil sharpener's over there, by the way."

I stubbed my pencil nib hard into my sheet, gouging the paper. That was a low blow. I'd *told* Miss Isaacs that I couldn't do joined-up writing, but did she care? Nope. Apparently, I'd have to use a pencil until I became *proficient*. I might as well have "RUBBISH AT HANDWRITING" stamped across my forehead. I had sticky thoughts of me without my pen licence as a grown man, never able to get a job, living in a cardboard box under a bridge.

"Go away, Luna," I snapped. "I'm not in the mood."

"I can't go away. This is my allocated seat. You're

just being a bitter quitter because your brother's going viral and you're not."

"*Keep that quiet*," I hissed, close to Luna's face. "If you tell anyone about that video, I swear I'll knock your—"

"What was that, Ethan?" The shadow of Miss Isaacs towered over me. "We don't use threatening language, do we? What's got into you? That's not like you at all."

"It *is* like him, Miss." Luna's face twisted into a fake cry. "He does it *all the time*."

Miss Isaacs raised her eyebrows. "Is that so? Do we need to have a chat with Mum and Dad about this, Ethan?"

"No!" I blurted out. "Everything's fine. I was just getting frustrated, that's all."

Miss Isaacs' expression softened a little, before she said, "If you need help, put your hand up or come to my desk. There's no need to take it out on your classmates. Now, can I leave you both to do your work without any fuss?"

"Yes, Miss Isaacs," I replied, bowing my head.

"You two are such close friends – you don't need to fight."

"We are." I smiled fakely at Luna. "Everything's fine."

"And what do we say, Ethan?"

"I'm sorry, Luna," I said, looking her in the eyes. I actually meant it too, because I would never actually knock anyone's anything off. That behaviour was reserved for the likes of Mason.

Miss Isaacs thanked us and left to check on our neighbouring table.

"Apology accepted, Ethan." Luna smiled. "But remember: in a world where you can be anything, be kind." She turned away and started chatting to Daisy. They paused for a moment, smirked at me, then carried on.

Arlo and Omar had already started on their worksheets and had filled in more answers than I had.

"All right?" I said, looking to them hopefully.

Arlo just smiled – like a half smile, not a real one. The kind of smile you give to someone who's annoyed you.

"Why weren't you at the conker tree?" Omar muttered. "We thought you'd skived off or something. I swear if it gets back to my mum that I was late, I'm finished."

"Seriously!" Arlo said. "I was stabbing in the dark out there."

"I'm sorry," I whispered.

"Well," Arlo said. "What's going on, then?"

Pressure rose in my head, like my eyes were going to explode.

"It's nothing. I just ... forgot, that's all."

"You – you *forgot*?" Omar spluttered.

I nodded weakly. "Yeah."

"You forgot to meet us at the conker tree, even though we've *literally* met there every morning for the past year."

I swallowed, but my mouth was too dry. "Still ... Blue Pencil Case Crew, right?"

Omar picked at his pencil case. "I've been thinking about asking my mum for a *Zombie Freakout* pencil case, actually. It's holographic and everything."

"Bro, I'm obsessed with that game," Arlo said. "Have you got to the bit with the modified baseball bat and the—"

Omar started making all these horrible splatting and groaning sound effects.

I hated the *Zombie Freakout* games and they knew it. They were too scary. Too much guts and gore and creeping down dark alleyways while zombies scuttered around in the shadows. Watching Mason play it sent shivers up my spine.

"Isn't *Zombie Freakout* for over-sixteens?" I said. "You shouldn't *really* be playing it, you know."

Arlo looked at Omar. They sort of smirked a bit at each other, but only with their eyes. Then they carried on chatting like they hadn't heard a thing.

Omar and Arlo hate me now.

The Blue Pencil Case Crew is over.

I'm NEVER going to get my pen licence.

17

Omar and Arlo didn't speak to me for the rest of maths, after my *Zombie Freakout* comment. When it was time for PE, they didn't even wait for me. I was practically running to keep up while they walked in double-long strides towards the changing rooms.

"Guys?" I weaved between two kids who were pushing each other into the wall displays. "Guys, wait up! Same teams, right?"

Everyone was buzzing because Mr Spickett had promised we'd be doing dodgeball in the sports hall rather than muddy, rainy football or muddy, rainy running laps round the field. I hated mud and rain. All those germs. It was the perfect recipe for sticky thoughts.

Even though I was worried about being hit, I was

excited to try dodgeball. I'd seen it online and it looked fun. I couldn't wait to hurl a ball as hard as I could and let some feelings out. If only I could be hurling the ball at Mason…

"Can you hear something?" Arlo said. "There's this buzzing sound in my ear."

Omar shrugged and kept his eyes forward.

"Come on, guys," I pleaded. "You're not seriously breaking up the Blue Pencil Case Crew over one tiny thing?"

"We got soaked through waiting for you," said Arlo. "I wrung my socks out in the toilets and about four pints of rain came out. So tell us what happened."

"I'm sorry," I mumbled. "My mum offered to drop me off at school … that's it."

"Nah," Arlo said, shaking his head. "Not buying it. Your house is only a fifteen-minute walk to the school gates. Plus, you'd be stuck for hours in the traffic on Upper Street."

He had a point. Mum and Dad always moaned about the traffic on Upper Street. The one-way system meant that it was the only road that led to school, and it was always being dug up for roadworks. During the morning rush, it took four hours to travel four metres. That's why I'd never been given a lift to school, ever.

"That was such a bad lie – you're obviously keeping something secret," said Arlo, a smirk creeping across his face. "I bet it's a girl. Come on, out with it."

"Oh no," said Omar disappointedly before I got the chance to respond. "That's a second BPCC violation. We agreed, no girlfriends until we go to St Hot Dog's. Even then, the school walk remains sacred."

"I do *not* have a girlfriend!" I retorted.

"Well, why didn't you wait for us?" asked Omar. "Did you walk in with Luna, is that it?"

My mouth flapped open in shock. "*Luna?* Are you serious?"

"I don't know," Arlo said. "Looked like you two were getting pretty cosy over the eleven times table earlier."

"As if! She was roasting me about my pen licence!" I huffed.

"I reckon it was a YouTube thing," Omar said. "Was your mum doing a walk-to-school challenge or something?"

My face reddened. Omar and Arlo usually ignored the whole *Meet the Laceys* thing, but sometimes it was too easy to use as a ribbing tactic. Whenever they mentioned the social media stuff, it felt way worse than when anyone else took the mickey.

I rolled my eyes. "You *know* it's not that. I would never *do* something like that."

"All right, Five B!" Mr Spickett suddenly appeared outside the changing rooms. "Let's get ready to DODGEBALL!"

Everybody cheered in unison except me. My dodgeball excitement had faded. I had too many other feelings tumbling around. It was like when all the poster paints get mixed together and come out as a horrible brown-grey splodge.

"That's the spirit!" Mr Spickett roared. "I trust everybody's remembered their kits for this very special dodgy day?"

Everybody cheered again. Except me. Suddenly my hands felt empty, and I remembered how light my backpack had felt on the walk to school. My stomach sank. I'd forgotten my kit. I pictured it, folded nicely by the dryer, exactly where Mum had told me it was, before Mason decided to ruin my morning and my life.

I raised my hand.

"Sorry, Mr Spickett," I said sheepishly. "I've forgotten my kit…"

"Ah, there's always one," Mr Spickett said jokingly. "Not to worry – there's a mountain of spares in the PE cupboard."

Other people's clothes give me the creeps.

The PE cupboard smells like mould and feet.

Those clothes smelled horrible and now I smell.

I can feel germs crawling all over my skin.

I shouldn't have accepted the spares. The shorts were as short as pants, and the T-shirt smelled weird. There were yellow sweat stains in the armpits and moth-bitten holes in the tummy. It wasn't nice and soft like when Mum does the laundry with the Blossom Orchard scented softener. I'd have to shower twice at home to get the particles off my skin.

Mr Spickett explained the rules, then the whistle shrieked and chaos began. Balls flew in all directions, thudding against the walls. Trainers squeaked on the floor. Yelling and screams echoed around the sports hall. I backed into the corner and cowered in a crouch.

I was pretty certain Luna was deliberately aiming at me. Every time she got a ball, she hurled it at me, overarm. I dodged the first few, but eventually one smacked me right in the middle of my chest, knocking me breathless.

"Lacey, out!" Mr Spickett blew his whistle. "To the bench!"

I walked over to the bench, chest stinging while Luna celebrated. Omar was there, having been knocked out the second the game started.

"Bad luck, Ethan." He patted my back, making the strange-smelling T-shirt touch my skin more. "She was gunning for you big time."

"Now do you believe that I didn't ditch you to walk to school with Luna?" I asked.

Omar smirked. "Fine. I believe you."

"Stupid dodgeball. It's not even a proper sport."

"I think it is, technically," Omar said. "There's leagues and everything. People going pro."

We fell silent as Luna and her crew eliminated Arlo with a throw so hard the ball whistled through the air before striking. Arlo dragged his feet to the bench and sat beside me.

"I could have won that game easily," he said. "Thought I'd give someone else a chance for once."

"Sure," I said. "How thoughtful."

Arlo smiled. "You're so *sensitive* today!" he said, tickling me in the ribs.

"I am *not* sensitive!" I squealed, which embarrassingly echoed around the hall, shrill as

Mr Spickett's whistle. Perhaps I was being a bit … sensitive.

Arlo and Omar burst out laughing.

"So what's going on?" Arlo said. "It's not a girlfriend. It's not a viral walk-to-school challenge. There must be a reason you're being so weird."

I looked at them both. "You really haven't seen it?"

"Seen what?" Omar said.

I sighed, resting my back against the cold wall of the sports hall.

"Mason's posted his first video on his channel."

"No way." Omar started bouncing, making the whole bench move. "I cannot wait to see this!"

"Man, I wish I had my phone right now," Arlo said, beaming.

"The thing is," I said, "the video's about me. The alien prank I mentioned. He's posted it. He got me good. Really good. Too good."

"Oh dear," Arlo said. "What happened, exactly?"

18

At break time, I kept watch while Arlo and Omar huddled in the corner of the playground to watch MasonMayhem's video. Phones were not allowed in school, and if mega-snitch Luna saw that Arlo had one, the three of us would be in detention for a week.

"How many views?" I said, not sure I wanted to know the answer.

"Um…" They were at the part where the TV had begun to blare out its official government warning of the impending alien invasion. They'd already seen me asking Alexa to play party music at volume ten. Cringe.

"Just tell me," I said.

"Two thousand and eighty-one," Omar said.

"No, it isn't!" Arlo said. "That says *three* thousand

and eighty-one. You need your eyes testing, mate."

Omar adjusted his frames. "I was *trying* not to freak him out, genius."

"Damn." I kicked my shoe against the playground floor, stubbing my big toe.

"That's nothing," Omar said. "Your parents get two hundred thousand every time they post a boring video of you opening a box of fidget spinners."

"Three thousand is like one per cent of that," Arlo said. "So literally no one has seen Mason's video. A drop in the ocean."

"It's literally not no one," I said. "It's *literally* three thousand and eighty-one people. That's more people than there are at this school! Do you know what *literally* means?"

"Pfft." Arlo shrugged. "Maybe it will go in your favour. You might get famous. You could become a meme!"

"I'm already a meme!" I groaned. "Surely it's someone else's turn?"

I pictured the embarrassing video of me as a toddler where I looked right into the camera, tensed my whole body, then promptly filled my nappy to the brim. Years later Mum deleted it after I begged her to, but it was too late. People had already put their own captions to it, like "When the coffee hits right" or "Me when someone asks how I'm doing" or "Mentally I'm here".

"How are the comments?" I asked.

"They're ... *fine*!" Omar said, trying to sound light.

"Read one out to me. Any comment. Just pick one."

"Um…" muttered Arlo.

I turned round to see him scrolling through the comments, obviously searching for one that was kind enough to read aloud.

"Pick one!" I snapped. "The one you're on now. Just read it!"

"*LOL, I can't believe how much he freaked out. This just confirms Ethan is the annoying crybaby we all thought he was. Mason is the GOAT,*" Arlo read aloud, before looking away awkwardly. "Sorry, mate."

I blinked away the tears I felt forming in my eyes. *Annoying crybaby*. I was not going to give them the satisfaction of being right.

"Read another one," I said.

"*OMG, Ethan really is a sensitive flower, isn't he?*" Omar read to me. "That's from an account called BinBagBoy2023, so I wouldn't worry about that one."

"*Why* does everyone keep calling me *sensitive*?" I growled.

It came out too loud. A group of Year 3 kids playing

tag all stopped and looked at me, mouths agape like goldfish in a bowl.

"I wasn't talking to you!" I shouted.

"Here's another comment. *Hey, isn't this Mason from Year Eight?*" said Arlo. "*Can't wait to rip on him for this. Cringe!*"

"Awkward," Omar said. "I thought he was the most popular boy at St Hot Dog's."

"He is," I said. "It's probably just a troll."

"Viral Buzz is popping off too," Omar said. "This MumPoweredByLaughter is obsessed. *Morning #LaceyHaters! Is anyone else loving the Mason/Ethan drama lately? I'm sensing some serious trouble brewing.*"

"Wow," Arlo said, shaking his head. "Grown-ups really do enjoy the weirdest things."

"Maybe don't look at the comments for now," Omar said.

"Yeah, or *ever*, more like," said Arlo. "Just ignore it. Touch grass."

I nodded, biting down hard on my bottom lip to prevent any *sensitive* feelings from slipping out and making things worse.

"Would you guys have fallen for it?" I asked.

"Um…" Arlo hesitated, then pretended his phone had vibrated.

"Is that a buzzard?" Omar wandered a few paces away and squinted at the sky. "I think it could be. Or a kestrel of some kind…"

"Hello?" I shook Omar's shoulders. "I'm freaking out here!"

Arlo sighed. "Let's be real. I've seen the prank before. It's one of the oldest tricks in the online trick book."

"Great," I said. A new, fresh heat was creeping up my neck. I turned to Omar. "And you too?"

Omar nodded, then looked at his feet.

"I am *such* an idiot," I groaned.

They didn't agree, but they didn't disagree either. They just went quiet. For ages.

"So what are you going to do?" Omar said eventually.

"What do you mean, *do*?" I shook my head. "There is nothing anyone can *do* about Mason. He's out to make my life a misery and there's nothing anyone, let alone us, can *do*."

"Oh, come on, Ethan," Arlo said, flicking my arm playfully. "You don't have to take Mason's attacks lying down, you know. Fight back. Get punchy!"

Arlo started jabbing the air and shuffling around like a boxer in a ring.

"Arlo's right. Hit him where it hurts." Omar said. "There has to be a weak spot. If there's one thing I've learned from playing *Zombie Freakout Four*, it's that the enemy *always* has a weak spot."

"He doesn't have a weak spot," I said. "Everything about Mason is tough. He's got so many friends; everyone loves him. He's bigger than me too."

"*Everyone* has a weak spot," Arlo said, nodding his head slowly like a villain from a film. "It's just a matter of finding what it is."

"What do you propose we do?" said Omar.

"I reckon we follow him," replied Arlo. "Sooner or later, he'll slip up. And then *BAM*. We post it online. Everywhere. For everyone to see. Goodbye, MasonMayhem, and perhaps he'll give our Ethan here a bit of space too."

"When exactly are we going to have time for that?" Omar said. "My extra-curriculars are really ramping up at the minute. I've got Algebra Ninjas on Tuesdays now."

"What about tomorrow?" Arlo said. "Before school?"

I smiled, just with half of my mouth. It was a nice idea. But it would never, ever work.

After the bell, we went to Omar's house to plan more.

I liked Omar's house a lot. His family didn't sit in

separate rooms with the doors closed – they left the doors open and actually talked. *To each other.* There were no cameras. Everything was relaxed. The only rule was you had to take your shoes off.

"Hi, Ethan," Omar's mum said. "Hi, Arlo."

"Hi, Mrs Omar's mum!" we both replied.

"Nice to see you both," she said, laughing. "Are you staying for dinner? You're more than welcome."

I wasn't expecting to be asked for dinner, but now that she mentioned it, I liked the sound of it. How could I want to go home, where the only food was horrible recipes made up for views?

"What are we having?" Omar said.

"Chicken kabsa," she said. "Your favourite."

"Sounds great," Arlo said. "But what *is* that?"

"Come and see." Omar's mum beckoned me and Arlo into the kitchen.

Whatever she was making smelled amazing. She opened the lid of a huge metal pot and showed us rice swimming in a deep, scented liquid. Then she opened the oven door and showed us chicken pieces, coated in something that smelled unreal.

"Add chicken to rice, top with herbs and nuts, simple," she explained.

"Wow," we both said.

"It's really good," said Omar, joining us in the kitchen. "Mum's kabsa is the best I've had."

His mum smiled. "You would say that. Boys, you're very welcome. The more, the merrier. Just ask your parents first, OK?"

"Nice," Arlo said, bounding to the front door. "I'll go and ask Mum. Back in a sec."

"Are you *sure*?" I said. "Won't I be in the way?"

"In the way of what?" Omar's mum said. "It's the evening – we're not doing anything. It's family time, and friends are always welcome."

"But won't your dad be annoyed if—"

"*No!*" Omar and his mum laughed.

I went red. I'd forgotten that not every family spent their evenings filming. If I brought Omar and Arlo over for Meal-Prep Monday, we'd have to hide them from view, edit them out of the footage, pretend they weren't there. Not to mention Dad would get into an almighty huff.

"I've got your mum's number, Ethan," said Omar's mum. "Shall I call her for you?"

"OK," I said. My stomach rumbled. "That would be great."

19

There's a weird atmosphere in the house.

I'd just eaten the best meal of my life. I didn't even have any news for Fidget. How could I worry when we were too busy talking to Omar's parents and sister, eating that amazing food, followed by a brilliant dessert called kunafa? I waddled home, full to the brim.

My house was eerily quiet. Everyone was in separate rooms and none of the main lights were on. The mood was like a smell in the air.

I took myself to bed without even saying goodnight. I had to get a decent night's sleep. Tomorrow was going to be a big day.

*

It felt like I'd barely blinked, before hints of sunlight started peeping through my curtains. My alarm clock said it was 6:58, a time reserved for grown-ups with jobs and Christmas morning. At least I was awake early enough to execute Omar and Arlo's not-so-master plan.

I changed into my uniform, then held my breath while I snuck across the landing. The coast was clear. Dad's snores blared from the spare bedroom, accompanied by Colin's sleepy grunts. Mum's bedroom door was shut. Mason could have slept through an earthquake, so I didn't need to worry about him.

Reaching the hallway, I exhaled. It was happening. Silently, I stuffed my shoes on, then swung my backpack over my shoulder. Avoiding Colin's squeaky toys, I crept towards the front door, slipped out and closed it behind me with a click.

I was out. A chill hung in the morning air. Fallen leaves were scattered across the lawn. I tucked my hands into my pockets and hopped carefully between the paving slabs, careful not to crunch the gravel driveway. Before sliding through the gate, I peered up at the house. Not a peep. Not a single light bulb shining.

Surely it shouldn't be *that* easy. But this was only phase one. It was going to take a lot more luck for our plan to work out. If either Arlo or Omar got caught or overslept, the whole plan was a dud.

I waited under the conker tree on Seabrooke Street. The conkers still hadn't fallen. Only a few had started to turn ripe, their spiky cases browning and becoming soft.

Come on, guys. My fingers were cold. A sticky thought about frostbite formed in my mind. We'd learned about it in science. A human being's body temperature was supposed to be around 37 degrees Celsius. Hypothermia could set in if it fell below 35. Continued exposure to extreme cold could result in damage to the external flesh and… I shook the thought away, along with the gruesome pictures I'd seen online.

St Hot Dog's was twenty minutes away on the 45A bus. Since we didn't have bus passes, it was a forty-five-minute walk. If we wanted to arrive before Mason and the other boys, we didn't have time to wait.

I heard Omar and Arlo before I saw them, their coats and bags rustling through the mist. When they appeared, they were giggly, with bright red cheeks and noses.

"That was close, lads," Arlo said, plumes of hot air flowed from his mouth with each word. "My mum got up for a wee while I was putting my shoes on. I swear she was *this* close to catching me."

"Did she suspect anything?" I said.

"Nah," said Arlo. "Mum's a zombie in the morning. She's working lates, so she's on autopilot unless she has two massive coffees."

Omar nodded. "It felt like *Mission Impossible*. I had to avoid the motion sensor on the burglar alarm, deactivate the petcam *and* not trigger the smart doorbell. Anyone would think we're stashing rare diamonds or something, the layers of security!"

Arlo acted out ducking and diving between lasers like secret agents do in films.

"What about you, Ethan?" Omar said.

"Easy." I shrugged. "Everyone's in a mood in my house. They're all shut away in different rooms. Nobody wants to get out of bed. Even Colin can't be bothered."

"Nice work, BPCC comrades," Arlo said. "This is some proper espionage, you know. Hey, maybe we could all be in MI5. When we're a bit older, obviously. Imagine it, Blue Pencil Case Crew still going strong, taking care of national security and stuff. It'd be fire."

"Right. We'd better move," Omar said. "If we want to get dirt on Mason, we'd better find a way in before the place is swarming with hot dogs."

"Good shout," Arlo said. "As the only people not dressed in hot-dog outfits, we're going to stand out like sore thumbs."

The closer we got to St Mark's School for Boys, the more hot-dog uniforms we saw on the streets. Brown blazers, mustard ties, all heading in the same direction.

"What is this, some kind of hot-dog convention?" Arlo wise-cracked.

"Don't," said Omar. "That will be us in two years. We ought to consider organized protest. A petition to get them to change the uniform."

"As if. St Hot Dog's is stricter than Edison Grove. They'd make the uniform *worse* in retaliation," I said. "If that's even possible."

Arlo and Omar shuddered.

"Pink spotty blazers," Omar said.

"Or lime-green trousers with reflective stripes down the sides," Arlo said.

"Now that you've said that, the hot-dog uniform doesn't seem quite so bad," said Omar.

The school lurked at the end of St Mark's Street.

Squat concrete buildings tucked behind overgrown hedges and tall metal fences daubed with greasy black paint to stop robbers climbing over. Pigeons nested along every ledge. Bird poo decorated every window. The school was as ugly at its uniform.

A sign outside read: WELCOME TO ST MARK'S SCHOOL FOR BOYS. But someone had crossed out MARK'S and written HOT DOG'S in spray paint. They had painted helpful illustrations of hot dogs all over, just in case it wasn't clear.

"Isn't it charming?" Omar said sarcastically as we reached the school gates. "St Mark's School for Boys should be considered the eighth wonder of the world, I reckon."

I felt for Fidget's arm in my pocket. "It looks a bit—"

"Depressing," Arlo said. "Evil almost. It looks like a prison. Where's all the *colour*?"

"I have no idea," I said, shaking my head.

Edison Grove Primary was bright with murals, most of them designed by the students, including our own self-portraits: three badly painted figures with blue rectangles in their wonky hands, representing the Blue Pencil Case Crew. Painted above us were rainbows, a smiling yellow sun and birds flying through the sky.

"I'm not certain I want to go to St Mark's now," said Omar. "Maybe taking the eleven-plus won't be so bad."

"You can't! What about our pact?" Arlo cut in. "Or did that mean nothing to you? Just a fart in the wind, was it? You'd hate grammar school anyway. You don't even *like* English that much, especially not grammar. Is that what you want, to study commas and conjunctivitis clauses the whole time?"

"That's not—" Omar sighed and put his hand to his forehead.

"He's right," I said. "You *did* promise us, Omar."

In Year Three we made a pact not to break up the Blue Pencil Case Crew, no matter what. We would tough it out at St Hot Dog's together: brown shirts, mustard ties, the lot. But then Omar got chosen for the Gifted and Talented programme, where all the clever kids got to go on a residential and do clever things like toasting clever marshmallows over a clever bonfire. Miss Isaacs told Omar's mum she should look into grammar school. Then his parents started pushing him to do the eleven-plus exam, buying books and highlighters, even hiring a private tutor so he could do *extra homework* in the evenings.

"How is it fair to hold me to something I said ages

ago?" Omar moaned. "I'm in Year Five now. Times change. People grow."

"No. They. Don't," Arlo said. "If you even think about sitting that eleven-plus, I swear I'll—"

"Guys," I interrupted. "We're here to spy on my evil spawn of a brother, remember? Now, shall we wait for him behind those bushes, then follow him?"

"Pfft." Arlo looked bemused. "Obviously not. We have to go inside the school grounds."

"Go inside?" My hands began to shake. I wasn't sure if it was because of the cold or a sudden sense of doom. "I thought we were staying *outside*. Wouldn't going *inside* break quite a lot of rules? Isn't it *illegal* to enter another school's grounds?"

Arlo shrugged and gestured to Omar. "I don't know, ask Gifted and Talented here."

Omar sighed. "It probably isn't smart. But illegal? Nah."

Without hesitation, Arlo zipped up his coat to hide his green Edison Grove jumper. "Only one way to find out!"

"No!" I reached out to catch his hood, but missed. "We'll get caught!"

"Can't catch me!" he called as he sprinted through the gates.

Omar steeled himself and zipped his coat up to the chin. Like a skydiver barrel-rolling out of a plane, he winked, then launched himself towards the gates, not looking back to see if I was following.

I watched, frozen, as they darted into the staff car park and ducked behind a car. Arlo beckoned to me from their hiding spot.

Two competing brains argued in my head: Bad Ethan Brain who wanted to break the rules vs Good Ethan Brain who didn't.

GOOD ETHAN BRAIN: Come on, we both know this is stupid. Let's just go back to Edison Grove and pretend none of this ever happened.
BAD ETHAN BRAIN: Stupid? This might be our only chance to get dirt on Mason. Remember Mason? Your brother who's trying to ruin your life?
GOOD ETHAN BRAIN: You won't have a life to ruin if you get caught sneaking into St Hot Dog's. You'll be jailed for life. The showers will be ... communal.
BAD ETHAN BRAIN: Jail schmail. The worst you'll get is a detention. This is your chance to get revenge.

GOOD ETHAN BRAIN: Maybe revenge is overrated. Why not sit down with Mason and have a civil conversation over a glass of squash?

BAD ETHAN BRAIN: There was nothing civil about that video, which, might I add, is being watched right now, as we speak, by people everywhere. You've already sneaked out before school – what's one more little broken rule?

"Fine," I said, caving in. "I'll do it."

Checking the coast was clear, I legged it through the gates. Thanks, Bad Ethan Brain – you win again.

20

"There he is!" I said, finally spotting Mason's floppy dark hair in the bustling group of human hot dogs surging towards the school gates. "That's Mason!"

"Is it?" Omar squinted into the crowd. "Where?"

"I see him!" Arlo said. "The one with the green backpack and the smug walk."

Rage bubbled in my body. My jaw clenched; my eyelid began to twitch. His swagger made me furious. Chest puffed out, arms swinging, a wide grin as if he had been appointed King of the Universe and Best Human Ever.

"Yeah, yeah, we all know you're the most popular boy in Year Eight," I muttered.

We watched as Mason crossed the zebra crossing

and went through the gates. His mustard-yellow tie swung with every step.

He approached a circle of boys and said something to one of them. The boy responded, then turned away. Nobody made space in the circle for Mason to join.

Still grinning, Mason walked off and went over to two boys who were kicking a football back and forth. He ditched his backpack and started hopping from foot to foot, anticipating a pass.

"Over here!" he shouted, darting left and right. "I'm wide open!"

The boys kept kicking the ball back and forth, back and forth, but never his way.

"That's cool," Mason called out as he picked up his backpack. "Another time."

"Did you say most popular boy in Year Eight?" Arlo said.

"I was thinking the same thing," Omar said. "Early field studies are indicating this may not be accurate."

I couldn't believe what I was seeing. Why was everyone ignoring Mason?

Spotting someone else, Mason held his palm up for a high five, only for his hand to go unslapped. He ran his fingers through his hair and kept walking, face reddening.

"Commencing Operation Mayhem, phase two," said Arlo. "Follow the subject to his natural school-time habitat, undetected. Over."

Omar rolled his eyes. "Great plan, but you don't have to say '*over*'. That's only for walkie-talkies. We're right next to you."

"I know," Arlo replied. "I just thought it would be funny. Over."

"Quick, he's getting away!" Omar pointed.

Mason was jogging across the courtyard, occasionally glancing over each shoulder. Something had changed. He wasn't acting like the King of the Universe any more. He was hiding from something or someone, desperate not to be seen. We scurried out from our spot and dashed along the boundary of the car park, careful to stay out of Mason's eyeline.

"Why's he running?" Omar wondered. "Did he see us?"

"No idea," Arlo said. "But we can't let him out of sight. Over."

Checking behind himself again, Mason dashed across a gravel path that led to the reception, then ducked below the office windows. Next, he cleared a low wall and disappeared into a shadowy space between two buildings.

"What is he doing?" I said. "Why isn't he going to the playground like everyone else?"

"*Playground?*" Arlo said. "No offence, but that's very primary school of you. My cousin who goes here told me there's two places where cool people hang out between lessons. The basketball court or the canteen. That dark corner over there is neither."

"Good intel," Omar said. "Do we follow him? It could be a trap."

"We follow," I said, spurred on by Bad Ethan Brain.

The three of us crept out of the car park and headed down the gap between the two buildings. We squatted behind a bush at the end of the passageway.

"There he is," Arlo whispered.

Mason was sitting on a bench just metres away, one foot kicking at the concrete floor, scrolling aimlessly on his phone.

"Probably liking all the mean comments about me," I grumbled.

Mason looked in our direction, brow furrowed beneath his fringe.

"Shhh!" Arlo cupped his hand over my mouth and dragged me deeper into the bush.

Then Mason sat up straighter. Someone was coming. A much taller, older boy, with shoulders as broad as a wardrobe. He was blazerless – his shirt was untucked, and his tie was loose and short. He wore Nike trainers instead of proper school shoes. He even had a moustache.

"Thought you could hide from me, did ya?" said the older boy.

Mason stuffed his phone deep into his pocket, then shifted along the bench.

"Hi, Karl," Mason said. He sounded weak, like he was scared.

The older boy, Karl, grabbed Mason by his mustard-yellow tie, lifting him slightly from the bench. "Answer me, then! Are you hiding from me or what?"

"N-no, I—" Mason's feet scrambled on the ground as he was raised from his seat.

"Good. I'm glad. I thought we could have a little chat," Karl growled.

Mason swallowed. "OK," he rasped.

"So go on. Ask me how I am."

"H-how are you, Karl?"

The older boy snarled. "Me? Oh, I'm *angry*."

"This is brilliant," Arlo said. He was filming everything on his phone, zooming in on Mason's crumpled face. "Exactly the dirt you were hoping for. Right, Ethan?"

I wasn't sure. My hands were shaking. That was my brother over there, getting held up by his tie. Part of me wanted to run up behind Karl and kick the back of his knee. Then I'd grab Mason, fling him over my shoulder and carry him to safety.

But who was I kidding? I couldn't lift Mason. I couldn't fight to save my life. Karl would flatten me like a fruit fly on a ripe avocado. *Squish*. Plus, would Mason do the same for me? Probably not. He'd probably film it and put it online and take the mickey, just like he did with the alien invasion prank.

I watched Mason blinking furiously. "Really? Wh-why?" he squealed.

Karl's face was close to Mason's. "Why am I angry? Let me tell you… I'm angry because you and your stupid little channel are winding me up. Did you or did you not fill the PE changing rooms with fart bombs?"

"What?" Mason gasped.

Karl pulled harder on my brother's tie, his knuckles turning pale as his grip tightened. "Don't mess me about, Lacey. See, the reason I ask is that one of those fart bombs leaked on my blazer, and now my mum's had to throw it away. So who's going to pay for a new one? They're not cheap, you know, those manky blazers! Anything to say for yourself, Lacey?"

Mason struggled. "I don't know what you're talking about!"

"Really?" Karl barked. "So tell me why you're the first name on everybody's lips when I ask them about it?"

"I don't know! Somebody's framing me!" Mason yelped.

"Archie Maxwell reckons he heard you filming in the caretaker's cupboard. *'I can't wait to see how the lads react to this noxious stench!'* Ring any bells?"

"No!"

"You calling Archie Maxwell a liar? Archie Maxwell's one of my top four mates, you know."

Mason swallowed.

"It doesn't seem like you're very popular around here, does it?" sneered Karl.

Mason shook his head quickly.

"I can't hear you!" Karl yelled.

"N-no," Mason spluttered. "No, it doesn't."

"Just because you're *famous*, it doesn't mean you can get away with winding everyone up."

Karl suddenly released Mason, and my brother landed with a thud on the bench.

"I'll let you off this time," said Karl. "You'd better pray your name doesn't come up again, Lacey, or I'll make the rest of your time at this school a living *hell*."

Mason panted and fumbled to loosen his tie. His Adam's apple bobbed up and down like in a cartoon. A red rash covered his neck.

"Now go on," said Karl. "Back to your little mates. Oops, I forgot. You don't have any."

With that, the older boy stalked off. Mason straightened his blazer, then sniffed and wiped away the tears from his eyes. The bell rang and Mason walked away, rubbing the back of his neck.

I looked at Omar and Arlo. Their faces were blank with shock.

"That," said Arlo, "was epic."

21

Back at Edison Grove Primary, concentration was off the cards. I felt paranoid, as if Arlo, Omar and I all had *"WE SNUCK INTO ST MARK'S THIS MORNING"* written across our foreheads in permanent marker. It didn't help that we'd arrived fifteen minutes late, flushed from cold and panting from running across town.

I pretended to take notes on history, but I couldn't stop thinking about what I'd witnessed. The tightening of Mason's school tie around his neck. The popping-out veins in Karl's fist as his grip constricted.

"Isn't that right, Ethan?"

What?

I looked up. Miss Isaacs had caught me off guard.

"It was the *fleas* that carried the virus, was it not?" she said.

"Um." I looked at the smartboard, scanning for clues. Nothing. Arlo nodded discreetly in my peripheral vision. "Yes?"

"Very good," Miss Isaacs said. "You're with us, after all. Thought we'd lost you. Off on adventures again, were you?"

"No," I croaked. "Sorry, Miss."

She continued: "That, everyone, is partly the reason why rats had a reputation as dirty, unsanitary creatures. Because they carried the fleas that harboured the virus. But attitudes have changed. Hands up if you've ever had a *pet* rat…"

"Adventures?" I whispered to Arlo and Omar, leaning away from Luna. "Do you think she knows?"

Omar looked alarmed. "How would she *know*?"

Arlo rolled his eyes. "She will *know* if you two keep whispering about whether or not she *knows*."

"Knows *what*?" Luna butted in. "If you're trying to keep a secret, you're being pretty obvious about it."

I shook my head. "It's nothing."

"It's not nothing," Luna retorted. "You boys are up to something. Coming in fifteen minutes late, whispering between you. I smell a *rat*," she whispered, then chuckled at her own joke.

"Hello!" Miss Isaacs clicked her fingers at our table. "What's so important over here that it needs to be discussed during class?"

"I was just explaining to Ethan about the fleas," Luna piped up. "He didn't understand. He wasn't listening properly, Miss. He was too busy playing with his toy, Fidget."

"Thank you, Luna, for helping. Ethan, it's time to be present in the real world, OK? Less *You*Tube, more *Me*Tube." She pointed at herself, then laughed.

I swallowed dryness. "Yes, Miss."

With that, Miss Isaacs turned round and literally opened YouTube on the smartboard. "Time to watch a video!"

Miss Isaacs played a "History Made Awesome" video about the plague. It featured close-ups of painful boils and flea-ridden rats and dark London alleyways – aka my worst nightmares. There were several clips of fleas jumping up and down inside a jar, which made me itch. I held my feet up off the floor so no fleas would climb up my legs and into my trousers.

When the video ended, I realized with horror that

my face was on screen looking back at me. The "watch next" recommendation was from *Meet the Laceys*: "Meal-Prep Mondays: Make 4-Foot-Long Burritos With Us!"

"Whoops!" Miss Isaacs swiftly minimized the screen before too many kids saw. "So, does anyone have any questions on the bubonic plague?"

I slid down in my seat. The close-up images of pus-filled boils and scurrying rats followed by the thumbnail of our video were inducing an off-the-charts cringe attack.

My legs began to jiggle up and down. I wanted to get up and sprint home. There I could tell Mum and Dad about Mason and him being bullied. Maybe they could tell the school, and the teachers could find that boy Karl and expel him for the rest of eternity.

Then I remembered the divorce. Mum and Dad probably wouldn't have time for my nonsense.

But there was also Bad Ethan Brain, the part of me that wanted to tell everyone what we'd seen, rub it in Mason's face, tell him that I knew he was the *least* popular boy at St Hot Dog's and blackmail him for ever. But that wasn't very *kind*, was it? We were supposed to be *kind*.

"What's the matter, Ethan?" Miss Isaacs appeared

beside me. She lowered her voice. "Your legs are going like the choppers. Do you need the bathroom?"

"Yes, please," I said.

I didn't really; I needed to be alone for five minutes. I needed to think. I needed to feed my new secrets to Fidget so he could work his magic and free up some space in my head.

"Off you go," Miss Isaacs said. "Just ask next time. No need to wait."

Gripping my pencil, I shot out of my chair and sprinted to the door.

"That goes for everybody, Year Five," Miss Isaacs boomed. "If you need the toilet, just put your hand up, OK?"

Everybody laughed, even Arlo and Omar.

"Guys," she groaned. "That's enough!"

In the toilets, I checked my uniform for plague-infested fleas. None spotted, only the odd suspiciously flea-shaped piece of lint. No red bites on my ankles, only indented marks where my socks dug in. I put my hand on my forehead. No symptoms of bubonic plague ... yet.

In the mirror, my eyes looked grey and baggy. My brain felt overfilled, like a Build-A-Bear with too much stuffing inside, bursting at the seams.

I needed a haircut. I looked a bit like Mason, but not much. We had the same dark hair, except Mason had a fringe. We both had brown eyes, although Mason's were always rolling and mine were still. Mason was stronger and taller, but I'd catch up one day.

But I wasn't sure if Mason *was* strong. Especially since I'd seen the size of Karl. If Karl was a T-Rex prowling St Hot Dog's School, Mason was a mouse trapped under a plastic cup.

I washed my hands five times (to be *sure* there weren't any lingering toilet germs). Then I sat on the changing bench and took Fidget from my pocket. I double-checked I was alone, then unzipped his mouth.

"Ahhhh." He let out a long, deep breath. "Fresh air at last. Thanks, big man!"

"What a morning," I said to Fidget. "You're not gonna believe what I've got to tell you."

"Sounds like you've got a lot on your mind, Ethan," Fidget said. "Why don't you feed your old pal Fidget some of your worries? You know they're my favourite!"

I nodded with relief. "That sounds like a good idea to me, Fidget."

I took a paper towel from the dispenser and tore it into thin strips. Then I began to scrawl.

> We followed Mason to school today.

> Mason is being bullied by a boy called Karl.

> I don't think he has any friends.

And then, because Miss Isaacs' video was playing on my mind:

> I think I've got the bubonic plague.

> I probably caught it at St Hot Dog's.

> What if Colin has plague fleas?

One by one, I took the strips and stuffed them into Fidget's zippy mouth.

"Mmmm," he said. "Delicious yummy secrets. Nom."

After he'd finished his starters, I set about writing the main course.

> I don't know what's happening with Mum and Dad.

> I'm too scared to ask any questions.

Mason is ruining my life.

"Mmmmm," Fidget said, swallowing the strips of paper greedily. He was always so hungry when I had big feelings. "Keep those secrets coming, Ethan!"

Part of me wants to ruin Mason's life too.

"Mm-mm-MMM. This is some top-quality grub!"

After he burped, I packed Fidget away in my pocket, feeling better and worse at the same time. Miss Isaacs said some big feelings take a while to fade away.

Before heading back to class, I washed my hands once more, just in case there were any plague germs on the paper towel or on Fidget. You couldn't be too sure with things like that.

22

I took my time walking home that afternoon, after leaving Arlo and Omar. I stopped off at the park by our house just to waste time. When I finally got home, the mood was thick like the gravy at Sycamore Village. The curtains were drawn and the TV was playing to itself. Colin padded towards me from the kitchen. He whimpered like he needed something.

"Hello, boy," I said, dumping my backpack and school shoes on the mat by the front door.

I scratched behind his ears and booped his wet nose. Funny how his ears made me forget about potential plague fleas. Colin looked to me, then to the patio doors at the back of the house.

"Has nobody let you out for a wee?" I said.

Colin yowled at the word *wee*, then stamped his

paw, his claws clattered on the wooden floorboards.

"Come on, then," I said, heading to the patio doors and unlocking them.

Colin sprang outside and scurried off to relieve himself by the disused climbing frame. Then he zipped around the garden, buzzing at his new-found freedom.

"Have you been left behind?" I asked. "That's not very nice, is it?"

Colin looked at me, but didn't say anything because he's a dog. Then he went straight back to zoomies.

I played fetch with him, lobbing his spit-covered toy so hard it hit the garden fence. I tried not to think about the spit, even when my hands grew slimy.

After a few throws, I stepped inside and washed my hands with antibacterial soap. Then again, just to be sure.

"Mum?" I called. "Dad?" I didn't bother shouting for Mason.

No response. It was quiet as the middle of the night, but it was only five o'clock. Nobody was cooking dinner. There wasn't even a note. They could have at least left a quick "*Popped out for five mins*" or "*Lasagne in the fridge x*" message like they usually do.

I tipped a mound of Frosties into a bowl, pouring a

generous glug of milk over the top. I paused, milk in mid-flow. I thought I'd heard a creak, like one of the stairs groaning under someone's weight.

"Hello? Mum, is that you?"

Nobody replied. Just the sound of the TV news presenter saying something about "*unexpected growth in the economy despite inflation*", which made me think of balloons.

I took my cereal to the bottom of the stairs. I looked around the hall. Something seemed off. Different, somehow. Like someone had been in and left again. Was the curtain in a different place, or maybe one of my shoes? Probably my imagination.

My eyes flicked to my school bag. Had it moved from where I'd dropped it on the doormat? Had the zipper been open before, gaping like a black hole in space?

"Did you do that?" I said to Colin, stupidly expecting an answer.

He gazed at me and licked all around his mouth.

"I'll give you dinner in a minute," I told him.

I looked closer at my backpack. The blue cover of my maths jotter was poking out. I set the bowl on the bottom step and fell to my knees, tipping the bag upside down. Everything dropped out: pencils, books, an eraser, a crisp packet, followed by a torrent of crumbs.

Everything except Fidget. I'd put him in my bag for safekeeping after Luna snitched earlier.

My stomach leaped into my mouth. *He must be here*, I thought. *He must!*

I patted myself down, checked every pocket of my uniform and coat. I ran to the kitchen, but he was nowhere to be seen. I even checked the garden.

My head began to pound. I couldn't have lost Fidget. Maybe he had fallen out in the park or somewhere on the walk from school?

I would have to retrace my steps, walk all the way back, check every single nook along the way. I zipped up my coat, a hard ball of fear swelling in my throat. It wasn't only Fidget that was gone. It was the secrets inside him too.

I turned my bag completely inside out, ran my hands through every pocket and compartment. That's when a single piece of paper fell out, gliding like a leaf falling from a tree. It was made of letters of all different sizes and fonts and colours, cut and pasted on to the sheet.

It read:

Dear Ethan,

Fidget has come to stay with me. I am sure we will get on like a house on fire. Let's hope he doesn't spill any of your juicy little secrets.

From

?

My pulse was in my eyeballs. He'd been kidnapped.

"NO!" I shouted to myself. It echoed around the house. "You ABSOLUTE FOOL!"

Colin cowered away, tail between his legs.

"Not *you*, Colin!"

I pushed my face into my coat and screamed. The sound was strange, like I was underwater.

An idea came to me. I'd seen films with super-smart

dogs who could find lost things. Sniffer dogs, led by detectives in trench coats with magnifying glasses. Dogs could find anything, couldn't they?

"Colin!" I took his lead from the coat hook. "Walkies?"

He bounded up to me, tail swaying left to right, ham-slice tongue drooping from his mouth. That's what I liked best about Colin. He forgave anything for a walk or a treat.

I held up my empty school bag to Colin's nose. Hopefully Fidget's scent would still be inside.

"You need to find Fidget, OK?" I nodded on Colin's behalf, helping him understand. *"FIND FIDGET."*

Some tracker dog Colin turned out to be. *Not.* He found everything *but* Fidget on the walk. In fact, here's a list:

1. Several trickles of dog wee, usually at the base of lamp posts.
2. A bag of dog poo hung neatly from a tree branch like a horrible Christmas bauble. Why do people do that?
3. A fried chicken bone, carried in his mouth for a good ten minutes.

4. A discarded packet of Wotsits, which he promptly stuck his face into. His nose was covered in cheesy orange dust.
5. A pigeon that was way past its glory days. So past them that I could only describe it as dead and covered in maggots. Sorry about that.

None of Colin's findings helped deflate the balloon of dread that was inflating inside me. Somebody had taken Fidget and it would only be a matter of time until they unzipped his mouth, revealing the contents of my brain for all to see.

Colin and I walked in circles, but there was no sign. Colin grew tired, and so did I. It was no use. Fidget was gone, and so were all my secrets. I had this hollow feeling inside. Whatever was about to happen surely couldn't be good.

"Come on, Colin," I said. "Let's go home."

"Where've you been?" Mum said as I closed the door behind me. "I thought Colin had escaped for a minute. Then I saw the lead was gone and figured you'd taken him out."

"Yep," I said. "He needed a wee and no one was home."

Mum's face clouded over. "Sorry. I had to go out for a bit. Are you all right? You seem strange."

"Yeah," I said. I didn't want to tell her about Fidget. "I ran with Colin, that's all. To give him some exercise."

"Oh, you are good," Mum said. "Did you enjoy that, Colin? You've been a bit neglected today, haven't you?"

Colin licked Mum's face as she bent down to kiss him.

She recoiled. "Oh, lovely…" Then she turned to me. "Ethan, I saw Mason's video. I can ask him to edit—"

"It's too late. There's no point." Then I pushed past her and stamped upstairs. There were worse things to worry about now.

"Charming," I heard Mum say as I slammed my bedroom door. "Another one enters the terrible teens early."

23

All night I dreamed of Fidget. He was tied up, blindfolded, in a cold dark room. Somebody was holding him hostage. They weren't even feeding him secrets, only fish heads and gruel. Then I would wake up, pillow damp with sweat. Patting around me, I'd find that Fidget wasn't there. It wasn't a nightmare. It was real.

The next morning was Flora's birthday party at Lumpy's Soft Play Centre. I had completely forgotten, and I wasn't in the mood. But Mum said it was rude to flake, and by the time she dropped me off, everyone was crashing around, screaming, touching the buffet with their hands, covering it with germs. My hand crept into my pocket on instinct, searching for Fidget to squeeze. I tried squeezing air, but it wasn't the same. It turns out that air can't be squeezed, even if you really want to. I stayed vigilant. The culprit was out there somewhere. Even the Blue Pencil Case Crew weren't above suspicion.

"Ethan," Arlo whispered while everyone sung "Happy Birthday". "You good? My readings are saying your vibes are off today."

"Yeah." Omar leaned in. "You keep fidgeting—"

"What was that?" I hissed, rounding on him. "What did you say about Fidget?"

Omar held his palms out. "Whoa, whoa, whoa, I'm just saying. You're jigging your knee so much you're shaking the whole table."

"He's right," Luna said. "Look at my card for Flora. It's all wobbly because of you. If you had a pen licence, you'd understand the importance of a stable writing surface."

"Sorry, Omar," I said, blinking through tears. "I thought you said something else."

At pick-up time, Luna bounded over with her friends, her top-of-the-range mobile phone in hand.

"Your brother's posted another video," she said in a sing-song voice. "It's about *you*."

"What? About *me*?" I asked.

"That's what I said, isn't it?" Luna said. "Maybe you need your hearing checked."

The girls all laughed as if that was the funniest thing ever.

"Let me see!" I reached for Luna's phone.

"No can do, I'm afraid." Luna snatched her hand away. "This phone is brand new and I'm not allowed to let anyone touch it."

"Don't be harsh," Arlo said. "Let him see it! Or at least tell him what it's about."

Luna pretended like she was mulling it over, then eventually she said with a smirk, "It's about that weird fidget teddy you carry around with you."

I felt like a football had smacked me in the face. *Mason*. My hands curled into tight fists. Mason took Fidget. He'd been in the house the whole time. I should have known. Obviously, I should have known.

"He can't," I muttered. "He couldn't—"

"What was that?" Luna flicked her eyes towards me.

"Maybe *you* should get *your* hearing checked," I snapped.

A long silence followed.

"That's so not OK," said Imogen. "We're going to have to tell Flora's mum that you said that."

"Yeah, that's too far," Daisy said. "If you can be anything in this world, be kind."

"But she said it first!" I blurted out.

Luna and her gang were already skipping away, yelling at the top of their voices.

"Here," Omar said, holding out his phone. "If you really want to see."

I tried to search for *MasonMayhem*, but my fingers kept slipping and pressing the wrong keys. Finally, Arlo took the phone from me. His eyes widened.

"How many views has it got?" I asked, frantic. "I *said*, how many views has it got?"

"Don't worry about the views," said Arlo.

"How can I not worry about the views?"

"Here you go, mate," said Arlo, passing the phone to me. "Just promise us you won't freak out, OK?"

"How can I promise that?"

It took a few seconds for my brain to register what my eyes were seeing. There was a thumbnail of Mason holding Fidget. My Fidget. My heart squirmed.

The video was titled "Secrets From My Brother's Anxiety Toy".

"No!" I stumbled, everything spinning around me. I didn't care in which direction I ran; I needed to get away.

"Where are you going, Ethan?" called Omar. "Don't drop my phone!"

"Leave him," I heard Arlo say. "He needs to watch it by himself."

Hiding behind a bush, I pressed "play".

The video opened with a mugshot, like the photos of criminals when they're taken to jail. There was a height marker drawn in pen that said "19cm". In front of that stood Fidget.

The view switched to Mason striding across his bedroom. He swung his desk lamp into Fidget's face so it lit him up like in an interrogation.

"Name?" Mason said in a gruff, bad American accent.

"*Fidget*," said Fidget, which was Mason doing a stupid high-pitched voice. It was the exact same voice he used to repeat whatever I said back at me.

MASON: Age.
FIDGET: I don't have an age. I'm not even real.
MASON: I see. Do you know why you're here, Fidget?
FIDGET: No. I ain't done nothing wrong, sir!

My molars began to grind. Fidget didn't have a cockney accent. Mason didn't know anything about him.

> MASON: You've been arrested for the charge of secret-smuggling.
> FIDGET: I never done it! I'm innocent. Innocent, I tell you!
> MASON: Our investigation has concluded that you are hiding important secrets from the authorities.
> FIDGET: Am not!
> MASON: Secrets belonging to our mortal enemy: one Ethan Lacey – aka Sensitive Ethan, aka Little Flower, aka LLB, Loser Little Bro.
> FIDGET: Ethan Lacey? Never even heard of him! Whoever he is, he sounds like a huge poo-poo head to me!

Burning heat spread through me like when I borrowed Mum's electric blanket. Everyone was going to think I was a baby.

> MASON: Well, I have to agree with you on that. Nevertheless, smuggling secrets is a crime of huge severity in Masonland!

FIDGET: I haven't done it, I promise! I never smuggled any secrets!

MASON: Oh, really? Then what are these?

In one quick move, Mason unzipped Fidget's mouth and shoved his fingers down his throat. Fidget screamed and gargled while Mason rummaged through the contents of his stomach, until he finally pulled out a tiny scrap of paper. My mouth went completely dry, like one of Grandad's biscuits.

"Bleurgh!" Fidget exclaimed. "What did you do that for?"

"Let the records show that a secret has been extracted from Fidget's stomach." Mason held the strip of paper close to the camera.

"I swear, sir. I've never seen that before in my life!"

Mason slowly unfurled the paper.

"*I'm scared I'll wet the bed at Omar's sleepover,*" Mason read out robotically. Then he smirked. "Is that so, Ethan? I wonder if there are more where that little gem came from?"

Mason tipped Fidget upside down while he screamed. More slips of paper fell from Fidget's mouth, tumbling and swirling in slow motion. Every little secret, worry or thought I'd ever fed to Fidget rained down and covered Mason's desk like snow.

"Wahey!" Mason pumped the air. "Is that a jackpot or what? Looks like Fidget's really spilled the beans on my kid brother. This is going to be one epic video, guys."

"Please, sir," Fidget said. "What's going to happen to me!"

"Prison!" Mason announced, banging his desk like a judge. "Prison for the rest of your days!"

"*Noooo!*" Fidget screamed. "*Please, sir, have mercy!*"

The next shot showed Fidget flying through the air in slow motion, spinning and spinning until he landed in Mason's bin with a thud.

The video cut to Mason at his desk.

"Guys, I'm just kidding. Fidget will live to see another day. Once he's served his sentence, that is. I'm a very fair judge."

My eyes burned. I'd spent all night looking for Fidget, and the whole time he'd been stuck at the bottom of Mason's bedroom bin with old banana skins and crisp packets.

Mason grinned at the camera. "Now's your chance to grab a snack and a beverage. Get comfortable. Because we're gonna be diving deep into my kid brother's deepest, darkest fears."

Omar's phone slipped from my hands and tumbled to the ground. It didn't smash, thankfully.

Mason's voice continued: "First of all, loyal *MasonMayhem* viewers, why don't you do me a favour and smash that 'subscribe' button down there? Then let the mayhem commence."

24

The video was twenty-five minutes long by the time Mason got to the final secret. He read them with glee, his grin widening with every word. By the time I looked up, Arlo and Omar were the only people in Lumpy's car park, waiting for me to walk home.

Here's just ten of the worst secrets that Mason spilled.

1. I'm scared I'll wet the bed at Omar's sleepover.
This annoyed me because I wasn't being serious. I hadn't wet the bed since … well, long enough for it not to be a concern. It was just a pesky little thought, like a sticker on an apple: annoying but easy enough to peel away.

2. *I HATE my brother Mason. I wish he would disappear.*

In fairness, I was glad Mason read this one, because it was true. Mum says "hate" is a very strong word, but when it comes to Mason, it's perfect. Not that he cared. He smirked, rolled his eyes, then moved on.

3. *Mum's shepherd's pie is the WORST.*

This one hurt. I felt guilty, like I never should have written it down in the first place. Picturing Mum spending hours in the kitchen, mashing potato and browning beef made my eyes sting, even though shepherd's pie made me gag. I think it's the carrot chunks. I crossed my fingers that she would never watch the video, but I knew she would. Everyone would.

4. *I HATE going on hikes with Dad.*

This one was just as bad. I didn't even know why I'd written it, probably just to be mean. I didn't hate the hikes, honestly. Sometimes walking up hills was hard, that's all. Sometimes I wanted to stay at home and watch TV. Is that a crime?

5. I stole Luna's invisible ink pen in Year Two.
I admit it, it's true. It was eating me up inside. I wouldn't have done it if I'd known it would still be preying on my mind three years later. I don't have a good reason: I simply wanted it. It was so cool – the way the UV light revealed the secret messages. Sometimes the memory of stealing the pen came to me at night and I would lie in bed, imagining the police circling above the house in a helicopter. Well, they'd definitely be coming for me now.

6. I think there's flesh-eating mould in the PE changing rooms.
Mason had a good old laugh. He really threw his head back so I saw the back of his throat. It's all well and good for him – they probably don't even have that mould at St Hot Dog's.

7. What if I never get good at Zombie Freakout 4?
This wouldn't have been such a big deal if I hadn't told everyone, including Arlo and Omar, that I'd completed it on hard. In reality, I always

died on the first level, even on story mode. I'd watched Mason complete it. Admittedly, I saw most of it through the gaps in my fingers.

8. *I'm going to fail my SATs next year and my life will be OVER.*
Mathematical reasoning was keeping me awake at night. I could practically hear Miss Isaacs saying "Show your work! Show your work!" Most of the time I wrote random numbers and symbols, crossing things out to make it look like I'd tried, even though I always gave up.

9. *Luna is a bully, but I can't say anything because our mums are best friends.*
If the previous Luna-related confession didn't make me want to change schools, this one did. Luna and her gang knew how to make life difficult, that's for sure.

10. *I don't want to be a part of Meet the Laceys any more.*
If Mum and Dad saw this one, it would kick off World War Three. I knew what Dad would

say. "If you're not a part of *Meet the Laceys*, you might as well not be a part of the Lacey family at all!"

"Is it bad?" Omar said.

He and Arlo stood a few paces away, as if they were scared I might explode.

I nodded.

"How bad are we talking?" Arlo said. "Life ruining or just a bit cringe?"

"The first one," I said. My voice sounded strange and tight. "It's bad."

"Well, we promise not to watch it," Omar said. "Don't we, Arlo?"

"Totally, totally." Arlo nodded. "We already see enough of you. Don't need to watch videos about you as well." He tried to laugh, but it sounded fake.

"Do you guys have to go home now?" I said.

"Nah," Arlo said. "As long as I'm back before dinner—"

"Same," Omar said.

"Good. I've come up with a plan."

"Wh-what kind of plan?" Omar asked.

"First, we get Fidget back. Then we take him down."

25

"Is it recording?" I asked.

We were in the park near my house. It was chilly, but we couldn't risk being overheard at home. I'd already found Fidget at the bottom of Mason's bin, sticky with residue and covered in crumbs. Now he was safe and sound in my pocket.

"I don't know!" Omar said. "It's too heavy."

Omar held Dad's expensive camera so shakily it made me wince. Dad made no secret of how much it cost. An eye-watering amount – more than some cars, apparently. I sometimes thought he cared more about the camera than me, the way he babied it and wrapped it up after every use. I hadn't had a hug from Dad in ages.

"There should be a flashing red dot. And *be careful*,"

I warned. "If that camera gets broken, it will take me the rest of my life to pay Dad back."

"I'm trying," Omar said. "It's my hands. They get so sweaty when I'm nervous."

"Give it here," Arlo said, wrenching the camera away. "You can be the director."

Omar looked relieved. "If it means I don't have to handle the sacred camera, then I'm happy."

We'd told Omar's and Arlo's parents that we were meeting for a Saturday hangout. We said we'd play video games at mine, go to the park, basically enjoy some wholesome fun. They said yes, obviously. Little did they know we had planned to record the most explosive online exposé of 2026.

Filming it was one thing; but posting it online was another. We would decide later whether or not to make it public. Arlo said that Mason's secret was gold dust, and we should keep our cards close to our chest for when Mason really crossed the line. I thought he'd crossed the line already, and I was ready to go, go, go.

"Have you thought about what you're going to say?" said Arlo.

I shrugged. I hadn't. I wanted to tell the truth. I couldn't keep writing everything down and stuffing it into Fidget, especially now. I felt like a glass of drink fizzing over; there were just too many secrets to keep inside.

"I think it's recording," Arlo said. "Action!"

"What the *actual*? You said I was the director. Directors say 'Action', not camera guys."

Arlo rolled his eyes. "Fine, Omar. You say it, then."

"Thank you." Omar raised his eyebrows. "Action!"

I took a deep breath, readying myself to change my family's life for ever. Then I burst out laughing. The giggles spread through us like a cold. First Arlo, then Omar folded at the waist.

"Cut!" Arlo said.

"Arlo! I'm the one that gets to say 'Cut'!" Omar huffed.

Arlo rolled his eyes. "Fine. On you go."

"Cut!" called Omar.

"Sorry," I said, still doubled over. "It's weird, that's all."

"I thought you were used to this kind of stuff," Omar said.

"I am," I replied. "Just not with you two around."

"Oh no," Arlo said. "Look who's here."

"What are you losers up to?" Mason was striding down the path towards us. "Giggling like a bunch of girls."

Arlo hid the camera behind his back. "Nothing."

"What's it to you, anyway?" Omar said bravely. "It's none of your beeswax what we're up to."

"Oh, is that so?" Mason said, squaring up to Omar. "It is my beeswax when I can hear your voices all the way across the park. Especially yours, Omar. *I'm the one that gets to say 'Cut'!*" He said the last part in a cruel, high-pitched voice.

Omar wilted.

"Leave us alone, Mason," I said. "If you don't go away now, I swear I'll—"

"Oh, if it isn't my sensitive flower of a little brother acting tough," he sneered.

"Don't call me sensitive," I growled. "I don't want anything to do with you. You're *not* my brother."

Mason blinked, then blinked again. "Is that so? Well, lucky me. My life just got ten times easier."

"Me too. Now go away."

"Sick. I'm going out with the lads anyway. Off to a party. Everyone will be there. Year Elevens and everything. Girls too. You wouldn't understand. You have to be *cool* to be invited."

With that, he turned on his heel and strode away.

"Sorry about him," I said. "Are you OK, Omar?"

"Yeah." He nodded, but his glistening eyes said otherwise.

"There's no party, is there?" Arlo said, shaking his head. "We all know there's no party."

We stood surrounded by the atmosphere Mason left behind like a bad smell.

"Right. Let's do this," Arlo said. He pointed the camera at me.

"Action!" said Omar.

I exhaled.

"Hi, guys, and welcome to my channel."

I spoke for an hour, until my throat was dry and my voice croaked. Once I started I couldn't stop. One time, I saw a viral video of some engineers unclogging a dam. The moment they released the valve, millions of litres of muddy water shot out at breakneck speed and almost destroyed a city downstream. That's what I felt like. My words were muddy water. My family were the city, going about their days with no idea what was about to hit them.

I didn't hold back. My feelings about *Meet the Laceys*, Mum and Dad's divorce and how they'd forced us to keep it secret. Finally, I doubled down on Mason, revealing how MasonMayhem was nothing but an act – how he's the most unpopular kid at St Hot Dog's School. I described in detail how that boy Karl grabbed him by the tie and yelled at him to the verge of tears. How Mason's feet had scrambled for footing while he was dangled above that bench.

When I finally stopped talking, the silence felt thick and murky.

"Wow." Arlo looked shellshocked. "That was—"

"A lot," said Omar.

"I don't have a choice," I said. "It's me or Mason. If I don't ruin him, he's going to ruin me. Who knows what he's planning next? It might even involve you two."

"You're right," Arlo said. "He needs stopping. We get that about Mason … but we didn't know there was so much other stuff going on."

I looked at the ground, words escaping me.

"Is that true about your mum and dad?" Omar said. "The … divorce and everything?"

"Because if it is, it doesn't have to be a big deal," Arlo said. "My parents aren't together and I don't even think about it. It just means I have to go bowling with Dad way more than before, but that's it."

I nodded. "It's true. But don't tell anyone until the video goes live. *If* it goes live."

"We promise. Don't we, Arlo?" Omar said, miming a zip across his mouth, just like Fidget's.

Arlo did the same. "We won't say a word."

"Not even to your parents, OK?" I said, looking them in the eye.

They both nodded. I noticed my hands were shaking. It felt good and bad to let it all out.

I sighed. "It doesn't exactly help that Mason's out to get me at the exact same time. It would be ten times easier if he wasn't constantly ragging on me."

"That's why we need to take him down," Arlo said. "Show the world he's not the Mr Popular that he pretends he is. He's nothing but a victim who takes it out on younger kids."

"You're right," I said. "Have you still got that footage of Karl nearly strangling him with his tie?"

"You bet I have," Arlo said. "It's backed up and password protected. Had to be sure."

"So what will you call your channel?" Omar said, changing the subject. "Mason's got *MasonMayhem*. What will you be?"

I shook my empty head. I hadn't thought about a

channel name. I didn't want a channel; I just wanted to tell my side of things. I could have borrowed Dad's laptop and uploaded the video to *Meet the Laceys*, but I didn't know the password. I'd tried to guess it before, when I wanted to delete an old video. The one where I fell over and badly grazed my forehead in this very park. It was so sore I cried for ages, with snot coming out of my nose and everything.

Anyway, I'd tried all the obvious passwords: *MeetTheLaceys*, *Password*, *Password123*, *Colin*, *GeoffLacey*, *DadOnTheRocks*. I even tried *Ethan*, plus every variation of my birthday. Wrong, obviously. Yet more proof he doesn't even care about me.

"What about *EthanExtreme*?" Arlo said.

"Nothing about me is extreme, Arlo," I said, rolling my eyes. "Except my extreme inability to do maths."

"What about *EthanExplains*?" Omar said. "Because you're literally Ethan, and you're … explaining everything."

A beat passed.

"I like it," I said. "I like it a lot."

Omar beamed. "Cool. How do we get it set up?"

"We need to lie," I said. "We have to pretend I'm thirteen – one of you needs to set up a fake adult account to give me parental permission."

"That sounds illegal," Omar said, his eyes widening in fear.

"It probably is," I said.

"Well, I'm out, then," said Omar.

"Wait a second," Arlo said. "Omar, don't you have YouTube on your phone?"

"Yeah," he said, taking his phone reluctantly from his trouser pocket. "Why?"

"By any chance, is your mum's account logged in?"

Omar tapped at the screen a few times, then squinted to look closer. "Yep. It's her account. 'Green Shakshuka Recipes' … 'Best of Korean Skincare 2026' … Yeah, it's definitely her."

"Fire," Arlo said. "This might be easier than we first thought."

26

Around five o'clock, Omar's mum phoned and said he had to come home for tuna pasta bake. She invited me and Arlo over too, but I said I had to have dinner at mine.

I stayed in the park to do some solo swinging. The back-and-forth motion helped me stop thinking, even if it did make me feel a bit sick. It would be my home time soon, not that anyone would notice.

I couldn't decide whether to post the video. On one hand, I wanted to teach Mason a painful lesson. And I wanted Mum and Dad to stop lying and realize what they'd done. On the other hand, once it was posted, it couldn't be unposted. The Lacey family laundry would be hanging out for the world to see, complete with pants with holes and poo stains and everything. Mum and Dad would never forgive me.

I took Fidget out from my pocket. He felt weird without his tummy full of paper secrets. He was empty, his fabric all baggy and loose. I felt guilty. It was my job to feed him, not anybody else's.

"*Please, Ethan,*" Fidget said. His voice was weak and feeble. "I'm so hungry."

"I'm sorry, Fidget," I said. "I can't."

"But why?" Fidget was pleading. Begging. "I'm *starving.* Even just a morsel would do… A tiny regret? A silly thought?" He coughed and spluttered, as if he was dying. "It doesn't have to be anything juicy…"

"I'm sorry," I said, squeezing Fidget's squishy arm. "What if Mason steals you again? Maybe I'm too old for this anyway. I'm ten now."

"But they're my p-p—" Fidget was starting to fade. "My primary food source!"

"I'm sorry!"

I stuffed Fidget into my pocket and zipped it shut. I could hear his muffled groans through my coat.

It was quarter past five. A breeze snaked up my sleeves and trouser legs, prickling my skin with cold. Still, I wasn't keen to get home. I shuffled back at a snail's pace, even walking to the dead end of Maple Close to waste time.

The real reason I couldn't go to Omar's for dinner was that Mum and Dad wanted us to film a video where we reviewed the top ten Christmas presents of the year. Companies had been sending things for weeks, and the spare room was starting to resemble a warehouse. I wasn't in the mood to think about Christmas, let alone be in a video where I'd have to smile and laugh and say how *amazing* everything was. *Amazing, amazing, amazing.*

Let's be clear: nothing was amazing.

"Cut!" Dad yelled. "What is going on with you boys?" He stood in front of the ring light, silhouetted. "Why aren't you smiling?"

"You do need to smile, boys," Mum said. "We can't exactly do a 'Ten Best Christmas Gifts of 2026' video with both your faces like thunder, can we?"

"Better?" I grinned sarcastically. "I don't feel like smiling. He just spilled my secrets to the whole of the internet, if you hadn't noticed."

"We've asked Mason to apologize," Mum said, "but it sounds like he hasn't."

"*Sorry*," said Mason cruelly. "Sorry you're so

sensitive you need an Anxiety Monster to store up your worries."

"Mason!" Dad said. "If you carry on like this, I'll be asking you to delete your channel."

"Just try it!" Mason said. "You don't know the password anyway!"

"It's probably MasonStinks1234!" I snapped.

The vein in Dad's forehead began to pulse. He sighed so deeply his breath rustled my hair. "Can you two pack it in, please? I know there's a lot going on right now—"

"Geoff." Mum raised a hand, interrupting Dad. "Maybe we're asking too much—"

"Don't put your hand up to me like that," Dad snapped. "You're always doing that. It drives me mad." He gave another massive sigh.

"Well, you're always sighing like *that*," Mum replied, sighing in an exaggerated fashion. "It's like living in a wind tunnel with you sighing all over the place."

"Oh, great. So it's all my fault now, is it?" Dad retorted.

"No." Mum rolled her eyes. "I was saying maybe we're expecting too much. All this content. There's a lot going on at the moment."

"Well, we need to keep filming," huffed Dad. "The content doesn't produce itself, does it? Or do you not want money and food and central heating?"

"I wasn't saying that," said Mum. "I meant—"

"They don't know how easy they have it, these boys," Dad continued. "Look at them! They can't even crack a smile."

Dad was always going on about how *easy* me and Mason had it, because he had to do a paper round and shovel horse poo at a stable when he was growing up. I would rather shovel horse poo than film "Ten Best Christmas Gifts of 2026" any day.

"Oh, here we go," Mason said, rolling his eyes again. "*I had to shovel horse poo from the age of seven*. Heard it all before, Pops. Change the channel."

"How dare you?" Dad turned the colour of a Royal Mail post box. "Get up to your room THIS INSTANT!"

"YOU DON'T HAVE TO SHOUT!" Mum shouted, standing up to face Dad.

Colin fussed and pawed at the door.

"I'll gladly go," Mason said, storming from the living room. "Anything to get away from you losers. You can stick your Ten Best Christmas Gifts up your—"

"Watch your mouth!" roared Dad.

Mason made sure to stomp as hard as he could on each stair.

"He's the loser," I muttered.

"Try to give him space, Ethan," Mum said. She looked tired. "He's just being a teenager. It's his hormones. If you've got something to say, feed it to Fidget."

"I *can't* feed it to Fidget!" I shouted, kicking a freshly unboxed Deluxe Foot Spa across the room.

"Don't you DARE kick that!" Dad picked up the foot spa, cradling it like a newborn baby. "That foot spa was *gifted* to us in return for an honest review. It's not a football!"

"Oh, shut up, Geoff." Mum kicked the empty foot-spa box. "If you love that foot spa so much, why don't you marry it?"

"Because *clearly* marriage is a waste of time," Dad snapped.

Mum burst into tears. Whatever she replied, I couldn't understand. Her voice was gloopy, her words all merged into one strange sound.

"Oh, for goodness' sake." Dad powered down the camera and lights. "So much for filming."

I wasn't sticking around. I made sure to slam the living-room door as hard as I could on the way out. I was no better than Mason.

27

Later that night, I listened to the sound of Mum and Dad fighting. Like a boiling pot, their pitch and volume only bubbled higher. Words like "ridiculous" and "stupid" and "Mason" and "Ethan" floated upstairs. Then there were other noises: a cup smashing, the front door slamming, footsteps crunching on the gravel driveway.

Afterwards, all I could hear was Mum's sobbing mixed with the zombie groans and gunfire blaring from Mason's computer.

I didn't know what to do. *Maybe I should go downstairs and find Mum*, I thought. *Make her a cup of tea with four biscuits on a saucer.* I knew her favourites: custard creams, bourbons, coconut macaroons and jam faces. But then I heard her crying harder and

I wondered if this situation was beyond four biscuits – or even a whole packet – and a cuppa.

I rolled over. Fidget was sitting on my pillow, watching me.

"It's all going to be OK," he said weakly. "If you're worried, why don't you write it down and feed it to me?"

"Stop it, Fidget. You know I can't do that. You're making me feel bad!"

I'm not proud of it, but I picked him up and launched him against my bedroom wall. He landed on the carpet with a thud.

"Ouch."

Guilt washed over me. What had I done? Nobody deserved to be thrown against a wall like that. Except maybe Mason. But *definitely* not Fidget.

I pushed my covers aside and picked him up, cradling Fidget as I walked back to the bed. He was winded. The urge to cry solidified in my throat.

"I'm sorry, Fidget," I whispered. "I'm so sorry."

"It's OK, Ethan," Fidget panted. "It didn't even hurt, honestly!"

"I didn't mean it. I'm a monster—" I couldn't catch my breath. My hands wouldn't stop shaking.

"You're no monster. I'm the only monster here," Fidget said. "It was fun. Like flying!"

I laughed, wiping snot from my nose with my forearm.

"Sure, it was a bit of a crash-landing," he said, "but Fidget's as tough as old boots."

I wasn't convinced. Without the secrets inside him, he looked baggy and sunken. One of his button eyes had come loose, hanging on by a thread. He was hungry. He needed to eat. But I couldn't feed him. Not with Mason around.

The doorbell chimed. Maybe Dad was back. I padded to the landing and waited in the dark. I heard Mum talking, then the front door clicking shut.

"Thanks," Mum said, sniffing. "Thank you for coming over. I didn't want you to see me like this…"

"Don't be silly." I recognized Oonagh's voice. "That's what mum besties are for. Plus, I didn't come empty-handed."

Mum laughed hoarsely. "Nothing a nice Pinot Grigio can't help with, I'm sure."

"I'll get the glasses." Oonagh's shoes clattered into the kitchen. "Where's Geoff?"

"I don't know," Mum said. "Gone. God knows where."

"Start from the beginning. What happened?" said Oonagh.

Mum sighed. "We were filming this *stupid* video. 'Top Ten Christmas Gifts'."

"*Nightmare*," Oonagh said. A cork popped and liquid glugged into a glass. "Just what you needed."

"The boys didn't want to film. I didn't either," Mum said. "But we have to upload it tomorrow, and Geoff gets so *stubborn* when it comes to deadlines."

"It's not an easy life, this influencer stuff," Oonagh said. "You know better than most. I'd say it's one of the hardest jobs in the world, actually."

"The boys weren't smiling enough," Mum went on. "None of us were smiling enough, apparently. Then he got all uppity about it and we ended up having a row."

"But you'll make up, won't you?" A pause. "Annabel? Is there anything you want to tell me, about you and Geoff?"

I held my breath. Was Mum about to tell Oonagh about the divorce? She couldn't! She specifically told us not to tell a soul.

"No, no." Mum exhaled slowly. "We're stressed, that's all. There's a lot going on behind the scenes."

"Such as?"

I crept back into my room, and found my notepad and a pencil on my desk. I was like a lion, hunting for prey. Hunting for Fidget's next meal. OK, he preferred to eat my worries, but surely someone else's couldn't hurt?

"I just feel so guilty," Mum was saying.

"About what?"

"About everything." Mum took a sip of her drink. "About Dad, for a start. He should be here, not at Sycamore Village. But I can't look after him."

I scribbled down:

> Mum feels guilty about leaving Grandad in Sycamore Village.

"You *mustn't* feel guilty—"

"And I wish the boys would get along." Mum was crying again. "They're always at each other's throats. They never agree."

> Mum wishes we would get along.

Oonagh made reassuring noises. "All siblings are at each other's throats. Me and my sister used to practically tear each other's hair out—"

"And I hate the channel," blurted Mum. "I hate what it's done to my life. I *hate* being recognized. I *hate* always being a product."

Mum hates the channel.

"Listen," Oonagh said. "Take a social media hiatus. All you do is post a screenshot from your notes app, something about needing a break for your mental health. The subscribers will lap it up and—"

"You don't get it," Mum said sharply. "I'm scared my family's falling apart."

Mum's scared our family is falling apart.

Neither of them spoke for ages.

"Right," Oonagh said at last. "I think you'll be needing another glass."

28

Dad wasn't home when I woke up the next morning. Hours passed, the especially slow and boring hours that belong to Sundays. Mason left his bedroom only to go to the toilet, slamming his door harder and harder with every return. Mum aggressively cleaned the house, scrubbing harder and vacuuming for longer than ever before.

Dad came home around one in the afternoon, his footsteps crunching as he approached the house. I heard the door click, then the vacuum cleaner powering down. Followed by an angry conversation, muffled through the carpet.

"Ugh. You smell like a brewery," I heard Mum say. "Where've you been?"

Dad said something about hiking with his friend Alan. They stopped somewhere for drinks. Something about a futon and how Cathy didn't mind.

"Oh, I should have known. *Alan…*" Mum replied, then I couldn't make out the rest.

I was confused. I thought Mum liked Alan and Cathy. Whenever they visited us, Alan and Dad watched football, while Mum and Cathy drank fizzy wine from thin glasses in the kitchen.

More muttering followed, then Dad began to climb the stairs, sighing as he reached the top. I got up and pressed my ear to the bedroom door. Dad's footsteps lingered outside his old bedroom, next door to mine, but then shuffled to the end of the landing to the spare room. The sofa bed creaked under his weight. It was not a comfortable place to sleep.

The front door clicked again. Now Mum was the one storming off.

Dad groaned – as did the springs in the sofa bed – when I turned on the light in the spare room. If I didn't know how a brewery smelled before, I did now. I didn't like it much. It was a weird smell that took over the room and made it stuffy.

"Ethan," he croaked. "Are you all right, buddy?"

"Yeah," I said, lingering by the door. "I've brought you a squash. Tropical fruit and orange."

"You're amazing," Dad said, shifting the pillows so he could sit upright. "Actual lifesaver."

I gave him the glass and watched as he drank it in four large gulps.

"Boy, did I need that," he gasped. "That's the trouble with hiking – it's thirsty work."

I chuckled, but I didn't really know what he was on about.

His eyes met mine. "Listen, I'm really sorry about last night. You shouldn't have to hear us argue."

"It's OK." I stared at the floor.

"And I'm sorry for storming off. I thought it might be best to take some time away from the house."

"Are you going to keep living here?" I asked, gesturing at the cramped spare room, which was full of boxes and stuff that didn't have a proper place in the house. Just like Dad.

"I don't know," Dad said. "I'm still figuring things out. Maybe once the van's finished—"

"You can't live in the van," I said. "It doesn't even have windows."

"It *will* have windows," Dad said. "Eventually. It'll be fully insulated and everything."

"Why can't you just go back to your normal bedroom with Mum?"

"That's not how it works, Ethan. Come here."

Dad patted the edge of the sofa bed, and I sat down. He ruffled my hair, which usually annoys me, but this time cheered me up.

"It's all going to be fine, Ethan," he said. "We just need to keep going for a while, for the sake of the channel."

"The channel?" I turned to Dad. "I don't *care* about the channel—"

"Well, you made that pretty clear last night," Dad said. "Barely cracked a smile, the pair of you."

"I don't want to do it any more," I muttered.

Dad sighed. I moved away from his brewery breath. "We're a family channel, Ethan. We can't be a *family* channel unless the *family* takes part."

"But we're not much of a family at the moment, are we? I haven't even seen Mason today. You're in here. Mum's gone out. Grandad's at Sycamore Village all alone."

"Grandad isn't *all alone*," Dad said. "He's having

a whale of a time at Sycamore Village. It's like one massive family there."

"Yeah, I guess."

Dad grinned. "That's the spirit. Meal-Prep Monday tomorrow. I suggest you go and practise that beaming smile. Go on. Show me your smile, Ethan."

"Fine." I smiled, but with my lips together, no teeth.

"Come on." Dad tickled my ribs. "I know you can do better than that!"

I smiled again, this time with teeth showing and everything. But only because I'm ticklish. Not because I was happy.

"That's more like it," Dad said. "There's my boy!"

"Dad," I said. "I'm going to go out for a bit. I fancy some fresh air."

Dad sank back into the bed. "Go ahead. I'm in no fit state to stop you."

29

"*Today we meet Elaine who thinks she may have found a priceless Victorian artefact while building a kitchen extension in Scunthorpe.*" The TV at Sycamore Village boomed through the walls. "*So, Elaine, tell us more about this wonderful candlestick.*"

I had walked all the way to Sycamore Village without really meaning to. Dad said it was like *one massive family*. I suppose I wanted to check.

I pressed the doorbell, and Sylvia's silhouette approached the door.

"Superstar!" she exclaimed as she opened the door. "And a day early too. What have we done to deserve this?"

"I fancied seeing Grandad," I said. "Can I come in?"

"Of course!" Sylvia ushered me inside and closed

the door behind us. The heat inside was tropical. "How's our little celebrity?"

"Not bad, thanks," I replied.

"I was watching you again the other day."

I smiled weakly. "Really? Which video?"

Don't be the prank video, I thought. *Don't be the Fidget kidnapping one either.*

"What was it you were making…? Barbecue hotdog spaghetti! Not *quite* my cup of tea, I'll admit, but it was entertaining!" She beamed at me. "Your grandad will be chuffed you're here. Off you pop!"

I set off down the corridor, then up the stairs to Room 227. Pushing open the door, I found Grandad staring at the wall.

"Ah!" he said, springing to life like a charged-up robot. "A *visitor*! What a delight. How can I help you, young man?"

"Hi, Grandad. It's me!"

"Hello, *Me*!" he said. He shuffled to the door and shook my hand. "Don't be offended, *Me*, but I'm having trouble remembering your real name…"

"Don't worry. It's Ethan. I'm Annabel's son, remember?"

"Ah, yes, Ethan. I knew it was *something* like that. Now come in – welcome, welcome."

"How are you doing, Grandad?"

"Oh, you know, plodding along. It's not much, this place, but it suits me down to the ground, especially with me being on my own. I've got the bedroom through there, kitchenette round the corner – not that I cook much."

I was about to say, *I've been here before*, like I usually did. But something stopped me. I wanted a normal chat, one that wasn't about filming or editing or content. One that wasn't an argument, wasn't a trick, wasn't a prank to go online. Nobody in the world knew I was here, except me, Grandad and Sylvia. It felt warm, and I don't mean because of the maxed-out central heating.

"That's brilliant, Grandad." I smiled at him. "Do you want to show me around?"

"I'd be honoured." He shuffled out of the living room and down the little hallway. "This is the kitchenette. My least favourite room because I'm a nightmarish cook."

The kitchenette was small and untouched. The surfaces were gleaming, free of crumbs and fingerprints. Two chairs next to a table, but only one had a bum indent.

"That doesn't sound good," I said, chuckling.

"You're quite right, it isn't. I could burn a salad, left to my own devices. Do you like biscuits?"

My stomach rumbled. "I *love* biscuits."

"That's sorted, then. A cup of tea and biscuits. Perhaps we could watch television?"

I grinned. "That sounds amazing, Grandad."

Grandad smiled. "Well, go on. Get comfortable, and I'll bring the tea in. The bathroom is just there, for tinkles and whatnot."

"Thanks, Grandad."

I slid into my usual armchair. It was plush and comfortable. There was a remote control on the side that reclined it. I lounged back with my feet in the air while I turned on Grandad's TV. He appeared with biscuits arranged in a spiral and two steaming cups of tea.

"What do you want to watch, Grandad?"

"Anything," he said. "Anything at all. It's such a treat to have somebody to watch it *with*."

I chose a nature documentary about a pride of lions in Africa. They lounged around in the sun, seemingly unaware of the cameras filming their every move. At one point, the two young lions started fighting to see who would be the new leader.

"Did you see that, Granda—"

He was fast asleep, chin tucked into his neck. I took the half-drunk tea from his hand, covered him in a blanket and let myself out of his flat.

30

"Did you post it?" Omar practically ran to meet me at the corner of Seabrooke Street the next morning. "I kept checking online, but I couldn't see anything."

Arlo trailed behind, less enthusiastic. It was Monday, after all.

"Not yet," I said, shivering. "I'm not sure if I should. Things at home are a bit…" I didn't know the word, so I just pulled an icky face.

How would I possibly tell them about the fighting, about Dad's brewery breath, about Mum's aggressive hoovering? That the frame around Mason's bedroom door was beginning to crack because of the constant slamming and slamming and slamming.

"It's been so hard to keep your video a secret," said Omar. "My mum kept asking what we'd got up to at yours. Apparently, telling her we played video games and hung out in the park wasn't enough detail. She's like an interrogator!"

"Yeah, in the end I had to step in," Arlo said. "Told her we formed a rap group called Blue Pencil Case Boyz. Spelled with a 'Z', obviously."

"Blue Pencil Case Boyz?" I said, raising an eyebrow. "Let me guess how you came up with that…"

Arlo nodded and grinned at me. "Divine inspiration, you could say."

"Well, now my mum's expecting a performance," Omar said glumly. "So we'd better hope she forgets. Or worse: we could actually make up a rap."

"I'm *not* doing a rap," I said. "Imagine if Mason found out. He'd destroy me all over again."

"Omar's mum will forget about it, don't sweat," Arlo said, swinging his football kit over his shoulder. "But I can spit some bars if it comes to it. You could say it's a talent of mine."

"Go on, then," Omar said. "Let's hear these bars you speak of!"

"Nah, nah." Arlo started to walk towards school. "I could if I wanted to. Just don't feel like it at the moment."

"Arlo." I patted his shoulder. "You're so full of rubbish sometimes."

"I know." He grinned. "Part of my charm though, isn't it?"

Omar smirked.

"Anyway, *we'll* be the ones destroying Mason," Arlo said. "Destroying him with our sick rhymes."

We walked to school without rushing, shoes smashing through piles of damp leaves. We laughed about Blue Pencil Case Boyz until it almost felt like a good idea. Omar stood on a slug, then a huge dog poo, which made him almost throw up, and we laughed even more.

Arriving at school with stinging red cheeks and tingling cold fingers, I felt as light as a cloud. I hadn't thought about home for a whole twenty minutes.

"Let's try again then, shall we?"

Back at home that night, Dad stood behind the kitchen island, wearing his *Dad on the Rocks* branded apron and surrounded by a huge pile of ingredients.

"Meal-Prep Monday!" He clapped his hands together. "A Lacey family classic. Today we're making eight-cheese pasta. This combination of cheeses is perfect for that viral cheese-pull moment." Dad stretched his hands apart like stringy melted mozzarella.

"Eight cheeses?" Mum said. "It's not exactly a healthy example, is it? Wouldn't four cheeses do?"

"Four cheeses is old news," said Dad. "Everyone does four cheeses. Eight cheeses? That's *pure internet gold*, Annabel."

Mum sighed and started putting on her apron. "Fine. Whatever gets the clicks, I guess. Don't all come crawling to me when you've got tummy aches. That includes you, Geoff."

Dad laughed, but not properly.

"Are you going to smile today, boys?" Dad said to me and Mason.

"Yes!" I said, grinning widely. If smiling was what was needed to avoid another argument, I'd smile all day long. "We'll smile, won't we, Mason?"

"Can anyone hear a mosquito?" Mason pretended to swat around him. "There's this annoying buzzing in my ears."

I flinched. Mosquitoes were one of my least favourite— Oh. I was the mosquito.

Mum's face went serious. "Give it a rest, Mason. Did you have a bad day at school or something?"

"Something like that," he said. "Science and maths in the same day should be outlawed. It's child cruelty!"

"You kids don't know how easy you have it nowadays—" Dad started.

Everybody groaned. Then we started to laugh.

"That's more like it!" Mum said. "Now, let's get going. This camera battery won't last for ever."

Mason and I obeyed, taking our positions.

One secret upside to Meal-Prep Mondays was the ingredients I could snaffle when no one was looking. Well, obviously someone was looking: the camera. There are a few videos where I can be seen scoffing a finger of cake mix or popping a chocolate chip into my mouth. Naturally I couldn't help but break off a corner of one of the cheese blocks and give it a nibble.

Dad joined us behind the counter. Once in position, he clapped to sync the audio.

"Hi, I'm Geoff!"

"I'm Annabel!"

"I'm Mason!"

"And I'm—" I started to sputter and wheeze.

The piece of cheese had gone down the wrong way. I coughed and coughed, doubling over at the waist.

"I'm…" I croaked, then my voice went.

"Cut!" Dad yelled. "Let's try that again, shall we? Hello, and welcome back to *Meet the Laceys*!" he said in his camera voice. "I'm Geoff!"

"I'm Annabel!"

"I'm Mason!"

My turn. But I couldn't speak. I couldn't breathe in

or out. I looked to Mason. He rolled his eyes.

"Come on, Ethan. Finish your mouthful." Dad winked cheekily. "You're not supposed to touch the ingredients until we start prepping."

I nodded and faked a smile. I would be fine if I pretended to be fine. I coughed, but my breath juddered like a car struggling to start. The cheese felt like a ball in my throat. I was going hot. Pressure grew in my head like a balloon inflating.

"Classic Ethan," Mason said. "It has to be all about *him*, doesn't it?"

"Come on, Mason," Dad said. "There's no need for that. We're trying to keep things upbeat today, aren't we?"

"Upbeat, right," Mason said, flicking his hair from his eyes. "It was very *upbeat* when you disappeared on Saturday night, wasn't it?"

Dad gave him a stern look. "Not now, Mason. This new attitude you've adopted is really starting to wind me up. What happened to the nice kid you used to be?"

Mason looked Dad dead in the eyes and slowly pushed one of the blocks of cheese off the kitchen counter. Then the packet of pasta, which scattered across the floor.

Dad's forehead vein bulged. "What on earth do you

think you're doing, Mason? Clear that up this instant." He sighed. "We'll have to edit this out."

"That's your solution to everything, isn't it?" Mum said. "*Edit it out, edit it out.* You can't edit real life, you know, Geoff."

"Well, maybe if we could, we wouldn't be at each other's throats the whole time!" Dad barked.

I stumbled away from everyone.

I could breathe, I told myself. *I COULD breathe.* I just had to focus. But air wasn't going in or out. Only gasps of sound were getting past the ball of cheese. I tried to swallow, but my throat wouldn't work. Sweat gathered on my forehead. The room went wonky.

"You know what." Mum had her hand on her hip. "We need some distance, Geoff. If we're going to keep the channel going, I suggest you find somewhere else to stay."

"I'm already in the spare room," Dad said. "Isn't that enough distance? Where do you want me? Australia?"

I stumbled into the middle of the kitchen, eyes streaming. I skidded on the pasta that Mason had spilled, falling and landing at Dad's feet.

"What are you doing, Ethan?" Dad said. "Now isn't the time to start messing about."

I clawed at my neck. My mouth gaped open and

closed like a goldfish, willing the air into me, willing the cheese out. My heart crashed in my ears like the sound of a gong. I really couldn't breathe. I couldn't breathe and nobody was helping me. I was going to *die*.

With my last bit of strength, I swung my arm hard into Mum's shin.

"*Ouch!*" she cried, lifting her leg away. "What did you do that for?"

"Mum…" Mason was kneeling next to me. "There's something wrong with Ethan…"

"Oh my God!" Mum shrieked. "Oh my God!"

The last thing I remember was Dad thumping hard on my back. Then my eyes began to close.

31

OK, maybe that wasn't the *last* thing I remembered.

I remembered the spit-covered hunk of cheese flying from my mouth like a bullet, then rolling across the kitchen floor. I remembered Colin eating it, which was pretty gross. I remembered my first few gasping breaths, air entering my lungs, the pressure draining from my head.

I remembered Mum and Dad's faces close to mine while they asked five million questions. Was I OK? Was I breathing? Was I in pain? What on earth happened? Was that everything I'd eaten? Was there anything else in there? Could I hear them? Why hadn't I *said* something?

How could I *say something* with a cheese boulder lodged in my throat? I wasn't exactly feeling chatty, was I?

Mason had watched from across the kitchen, eyes wide.

Mum phoned 111 and they said I had to go to hospital to get checked over, even though I was fine. I remembered the silent car ride where Dad drove and Mum sat in the back with me, stroking my face, and I remembered the dull pain in my upper back. I remembered the lit-up "ACCIDENT & EMERGENCY" sign at the hospital. I remembered sitting in the waiting room. I remembered the doctor looking down my throat and gently touching my neck.

Once it was clear that I was going to be OK, it didn't take Mum and Dad long to get back to bickering. They pulled the thin hospital curtain round my bed and began to argue in quiet whispers and hisses on the other side.

"We should have noticed," I heard Mum say. "God, that could have been really bad. I mean, *really* bad, Geoff."

"It was an accident, Annabel. There's no use blaming ourselves. These things happen, you know. They happen every day, all over the world."

"Our son nearly choked to death and we were too busy fighting. I think now might be a good time to blame ourselves, don't you?" said Mum.

"No, actually. I don't," Dad replied. "I think we should be thanking our lucky stars that Ethan's going to be OK."

"Are you implying that I'm *not* thanking my lucky stars? Because of course I am. You're the one that's acting like nothing's even happened."

"Annabel, if we *both* start freaking out, it's not going to do anyone any good. Especially not Ethan."

"I'm *not* freaking out!"

"He can probably hear this. This curtain isn't some impenetrable soundproof metal wall, you know."

"Oh, great time to be a smart-arse, Geoff."

I rolled over in bed. Fidget was watching me curiously from his place on the visitor's chair.

"That was a close one, big man," he said. "You really had me going. I thought, *Nope. That's it. He's a goner*."

"Thanks, I guess," I said. "I probably won't be eating cheese for a while."

"Oh, you mustn't let it put you off. Cheese is brilliant! Not as good as secrets though…"

"If you say so."

I was already planning how to avoid cheese for the rest of my days. Pizza wouldn't be the same, but I'd survive.

"Don't be scared, Ethan," Fidget said. "Everything's OK now. You can breathe easy."

I took a long, slow breath in through my nose. My back ached where Dad had thumped it, trying to dislodge the cheese. I reached over and brought Fidget to the bed, tucking him under the thin white sheet. I wasn't staying overnight, but I was desperate to sleep.

"Goodnight, big man," Fidget said. "I think you've earned a jolly good nap."

"Goodnight, Fidget."

Just as I closed my eyes, the curtain whipped back. It was the doctor.

"Ah, here he is," she said. "The tough young man. How are we doing?"

"Fine," I croaked. "A bit sore."

Mum and Dad appeared at the end of the bed. Mum's eyes were teary and puffy. Dad's neck was blotchy red like a toadstool.

"That's to be expected," the doctor said. "Any discomfort should fade over the next day or so. Everything's all clear on the X-ray, so you're free to go whenever you're ready."

"Thank goodness," Mum said. "You've been very brave, haven't you, Ethan?"

"Is there anything we should look out for?" Dad asked.

The doctor shook her head. "I wouldn't have

thought so. He'll likely be a bit tired and shocked. These things can take it out of the young ones."

The doctor took a form from the end of my bed and began ticking and signing various sheets. Suddenly she gasped and stopped dead, her pen floating in mid-air.

"I knew it," she said.

"What? What is it?" Mum was wide-eyed.

"I knew I recognized you." The doctor gestured to Dad. "Aren't you guys … *Meet the Laceys*? From YouTube? My girlfriend and I watch your videos *all the time*!"

32

It was only fair that I got Tuesday off school, wasn't it? Mum and Dad agreed. The doctor did say I would be tired. I *had* almost choked to death on a clump of medium-strength Cheddar. The least I deserved was a rest.

None of that stopped Mason from whining.

"That's so unfair!" He dropped his cereal spoon on to the table. "He's fine! He's literally smiling right now!"

I quickly straightened my face before anyone saw.

"Mason." Dad spoke in a calm tone, despite his forehead vein betraying him. "Your brother had a traumatic experience last night. He needs to relax."

Mason huffed, sending his nostrils flaring. "I wish I could choke and get a day off for no reason."

"I wish you'd choke too," I croaked under my breath.

"Did you *actually* hear that?" Mason looked around like a footballer who'd been badly fouled.

"Why do you want a day off so badly, anyway?" Mum said. "So you can waste more time shooting zombies?"

"No." Mason rolled his eyes. "I've got corporate burnout, that's all. I watched a video about it the other day."

"You don't—" Dad sighed. "You can't have corporate burnout at thirteen, Mason."

I knew why he really wanted a day off school. It was because Mason was universally hated, looked ridiculous in his hot-dog uniform and was being intimidated by an older boy who was nearly as tall as a lamp post.

"Why don't you invite some of your school mates round for a play date, Mason?" Mum said. "We never seem to meet any of them."

"*Mum!* We're in Year Eight – we don't have play dates!"

"OK, OK. Well, I'm just saying, ask them round. I can do pizza, nachos or whatever the cool kids are eating nowadays."

"Eight-cheese pasta?" Dad offered.

Mum rolled her eyes. "Not funny, Geoff. In fact, I really don't appreciate you joking about that."

Dad sighed and went back to his phone. He was replying to comments on the channel. It was good for engagement, he said. He engaged with the comments more than with us half the time.

"And that's exactly why I'm not inviting my mates over," Mason said through a mouthful of cereal. "You're always arguing."

"Can I have some more hot chocolate, Mum?" I said feebly. "I'm *really* thirsty all of a sudden."

"Of course, sweetheart," Mum said. "Can I interest you in anything to eat?"

I shook my head and swallowed. The thought of solids scared me. "Just hot chocolate will do. With whipped cream if you have it…"

"Oh, come on!" Mason slammed his hand on the table. "He's rinsing it now!"

"That's enough, Mason," Dad said. "Get ready for school. Your bus leaves in thirteen minutes. Correction: *twelve*."

"Fine." Mason left the table, flicking his fringe from his eyes. As he passed me, he muttered, "You'll pay for this, attention-seeker."

"Have a nice day!" Mum called. Then she waited for his thudding footsteps to climb the stairs. "I do worry about him sometimes."

"Typical teenagers," Dad said. "Remind me never to have any more."

"I think that ship's long sailed, don't you?"

"Well, Ethan's next in line. We should make the most of him before he turns into a demon as well," Dad said, looking back at his phone.

Being off sick from school wasn't as good as I expected. It was exciting for the first two hours. I couldn't help but smile thinking about what boring lesson Miss Isaacs would be teaching. Mental arithmetic, Aztec rituals, acrostic poems; there was nothing I'd rather be doing than sitting at home in my dressing gown, nice and warm while I watched TV.

It got boring pretty quickly though. The day felt utterly endless. Each hour took a month to pass. I skipped through the apps on our TV, but choosing something to watch was impossible.

I missed Omar and Arlo. What were they up to without me? What if the funniest thing ever happened in class while I was at home? What if they were recruiting for a replacement member of the Blue Pencil

Case Crew? They'd be holding open-call auditions in the playground. Miss Isaacs might have reallocated my chair to Flora, who was always begging to sit next to Luna.

I wished I could tell the boys about the choking incident. Omar would say something reassuring. Arlo would have some extreme survival story about a time he choked on a whole French stick.

Turning the TV off, I went upstairs to see Fidget. He hadn't had much to eat since I'd fed him Mum's worries. I'd been too nervous to write my worries down since Mason read them out, but I figured he'd give me a break now, especially after last night.

In my room, I tore a page out of my notebook, which I then tore into strips. I began to write.

I'm cringing that I choked on cheese.

I'm too scared to have breakfast.

What if Omar and Arlo replace me?

Why can't Mum and Dad stop bickering for five seconds?

As I was folding up my worries and stuffing them into Fidget's open mouth, I heard the sound of Mum's phone vibrating downstairs.

She answered it immediately. "Hello – oh no. Vomiting, you said? *And* a temperature? Goodness, that's come on quick. He was fine this morning."

I crept to the top of the stairs to listen.

"Right, right." Mum's car keys scraped across the table as she picked them up. "I'm on my way. I'll be there to collect him in twenty minutes or so."

She ended the call and sighed. There had been a lot of sighing lately.

"Ethan!" Mum called to me. "Mason's feeling sick, apparently. We need to go and get him from school."

My heart sank. I knew there was nothing wrong with Mason; he just wanted to come home and ruin my sick day. I shuffled downstairs. Mum was already putting on her coat.

"Sorry, Ethan. You'll have to come with me so I can keep an eye on you. You don't have to get out of your pyjamas; you can just stick your shoes on and wait in the car."

"There's nothing wrong with him!" I protested. "Why can't he let me have one day off without him having one too?"

Mum sort of shrugged, like she wanted to agree but couldn't. "If they're saying he was vomiting, then I have to collect him. Those are the rules, I'm afraid."

"I hate the rules," I said.

But I didn't really. I just hated that *particular* rule – which made this particular day particularly worse.

33

I waited in the car while Mum went inside the reception of St Hot Dog's. The windows steamed up from the cold, so I wiped a lookout hole with my dressing-gown sleeve. I glimpsed the shadowy gap between the buildings, where that boy had grabbed Mason by the tie.

A few minutes passed before Mum appeared with Mason in tow. He was acting glum, walking slowly and bent at the waist as if doubled over in pain. He held a large metal bowl in one hand, a wad of green paper towels in the other. I pressed my face against the window for a better look. He wasn't even pale.

"Get in the back," Mum said, opening the door for him. "And you've got your bowl in case you feel sick, haven't you?"

"Yes, Mum," Mason croaked, climbing in. "Thanks for picking me up."

I stared at Mason as Mum got into the front seat. His head drooped into the metal bowl. His fringe covered most of his face, but I could have sworn I saw a sly grin, even a wink.

"Right then, I've got two patients on my hands now," Mum said, "so I'll try to drive nice and carefully."

"Mum?" Mason put on his most angelic voice. "Can we have McDonald's on the way home? I really think some fries and a milkshake would settle my stomach. I don't want a burger or anything…"

In the rear-view mirror, I watched Mum's eyes narrow.

"I don't think that's necessarily the best idea—"

"Oh, *please*, Mum," Mason pleaded. "It's literally the only thing I can stomach…"

"Fine," she said. "If it'll make you feel better. Maybe you can have something solid too, Ethan? You can't survive on hot chocolate for ever."

"He needs a happy meal," Mason said. "Maybe it'll cheer him up a bit."

I scowled at him, wishing my expression had the power to twist his arms or pull on his irritating curtain of a fringe. "Whatever."

"I suppose I could get a salad," Mum said.

"Sick!" Mason punched the air with his fist. "We're going to McDonald's! We're going to McDonald's!"

"Oh, feeling better all of a sudden, are we?" Mum said.

"No. Not really." Mason put on his croaky voice, before bursting into a fake coughing fit. "I was just rallying, that's all. It's still touch and go."

I looked back as the car moved off. Two older boys in St Hot Dog's uniforms were pointing at our car, pretending to hold up a phone and talking to it, moving it around like Mason did. When they saw me staring, they just started laughing.

Mason carried his large double-cheeseburger meal with fries, Coke, mozzarella dippers and an extra cheeseburger "for the side" to his bedroom with glee. His door slammed, and sounds of machine guns and splattering zombie guts soon followed.

"He could at least *try* to fake it," I muttered, parking myself on the sofa.

I only ordered a small fries and a Coke. I still felt scared of solid food, and I really didn't want to go back to hospital with a mouthful of cheeseburger stuck in my throat. That would have been even more embarrassing than the cheese chunk.

Cautiously, I chewed a fry and washed it down with a mouthful of Coke. It tasted nice. Really nice. I gobbled the rest of the fries in seconds. Mum looked happy as I placed the empty packet in the recycling. Then she was even happier when I took a stack of biscuits from the jar.

34

After dinner, Dad's phone vibrated. I didn't think anything of it, until I heard him say, "Cindy! What a nice surprise!"

Cindy was our manager. It was her job to get us new and exciting brand deals and collaborations. Companies came to her, then she came to us, and Mum and Dad said yes or no to the deal. Except they only ever said yes, even when the brand deal was Nits B Gone headlice lotion and I had to pretend to have nits for a video.

Cindy worked in a cool office in London that had arcade games and beanbags and a fridge where you could take as many fizzy drinks as you liked, *within reason*. Everyone who worked there was cool. They all had funky hair and tattoos, and didn't look like they were doing any work.

I crept on to the landing to listen.

"Not bad, not bad," Dad said. He sounded more cheerful than he had in ages. "Keeping the Lacey cogs whirring. Oh, here's Annabel – let me put you on speaker."

"Hi, Cindy," Mum said. "Everything OK?"

"Annabel! *Mwah, mwah* – phone kisses!" Cindy said. "I have to say, guys, you are *slaying* the game lately. That barbecue hot-dog spaghetti *ate and left no crumbs*, as the kids say. No cap."

"Oh," Mum said. "I wasn't so sure—"

"Absolutely, it's what the people want to see," Cindy cut in. "Wholesome content from everybody's favourite family next door!"

"Viral Buzz doesn't agree about the favourite part," Mum said.

"Bottom feeders, the lot of them," Cindy replied. "You two are *creatives*. You're *geniuses*. You're *mavericks*. You're making major bank. Who cares what Anonymous37208 thinks."

"That's what I've been telling her," Dad said. "We should just ignore the hate and keep on posting."

"Spoken like a true industry professional. You'll be coming for my job next!" Cindy did this weird fake laugh. "But listen – I have an offer I'd like to float. A big one. I'm talking life-changing stuff here."

"Go on," said Dad. "What's the brand?"

"This is no brand deal, Geoff," said Cindy. "This is traditional media. This is crossover. This is *television*. Imagine the Laceys broadcasting into every home, nationwide."

"TV?" Dad sounded delighted.

"That's right. We've had contact from the producers at *Rise and Shine*. They're looking for a married couple to do a daily segment on family life. We're talking marriage, parenting, cleaning hacks, parents' evenings. We're talking a *seriously* big pay cheque, guys. There's even scope to get the boys involved during the school holidays."

My heart pounded. They would say no, wouldn't they? After everything that had happened? *Surely* they'd say no. They couldn't pretend to be a happy couple *on TV*, could they?"

"*Daily segment?*" Dad said. "That's quite a commitment."

"It would be. You'd be travelling to London to film. But it's nothing you can't handle. You already upload daily, and at least with TV you don't have to do the editing yourself."

"Well, that does sound nice," said Dad. "Maybe we could relocate? Make a proper go of it."

"I'm not sure," Mum said. "I don't know if it's the type of thing we would do."

"Of *course* it's the type of thing you would do," said Cindy. "You're every woman's online mum bestie, Annabel. You too, Geoff, you're the dad next door. The boys will be natural TV stars. Mason clearly has charisma, and Ethan's just so charming. Everybody *loves* Colin, as you know."

"We'll need to think about it," Mum said.

"Annabel, come on. You should be *excited*!" Cindy said. "Remember, there are countless other family influencers they can approach. Donna And Clive Plus Five would bite my hand off for this opportunity. So would Tripping Over Triplets."

"We *are* excited!" Dad chimed in. "We're very excited. Annabel's just nervous, that's all. But I think, screw it. Let's do it. What's the worst that can happen?"

"Geoff—" Mum whispered. "No. Shouldn't we at least talk to the boys—"

"That's the spirit!" said Cindy. "I'm over the moon. Obviously there will be screen tests, paperwork and so on. Let's aim to get you all up to London soon to get things in motion."

"You're the best, Cindy!" said Dad.

"I know, I know," she replied. "More to come from me. Toodles! Aaron, tell *Rise and Shine* the Laceys are keen. Where's my oat flat white—"

My body vibrated with anger. I heard a sound beside me. The floorboard creaking under Mason's foot. He'd heard the whole thing too.

35

The atmosphere downstairs was thick like fog as Mason and I marched into the living room. Mum wasn't looking at Dad and she didn't look at me or Mason either.

"What's this about a TV show? We heard the whole thing," I said. "Didn't we, Mason?"

"Yep," Mason said. "I'm buzzing, TBH. Finally, MasonMayhem hitting the big time. About time, if you ask me."

"Don't get excited," Mum said. "I've decided we're not doing it. I'm going to phone Cindy right now and call the whole thing off."

Dad looked gobsmacked. "You'll be doing no such thing! This is the biggest opportunity of our lives, Annabel."

"I don't care!" Mum replied. "How can we do a segment on marriage and parenting when we're getting divorced and our own kids don't like us!"

Dad's face clouded over. "We'll make it work. We are *not* turning this down. We made a plan. Think of the brand."

"*Brand*." Mum shook her head. "When did we become a *brand*? I only started posting for fun. Who'd have known it would turn into all this mess."

Dad carried on talking. "All we have to do is stick to our plan and act like a family—"

"Do you even hear yourself?" said Mum, her voice sharp. "*Act* like a family. I'm sick of *acting*, Geoff."

"People are noticing the lack of content, Annabel," he said. He waved his phone. "Top comment on our last post: '*Does anyone else think they seem awfully quiet?*' Four hundred and eighteen likes, that one. And it's all kicking off about us on Viral Buzz too."

"Don't engage with it, Geoff." Mum went to the kitchen and poured a glass of wine. "You heard Cindy," she said as she came back into the living room. "Bottom feeders."

Dad wasn't listening. "SpookyQueen8790 says, '*Has anyone else noticed the lack of uploads recently? I need my Laceys fix!*'"

"They'll have to wait, then," Mum said. "The world isn't going to end if we stop uploading."

Dad continued: "MacaroniPeas replied, *'I think something's going on behind the scenes. The channel has been super inconsistent lately. The only one posting is that brat, Mason. He gives major narcissist vibes.'*"

"What the—?" Mason said. "Show me who said that."

"What's narcissist vibes?" I said. Nobody answered.

Dad carried on with the commentary. "LegendOfHelga says, *'The whole family gives me the creeps. There's no way everything is so sunny and perfect behind the scenes. You can see it all over Ethan's face.'*"

"Then MinekoGnocci says, *'They live near me. I have it on good authority that their beloved grandad has been left to rot in a home while they live in luxury. I'm sick to the back teeth of the blinking Laceys.'*"

"OK, Geoff." Mum sounded tired. "There's no need to read them all out."

But Dad didn't stop.

"CrispinChicken says, *'There's something going on for sure. They barely post any more. No Meal-Prep Monday vid this week, SMH. BTW hasn't Geoff been renovating that van for like four years now? LOL.'*"

"MumPoweredByLaughter: *'I have it on good authority that Annabel and Geoff have hated each other's guts for years. Even the boys aren't on speaking terms. And I can clear up the mystery of this week's Meal-Prep Monday. They're negligent too. Ethan choked on a chunk of cheese and had to go to hospital.'*"

"Wait – that last one's strange," Mum said. "I've barely told anyone about Ethan choking on that stupid cheese."

Dad sighed. "It'll be someone from the hospital. People recognize us. Even the *doctor* recognized us. The point is, we need to keep the plan going."

"It's a stupid plan," Mum said.

"Very mature, Annabel. Very mature indeed."

"*I'm* immature?" Mum snapped. "I'm the only one facing reality here! It's over, Geoff. *Meet the Laceys* is over! I've got half a mind to log on to my laptop and delete the whole channel right now. Just wipe it all in one fell swoop!"

Dad went white. "You can't do that. I need this. I'm not going back to my old job, Annabel. Do you really want me making cold calls to accounting firms? You heard Cindy, I'm a *creative*. I can't go back to that!'

Mum stared at him, not saying a word, then she

turned and walked into the kitchen. A few minutes later, we heard a smash.

I knew what the sound was. It was the wine bottle, hitting the wall.

A silence as cold as metal stretched out for ages.

36

Upstairs in my room, I loaded the Viral Buzz forum on my tablet and went on to the *Meet the Laceys* subforum. There were plenty of threads dissecting our lives:

- LaceyHaters HQ – Introduce Yourselves!
- Meal-Prep Mondays – Opinions?
- Is it me or is Annabel more absent nowadays?
- What's the deal with this *MasonMayhem* stuff? Cry for help?

Each of the threads had countless comments. People agreeing and arguing, talking about their least favourite vlogs and guessing what was going on behind the scenes.

I found one of the comments Dad had read out.

@SpookyQueen8790: Has anyone else noticed the lack of uploads recently? I need my Laceys fix!

I scrolled through the comments beneath. Something felt strange. Most of the stuff they were talking about had been posted online, but some of it was about real life. MumPoweredByLaughter was saying I'd been to hospital for choking on a chunk of cheese, for instance. How did they know? This weird feeling spread through me. Were we being watched?

Something snapped in my brain and suddenly I'd had enough. I was going to upload my video about *Meet the Laceys*. About everything.

I logged in to my *EthanExplains* channel. No content, no followers. The "About Me" section was empty, and the profile picture was the default grey circle with a blank white silhouette in the centre.

Using the camera at the top of the tablet, I took a blurry picture of my face and selected "Upload".

"There," I said, watching the progress bar slowly creeping along. "That's better."

In the end, it was an easy decision to make. I'd had

enough of arguments. I'd had enough of pretending. I'd had enough of smiling for the camera until my jaw ached. I'd had enough of Meal-Prep Mondays and unboxing junk and family-day-out vlogs where nobody really enjoyed themselves, where anything that didn't happen on camera never really happened at all.

I was tired of bottles smashing and Dad hiding in the garage working on the never-ending van renovation just to get away from Mum. I was tired of saying, "It's amazing!" Nothing was amazing.

I was tired of being edited. Having my words and actions chopped and erased like a spelling mistake in a school jotter. Being threatened that I'd be edited out if I didn't play along.

Well, they wouldn't be able to edit me out of this video, would they?

I went downstairs to the office and plucked the memory card from the camera I'd used to record the video. I slotted the card into the bottom of my tablet. Then I selected "Upload video" on my channel's interface. I breathed deeply, my fingers trembling as I selected the footage that Omar and Arlo had recorded, the video where I spill everything about *Meet the Laceys*.

My finger hovered over the "Post" button, then recoiled. I couldn't post it now – not while I was at home. Mum and Dad would eat me alive. I decided I'd wait until school tomorrow. That way, I'd be safe in Miss Isaacs' class where nobody, not even Mum and Dad, could get at me.

I selected "Save to Drafts" and put my tablet to one side. Then I turned to Fidget.

"How's it going, big man?" he said.

"Not so good," I said. "But I think I have a plan."

"A plan? It's always good to have a plan!"

"Hmmm, maybe not this plan," I said, chewing my lip.

"Are you going to tell your old pal Fidget? You can write it down if you want."

I crossed the room and tore a strip from my notebook. Then I wrote the juiciest secret I would ever feed to him.

"Here you go," I said. "Enjoy it. That's some pretty serious stuff right there."

"That's what I'm here for!" He swallowed down the strip. "Ah, delicious! Now you can rest easy. A problem shared is a problem halved, remember!"

"Maybe not this time, Fidget."

I'm about to destroy Meet the Laceys.

37

It was a straightforward morning routine:

- Brush teeth
- Put on uniform
- Post life-ruining video about my own family online

So that's exactly what I did. Just before I left the house, I opened up my drafts on my tablet and selected "Post".

I knew it would go live while I was at school, our lives exploding while I sat struggling to understand fractions. Speaking of fractions, I supposed a fraction of me hoped something would go wrong with the upload. But three-quarters of me wanted to do it.

So the day rolled on. Occasionally, anxiety broke

through and scattered my concentration. I hadn't told Omar and Arlo what I'd done. I'd wanted to enjoy one last walk to school before everything changed.

During RE, Miss Frame the teaching assistant appeared at the classroom door. Usually that meant somebody's parent had dropped off a forgotten lunch or PE kit. This time she passed Miss Isaacs a note, then they both looked at me. My heart paused. My blood turned icy.

"Ethan Lacey," Miss Isaacs said. "You're wanted in reception."

Gravity felt stronger all of a sudden, especially in my stomach. Arlo and Omar looked at each other, then me, like, *What?*

"Wh-why?" I managed to say, even though I knew what was happening.

Miss Isaacs looked at the note. "It doesn't say," she said, "but you can take your things."

I swallowed. Taking my things meant I was never coming back.

The sight that met me was horrifying. Dad was in reception, pacing a tight circle. He looked pale and agitated – not like he'd seen a ghost, more like he'd *become* one. I hung back at the door. Maybe if I ran back to class, Miss Isaacs would let me stay. Maybe I could live in our classroom, sleep under the table and drink water from the hand-washing tap in the corner. I could use the curtains as a blanket. Omar and Arlo could feed me scraps from their lunches. It wouldn't be so bad.

"Here he is!" Miss Frame said. "Enjoy the dentist, Ethan. No fillings, I hope!"

"Bye," I said feebly to Miss Frame.

The door to reception swung shut and her footsteps faded.

"What have you done, Ethan?" Dad gripped my shoulders. His eyes were shining like glass. "*What the hell have you done?*"

"I don't know what you—"

Sweat beads glistened on his forehead. "Why did you post that video? *Why would you do that to us?*"

I tried to step back. "What video—"

"There's no point lying. It's too late – it's online. It's everywhere."

I swallowed. "Is it?"

Dad stared at me, wordless. There were more wrinkles around his eyes than before. I didn't know it was possible to age so much in one morning.

"Well?" he said harshly. "Anything to say for yourself?"

Mrs Fletcher the receptionist cleared her throat. She was looking at us curiously over her computer screen, her glasses reflecting the glare.

"He gets nervous," Dad said. "About the dentist."

Mrs Fletcher nodded and carried on typing.

I stared down at the shoe-scuffed floor. I wasn't going to tell Dad I was sorry, because I wasn't, not really.

Dad pulled me in close. For a second, I thought it was going to be a hug. He was going to say sorry for overreacting, that he understood, and that everything was OK.

I put my arm around him and patted his back. I let out a deep breath. I'd fixed everything, finally, with my video. Dad would take me home to celebrate. Mum would be relieved too, and Mason would have deleted his *MasonMayhem* content and we could go on holiday. Like to Center Parcs or something, or somewhere with a world-cuisine buffet like I'd seen online.

"Ethan," Dad whispered close to my ear. "You have no idea what you've done. You have single-handedly destroyed this family."

My body flooded with stone-cold fear. I scrunched up my mouth to stop my bottom lip from shaking.

"Don't bother getting upset," he said, releasing me from his hold and dragging me away by the hand. "There'll be plenty of time for that later."

Cindy was on speakerphone when we got home. She didn't sound happy.

"This is serious," she was saying. "I'm sorry, Annabel, but I'm going to have to pass you over to our crisis management team."

"Fine," Mum said. Then she saw me and walked away.

Mason's cheeks were red and puffy, like they'd been smacked. He was sitting at the dining table, scowling into space. The second he saw me he charged at me, fists pulled back, ready to punch.

"Hey, hey, hey." Dad half-heartedly stood between us.

"Let me at him!" Mason snarled. "I'm going to turn him into pulp!"

Flecks of Mason's spit landed on my cheek. I pressed my back against the front door, desperate for a few extra centimetres between me and him.

"He's a *liar*!" Mason screamed. "Why did you lie that I'm getting bullied? I'm the toughest boy in the whole of Year Eight and anyone who says otherwise—"

"You *are* being bullied at school!" I shouted. "I saw it. We all saw it – me, Omar, Arlo. We snuck into St Hot Dog's and watched Karl get you by the tie and pull you up off the bench!"

"Is this true?" Mum was standing in the hallway now. "Is someone bullying you, Mason?"

"No!" Mason shouted. "He's talking crap!"

"Karl said you got stink-bomb juice all over his blazer and his mum had to bin it! All because of your stupid prank channel!"

"We were playfighting!" Mason's voice cracked, as though he was on the edge of tears. "It was a game!"

"Why were you crying afterwards, then? We have it on video! You were crying and wriggling like a worm in your little hot-dog uniform!"

Mason lunged for me, his arm twisting under Dad's armpit as Dad tried to block him. I felt Mason's nails gouge the skin on my cheek and I sprang forward too, my arms and legs kicking and grabbing and clawing until my foot finally made contact with his shin. I felt the hard bone through my school shoes.

Mason shrieked and fell to the floor, clutching his leg, letting out gasping sobs and stuttered cries. Big tears crashed from his eyes. Snot streamed from his nose; spit strung between his lips.

"Not so tough now, are you?" I said, my voice shaking.

Dad looked horrified. "Ethan, what have you done?"

"What has happened to you?" Mum stared at me like I was a stranger. "This isn't like you, Ethan."

My pulse roared through my body. Why were they blaming me? None of this would have happened if they hadn't forced us to lie and let Mason do whatever he wanted. Why did I always pay the price for everyone else's decisions?

Mum crouched down and cradled Mason. "Shh. It's OK."

"H-h-he attacked me!" Mason sobbed. "He's broken my leg clean in two!"

"He deserved it!" I roared, my words painful in my throat. "You all deserve it!"

I pushed past Dad and stomped upstairs. Nobody came after me. I hoped they never would.

38

I HATE MY FAMILY.

Mason deserved it.

I'm leaving home and I'm NEVER coming back.

Mason's leg was only bruised. But it was *badly* bruised, according to the A & E doctor. That's what Mum said when she got back from her second hospital trip in as many days. I crept on to the landing to hear. It was the same doctor who'd checked my throat after the cheese incident. She'd recognized Mum again.

Mum said Mason would have to take it easy for a bit. She sighed, and I heard her slump on to the sofa.

Dad said, "Right," then went quiet. "They're having a field day about us on Viral Buzz."

"Of course they are."

"We're even on the *Daily News* website. The headline goes 'Is it curtains for popular vlogging empire *Meet the Laceys*? Son's explosive exposé tears family apart.'"

No response from Mum.

"Cindy says *Rise and Shine* retracted their offer," Dad said.

"Good," Mum replied.

I went to my room and closed the door. Mason was limping up the stairs and who knew what would happen if we came face to face. Whether it was him or me injured, Mum would definitely be making a third trip to A & E.

I went back to packing my things. I'd emptied my backpack of all my school stuff, replacing it with everything I'd need for a life on the road. Socks, jumpers, nine pairs of pants. Then I added my tablet, a charger and £32.70 in pocket money that I'd saved up, mainly in coins. Oh, and Fidget, of course, but he would live in my pocket like usual.

I didn't know where I was going to live. Omar and Arlo's houses were off-limits, even though they would happily hide me in their wardrobes. Eventually I'd be found and their parents would end up phoning Mum and Dad, and I'd be back at square one. Then I'd be confined to my bedroom for eternity, scratching a tally into the wall until I became an old man with a long grey beard.

I'd seen a film where some guys lived under a motorway bridge, huddled around flaming metal bins, wrapped up in hats and scarves. The problem was: I wasn't sure how to get to the nearest motorway bridge nor how to start a fire in a metal bin. Plus, it looked quite grubby in those places. I'd have dirt under my nails the whole time.

Like all great explorers, I would figure out the details later. The most important thing was to leave. Backpack, gloves, trainers and gone.

I snuck downstairs for one final glass of squash before I left for ever. I wouldn't be saying goodbye, not out loud anyway. I would say it in my head by looking around the house, taking pictures in my mind. I'd done it since I was little. I imagined a clicking camera sound in my head, closed my eyes and the picture was saved. Most of the time it worked.

The living-room door was ajar. Behind it, Mum and Dad were still talking.

"Viral Buzz are calling us liars!" Dad said. "Saying the whole *Meet the Laceys* brand is nothing but a con."

"I don't need to hear this, Geoff," Mum snapped. "My phone's blowing up. Oonagh won't stop calling."

"Great," Dad said.

"Oonagh." Mum answered her vibrating phone at last. "Yeah, I've seen it. I'll have to talk later – it's all kicking off. Yes, a drink would be good. OK. Bye."

"This @MumPoweredByLaughter account is really gunning for us," said Dad, obviously still scrolling through Viral Buzz. "They know so much. Get this: '*Their youngest got taken out of school early today.*' Isn't that weird? Do you think it's one of Ethan's teachers?"

Mum sighed. "I don't know. News travels fast. Parents talk. Playground gossip."

"I've got four emails from Cindy," Dad went on. "She's freaking out. Each one's about another brand dropping us. Organic wet wipes: gone. Kid-friendly supplements: gone. Mountain-trail hiking boots collab: gone. We're over."

"Don't be dramatic."

"We could have paid the mortgage for two months with that hiking shoes video I was working on. Now we'd be lucky to get an offer for Top Ten Bin Bags…"

"What do you want me to do about it exactly?" Mum sounded irritated.

"I want you to help me manage this PR crisis, Annabel!"

"PR? Seriously? Are you not more worried what our friends and families must think?"

I crept down the hallway, past the living room, and quietly made my squash in the kitchen. Tropical fruit and orange had never tasted so bitter. I was underneath Mason's room. It sounded like he was punching something, his pillows maybe, or his mattress. Whatever it was, I knew the punches were aimed at me.

"Friends and family forgive," Dad said. "But subscribers? Never."

"Oh, Christ," Mum said. "You sound like Cindy. Dad will be pulling his hair out."

"Don't worry about him. He doesn't know if he's having a boiled egg or a haircut half the time."

"*Don't* you dare talk about Dad like that," yelled Mum.

Grandad! The electric buzz of an idea shot through my body. I would go to stay with Grandad at Sycamore Village. Sure, I probably couldn't stay for ever, but one night, maybe two. I could sleep under his bed or in the kitchenette, hide from the staff when they did their hourly checks.

I put on my coat and backpack, before slipping on my trainers.

"Come on, Fidget," I said, picking him up and looking into his button eyes. "We're moving out."

Before I left, I padded to the back door and found Colin's bone chew. I patted his head and gave it to him on the rug. He began to crunch, his teeth chomping on the bone.

"That's it, boy," I whispered, leaning close to him. "Enjoy your chew. We can't have you barking when I go, can we?"

He dropped the bone and looked up at me, covering my face in warm, wet licks. I scrunched my eyes shut, but didn't push him down like I usually did. Germs didn't matter now. It might be the last time he ever licked me.

"Go on, Colin," I said quietly. "Where's your chew? Find your chew!"

He returned to his crunching as my eyes began to water. Colin was the only member of this family I was going to miss. I only hoped he wouldn't miss me too much. That thought made my eyes sting.

I didn't even bother sneaking away. I just walked out as if everything was normal, letting the door slam behind me.

Mum and Dad's argument had reached boiling point, so they didn't hear.

After the door slammed, I was alone in the front garden, feeling the rush of cold air against my hot, flushed face. All was black except the orange cones of light beneath the lamp posts and the dinner-plate moon. The night was a little too quiet. The bare trees sent spindling shadows across the ground. It was creepy.

"You've got this, big man," Fidget said from my pocket. "Be brave. I know you can!"

"Thanks, Fidget." I shivered – from cold or fear, I wasn't sure.

"You know the way," Fidget said. "Same way as always."

The end of my nose was numb. I stuffed my hands into my pockets and counted my steps. By the time I'd reached seventeen steps I was at the front gate. I closed it behind me and looked back at the house.

From the road, I could hear Mum and Dad's voices, muffled by the walls. I watched their silhouettes through the curtain. Mum's hands gesturing. Dad leaning over the table.

Shadows and lights flashed through Mason's bedroom curtains. Zombies getting splatted into paste. The other windows were dark, like teeth missing from a smile. Nothing going on, just empty.

It was 9.16 p.m. It was the latest I had ever been outside alone. I began to walk, fallen leaves crunching under every footstep.

39

Even though I knew the way to Sycamore Village, being out on my own at night felt like walking through another world where everything was opposite and eerie. Alleyways and corners that I walked past every day felt evil, filled with dark that was darker than normal dark. A dark so thick that anything could be hiding in the shadows.

My footsteps echoed too loud. A car alarm. A flickering lamp post. I peered over my shoulder. Was somebody there? Oh yes, that would be my shadow, always lingering just behind me.

Now was really not the time for sticky thoughts.

On Seabrooke Street, a black cat sat beneath the conker tree. Its green eyes reflected the light as a car swung past. Two glowing gemstones in the gloom.

A shiver trickled down my spine and I squeezed Fidget.

Go back home, Ethan, I thought.

I stopped walking, allowing the foolishness of my actions to sink in. This was beyond dangerous. Mum and Dad would hit the roof. The police could be looking for me. A national manhunt. I might be on the news: *"Ten-year-old influencer kid missing after online meltdown."*

But I couldn't go home. Mum was upset. Dad couldn't stand the sight of me. Mason would put me in hospital in revenge for me telling the world he's being bullied. Maybe it was time to forget my family. Maybe I could find a new one. A family who didn't film everything, who didn't care about followers and comments and forums and what other people thought.

The cat yowled at me. A loud, screeching sound that made my skin go tight. I ran away into the night.

Life was tough on the road, but we'd get used to it, Fidget and me.

40

I didn't know how I would explain to Grandad that I was moving into Sycamore Village. Maybe I wouldn't explain. Maybe I would just stay and never leave, living off biscuits and tea and sleeping in the armchair.

Sycamore Village looked to be asleep. The lights in the communal sitting room were off. The only illumination was cast by occasional flickers of a television playing to nobody. Nobody awake, at least.

My footsteps crunched as I walked up the path. I took a deep breath and prepared to ring the doorbell. With any luck, Sylvia would answer and get distracted by talking about *Meet the Laceys*. Hopefully she hadn't seen my video. Then I could slip past under the guise of visiting Grandad. Once inside, I would hide.

It was only as I went to press the buzzer that

I noticed the front door was ajar. I pushed it open. People in Sycamore Village uniforms were rushing this way and that, quietly scuttling between rooms, speaking in sharp, hushed tones to each other. Clearly things weren't as sleepy as I'd thought.

"Not in here," one carer whispered to another. "Are you sure you've got the headcount right?"

"*Yes*," the other carer hissed. "I can count, you know. I've checked four times. He's not here. Not unless he's hiding in a cupboard somewhere."

Sylvia appeared from round a corner. She seemed flustered. "He's not in his room. Somebody check the CCTV tapes. If he left through the front door, it'll be on video."

"Good idea, Sylvia," said a man before he rushed down a corridor.

"He must have gone to his family's place," said Sylvia, "but we'll have to alert the authorities if we don't find him soon—" Her eyes widened the moment she noticed me. "*Oh* – Ethan, thank goodness!"

Two other carers turned and stared at me. Several looks passed between them. Confused, relieved, concerned, then confused again. A few seconds of silence passed.

"I'm here to see Grandad," I said. "Is he awake?"

"A-awake?" Sylvia steered me gently into the communal living room. "Do you mean to say he's *not* at your house? Is that not why you're here?"

I frowned. "Why would he be at our house? Can I go upstairs? I won't wake him up. Just don't tell Mum and Dad I'm here."

"Your mum and dad don't know you're here?" Sylvia ran her hands through her purple hair. "It's almost ten o'clock at night, sweetheart!"

"I know," I said. "I really need to see Grandad without them knowing I'm here."

"But they'll be worried about you!" exclaimed Sylvia.

I shrugged. "They probably haven't even noticed I've gone. Even if they have, they wouldn't care."

"Aw, Ethan." Sylvia's knees clicked as she crouched in front of me. "What do you mean? Of course they'll notice."

"No, they won't." My lip started to wobble. "But it doesn't matter because I'm coming to live with Grandad."

It was Sylvia's turn to frown. "Right, about your grandad. He's definitely not been to your house this evening?"

"Are you saying he's gone missing?"

Nobody spoke.

Sylvia sighed and turned to the other staff. "I think we have a few phone calls to make."

Mum and Dad showed up before the police, which was lucky. I would have got arrested for running away if the police had got to me first. I really didn't want to get arrested.

Car doors slammed shut, and footsteps hurried down the path. I squeezed Fidget hard.

"It'll be all right, big man," he said. "It'll all be fine."

Mum and Dad did not look happy. Not one bit.

"What on *earth* were you thinking?" Dad said the second he entered the room. "How could you be so careless? Going out on your own in the middle of the night. You're ten years old!"

"I know." I stared at the thick patterned carpet, hoping to disappear into the colours and shapes.

"Care to explain yourself?" said Dad.

"I was moving out." I lifted my backpack to show him. "You didn't even notice me leaving."

"Moving out!" Dad did this weird dry laugh. "What did you plan to do exactly? What if someone had snatched you off the street? What if you'd been hit by a car? How would we have known?"

I admit that I started crying, which was kind of

embarrassing with everyone around. I wanted Sylvia and the carers to leave, but they kept staring.

"Geoff," Mum said. "That's enough. I think he gets the message."

She pulled me into a hug and I buried my face in her coat. I couldn't remember the last time anyone had given me a hug. It had been ages.

"Oh, my darling." Mum stroked my hair. "It's all OK, Ethan."

Dad patted my shoulder. "Look, we're sorry. Aren't we, Annabel? We know things haven't been great."

"Yes." Mum's voice cracked. "We're really sorry."

"And I'm sorry we didn't notice you leaving," Dad said. "We were distracted. There's so much going on. Everything with the channel, with us, with you and Mason, with Grandad."

Mum let out a long sigh. "You can say that again. I feel like the worst mum in the world, and the worst daughter."

"We've taken our eye off the ball," Dad confessed. "Off you, and Mason. You two should be the main priority."

"Mason hates me!" I said, my voice burning in my throat. "And I hate him!"

"*Hate* is a strong word," Dad said. "You don't mean that."

"I do mean it! I really do mean it!" Tears soaked my eyelashes, and I covered my eyes with my sleeve. "I'm never, ever, *ever* speaking to him again!"

Dad looked at Mum, then back at me. "We'll work on that, OK. Together. It might take some time, but we'll work on it."

A car pulled into the car park. Blue flashing lights danced across the walls. We watched as two police officers climbed out and approached the building. I swallowed.

"It's all right," said Mum. "They're not here for you."

"It's about Grandad," Dad said. "Seems you weren't the only family member to go wandering tonight."

Sylvia entered the living room with steaming cups of tea. "Here you go, folks. I thought you'd be needing these. One sugar, Annabel, like usual."

"Cheers, Sylv," Mum said. She clasped the tea with both hands and stared down into it like it held all the answers she needed.

41

I'm pretty sure Dad was speeding as he drove me and Mum home, hurrying to get back to Mason and to check for Grandad. Headlights rushed past the window.

"I don't know what to do," Mum said. I wasn't sure if she was talking to us or to herself.

"For now, do nothing," said Dad, eyes fixed on the road ahead. "The police know what they're doing."

"I know," Mum said. "I can't stop thinking about him falling down a manhole or being stuck in a ditch somewhere in the dark…"

I squeezed Fidget hard. "A ditch? What ditch?"

"Don't worry, Ethan," Dad said. "Mum's just catastrophizing, that's all."

"Catastrophizing?" Mum said. "What else am

I supposed to do? This is *literally* a catastrophe, if you hadn't noticed, Geoff."

"Sorry. But let's keep a level head," Dad said. "Worrying doesn't help Grandad. No wonder Ethan is so anxious."

"Oh, great. Now you're blaming me for Ethan. Perfect timing for a dig, as usual," Mum hissed.

"STOP IT!" I shouted, squeezing Fidget in my fist. "Can we *please* not argue for once?"

The silence that followed was thick like syrup.

"Sorry, Ethan," Mum said. "You're right."

"You need to focus on finding Grandad," I told her. "Argue about it later."

Mum's phone started ringing. The car's dashboard screen read "MASON" below his pixelated face.

"Did you find him?" Mason said, his voice on speakerphone. "I mean Grandad, by the way. I couldn't give a—"

Mum cut him off. "We've got Ethan but not Grandad."

"Smart move, Snot Monster," sneered Mason. "Running away in the night. Real smart."

"*Mason*," Mum said in a warning tone.

"Sorry, Mum. So you didn't find Grandad?"

"I'm afraid not," Mum replied. "He's definitely not

at Sycamore Village. He hasn't turned up at home, has he? The police are coming to check."

"Nope," Mason said. "Not that I know of."

"We'll be home shortly," Mum said.

"Got it," Mason said. "Mum…?"

"What?"

"Any chance you can stop by McDonald's on the way back? It's been a really long night and I think we all deserve—"

"Not now, Mason," Mum and Dad said together.

"Fine. What about after we find Grandad?"

Two officers came to the house, a man and a woman. It only took them five minutes to check that Grandad wasn't there. They looked in the weirdest places. In the bathrooms, in the garage and inside Dad's van. They even checked the garden shed, shining torches into every spider-ridden corner.

"Nope," the man said, coming into the living room. "He isn't here."

Mum nodded, staring down at the carpet. Dad had his arm around her. Mason was perched on the edge of the sofa, eyes wide with worry.

"Is he going to be OK?" Mason said, his voice wobbly and quiet.

"Of course he will." Dad rubbed Mason's back.

"So do you have any ideas where he could be?" said the other officer. She scanned our faces. "Anywhere he'd spoken about visiting? Any friends or family he could've gone to?"

Mum shook her head. "All his friends are at Sycamore Village."

"Any acquaintances, old work colleagues?"

"Not that he mentioned." Mum cleared his throat. "He's a bit forgetful. He gets confused. That's why he lives there."

"Did he have a partner?"

"Christ, no," Mum spluttered.

The officer scratched something in her notepad. "Has anyone noticed any strange behaviour?"

"I don't think so," said Mum slowly. Her eyes filled with tears. "I've just been so wrapped up in…" Her breath caught in her throat. "In…"

"It's OK." Dad squeezed her shoulders. "We know, love."

Love? Mason and I locked eyes for a second. Did that mean they were getting back together?

"He could be anywhere by now," Mum sobbed. "He doesn't know where he's going. He'll be lost, wandering around aimlessly."

The other officer said, "We'll be contacting local hospitals, of course. In case he's turned up there somehow."

"*Turned up there somehow*," Mum repeated, shaking her head. "I can't stand this. Talking about Grandad like he's a lost sock or something."

"I'm sorry," said the female officer. "We'll do all we can to help you. Do keep in touch. If you have any ideas, even if they seem silly, let us know."

The officers left, their shoes clumping down the hallway. We sat in silence until we saw their headlights move off outside.

"Do you think we should post something on the channel?" Dad said. "A video asking people to help us look for him, perhaps?"

Mum shook her head. "Nobody will want to help us, not now. We're public enemy number one online after…"

Everyone glanced at me, then looked away. I sank down into the sofa, trying to disappear.

"Sorry," I croaked. I never would have posted that stupid video if I'd known we would need the channel to help Grandad.

"We should call everyone we know," Dad said. "The more eyes open, the better. Surely someone will see him wandering around. It's a small town."

Mum let out a puff of air. "You're right. We should. I just don't know how I'm going to face everyone. This last week has been embarrassing enough without us misplacing a member of our family."

"Go to bed, Annabel," said Dad. "Let us take care of this. You need to be well rested in case we need to search for him tomorrow. The boys will help, won't you, lads? You can have the day off school, seeing as it's going to be a late one."

"*Yes!*" Mason punched the air, before catching himself. "Sorry. I didn't think."

"Fine," I said.

Neither of us made eye contact.

42

Talking on the phone makes me nervous.

Mum says Grandad might be lying in a ditch.

Please, please, please let Grandad be OK.

Dad set me and Mason up in the living room with two mobile phones and a list of phone numbers he'd printed out. Some of the names were people we knew: Alan and Cathy; Dad's friend Steve; our Uncle Dan who wasn't technically our uncle, just one of Dad's football friends. Even Arlo and Omar's parents were there.

There were others I'd never heard of: Mr Patel; Rumble Tumble Laundrette; somebody called Fiona

Colin, who, it turned out, was the breeder we'd bought Colin from five years ago.

Mason and I sat at opposite ends of the dining table and practised our scripts.

"*Hello, I'm sorry to bother you so late. My name is Ethan Lacey, and I'm calling—*"

"You sound stupid," Mason said. "Like those people who call and try to get Mum and Dad's bank details."

"You do it, then, if you're so good on the phone."

"Fine," he said, clearing his throat. "*Hey, what's up, you guys? It's your boy, Mason Lacey, and I'm blowing up your line tonight to ask if you've seen my grandad—*"

"It's not a video, Mason. This is serious," I cut in. "You don't *have* to talk like that."

Mason scowled. "Whatever. Let's just get this done, then we can all go to bed. I'm tired."

"I'm *not* tired," I snapped, stifling a yawn.

I picked up my phone and dialled the first number.

It didn't go well. It was past eleven o'clock and most of the calls went unanswered. Every sane human was in bed. I tried to leave a voicemail for not-really-Uncle-Dan, but fluffed my words, and pressed "End Call" before I'd finished the message. I put a question mark next to his name – one for Dad to try later.

I ran my finger down the list, looking for an easy

one. Maybe Arlo and Omar would answer. Arlo was always bragging about how he didn't have a set bedtime and had once stayed up for eleven days straight.

I dialled Arlo's landline and listened. It rang for ages, then a gruff man's voice answered. Arlo's stepdad.

"'Ello?"

"Good evening," I began. "I'm so sorry to bother you—"

"BOG OFF!" he replied. "Have you any idea what time it is? My stepson will be cranky now you've woken him up!"

The line went dead. I returned to scanning the list while holding in a smirk.

The name Oonagh O'Malley jumped out. Even though I didn't like Oonagh and Luna much, I wasn't scared to call. She was Mum's best friend, after all; she had to help us. She could even drive around town looking for Grandad in her red convertible with that "Powered by Family and Laughter" bumper sticker on it—

I froze. Two thoughts rushed together like magnets in my brain. That cringe bumper sticker. *Powered by Family and Laughter.*

"Mason," I said. "What's that account called on Viral Buzz? The one that's writing all the comments about Mum and Dad. The one who knows loads of private stuff about us."

Mason shrugged. "MumPoweredbySomethingStupid. Cringe." He picked up his tablet and scrolled. "This is it. MumPoweredByLaughter."

A window opened in my brain and I saw through it.

"I know who it is, Mason," I said. Chills shot up and down my body. "I've figured out who it is!"

"Hello?" Oonagh sounded croaky and half asleep. "Do you know what time it is? A girl needs her beauty sleep!"

"It's Ethan." My heart hammered so loud I was sure she would hear it through the phone. "Ethan Lacey. I'm sorry to bother you, Oonagh."

"Ethan?" I heard Oonagh sitting upright in bed. "What's the matter? Is everything OK?"

"We're a bit worried at the moment," I said, looking at Mason.

Mason nodded and gave me two thumbs up.

"Oh no," Oonagh said. "What's going on? Do you need content advice from Aunty Oonagh, is that it?"

"It's Grandad," I said. "We can't find him anywhere. He's gone missing."

Oonagh gasped. "You're serious? And you don't have any idea where he's gone?"

"None at all. He disappeared two days ago," I lied. "That's why we're calling, to ask you to keep an eye out."

"Of course," Oonagh said. "Poor Annabel – I bet she's tearing her hair out."

"She can barely get out of bed," I told her. "She's done nothing but stuff her face with chocolate biscuits and cheese triangles these last couple of days."

"Oh, bless. Who could blame her? What about your dad?"

I hesitated and my gaze flicked to Mason.

"Say it," he hissed.

"Dad's gone. Moved out," I said, wincing at the lie. "He's got a new girlfriend, you see. She's … Swedish."

"He *never* has!" Oonagh said. She sounded almost delighted. "*Swedish?* Oh, that little rat. Probably traded Mum in for a younger model. Men – you just can't trust them."

I didn't know how to respond to that, so I just said, "So will you keep an eye out for Grandad?"

"Of course I will, sweetheart. Kisses to Mum for me. I'll see her for a coffee soon, no doubt. Ciao!"

I ended the call and dropped the phone like a red-hot lump of coal. My pulse thrummed through my fingertips. I couldn't believe I'd just lied like that.

"Nice work," Mason said. "But where did the Swedish girlfriend come from?"

"I panicked, OK?"

Mason nodded. "We've done the hard part. Now we wait. If any of that ends up on Viral Buzz, we've got her. Especially that Swedish girlfriend stuff."

"I'm going to prison for lying, aren't I?" I placed Fidget on the table and looked into his button eyes. "I won't cope well in prison, Fidget."

Mason rolled his eyes. "If anyone finds out, I'll take the blame. I'll say I made you do it."

"Seriously?"

Mason shrugged. "Nothing to lose now, LLB."

"Can you *please* stop calling me LLB?"

"OK, Snot Monster."

"That's not—" I sighed. "Whatever.

43

The next morning, I woke up to find Mason in my room. I don't need to tell you that he didn't say "Rise and shine, porcupine" like Mum did.

"Get up, Snot Monster." He whipped the curtain back. "It's important."

I groaned. My eyes felt glued together. Sleep had only come in crumbs. All night I'd dreamed of Grandad. I saw him staggering around in the dark, his elbow-patch cardigan sopping with rainwater. In the dream he turned to face me and I'd woken with a start, sweat trickling down my forehead.

"What have I done now?" I mumbled.

"It's happened! You were right, about MumPoweredByLaughter. Look at this."

I sat up and took Mason's phone ... and there it was.

The newest post on the *Meet the Laceys* subforum:

> @MumPoweredByLaughter, posted at 23:57 yesterday
> 903 likes
> OMG #LaceyHaters, do I have news for you! Turns out the whole family is in such a shambles, even Grandad wants out. Remember when they packed him off to a home? He's gone walkabouts. Apparently no one's seen him in two days. Even the police are involved! Get this, Geoff's treated himself to an upgrade too. No, not a new van. A new GIRLFRIEND. Swedish and blonde apparently. Annabel is eating her feelings, chocolate biscuits and cheese triangles aplenty. Oink! Thank me later. X

I handed the phone back to Mason, my mouth hanging open.

"I know." He punched his fist into the palm of his other hand. "I've got half a mind to go over to her house right now and—"

"Don't, Mason," I pleaded. "We need to think of a plan—"

"Morning." Dad stuck his face through the gap in my bedroom door. His hair was ruffled. So was his skin. "Good to see you two getting on. There's nothing like a crisis to bring a family together."

Mason hid his phone behind his back and grinned.

"Keep it up, guys," said Dad. "We'll need that team spirit for today's search. I'll make breakfast, if you can stomach it. I'm not sure I can."

We listened as Dad's footsteps travelled downstairs.

I turned to my brother. "*Don't say anything*, Mason. Not till we decide what to do. Promise me. Mum's got enough on her mind without finding out Oonagh's a—"

"Total witch," Mason said. He was pacing around my room, tossing his phone from hand to hand. "A liar. A bully. How could she? Post someone's private life all over the internet like that?"

"Yeah, *who* would do something like that, Mason?"

I glared at him while cogs whirred in his brain. Eventually he realized and went a bit pink. That was the real Mason, not MasonMayhem.

"Sorry about the whole Fidget thing," he said. "And the alien prank. It was harsh."

"Thanks," I said. "Now apologize to Fidget." I propped up Fidget beside me on the bed.

"Nah, nah." Mason recoiled. "I'm not doing that."

"Fine, then." I lay down in bed. "Apology rejected."

"Fine! I'll do it." Mason rolled his eyes. "I'm sorry, Fidget."

"*That's OK, Mason!*" I said in Fidget's voice. "*Everybody makes mistakes!*" Then in my own voice I added, "I'm sorry too. Sorry for putting that video up. Even though it was in retaliation, and you *did* deserve it."

I stuck my hand out for a shake and Mason sort of slapped it. I couldn't be certain, but I was fairly sure we'd just made up.

44

Neither the police nor Sycamore Village had found Grandad. Mum rang Sylvia, who told her she'd stayed up all night waiting, hours past the end of her shift. Sylvia had even checked the whole of Sycamore Village again that morning, and had walked in on Grandad's tea-making alarm clock pouring a cup out for no one to drink.

The police had checked the CCTV and found grainy footage of Grandad simply letting himself out of the front door, then disappearing into the dark. Picturing it, I felt punched in the tummy.

Colin, Mason and I sat in the seats at the back of Dad's van while Mum finished talking to Sylvia. Mason was on his phone, reading Viral Buzz. The likes on MumPoweredByLaughter's latest comment had multiplied.

"*Mason*," I hissed, and shook my head. If Mum and Dad caught him on Viral Buzz, the fallout wouldn't be survivable.

"Sorry." He stuffed his phone into his pocket.

"Thanks, Sylvia," Mum said. "We'll keep you posted too."

"Nothing?" Dad said as she hung up.

"No news," Mum said. "I'm worried. It's freezing outside. What if he's trapped somewhere?"

"He won't have got trapped," Dad said. "Knowing him, he'll have found somewhere warm for a chat and a cup of tea."

"For twelve hours?" Mum was wringing her hands. "Charming as he may be, he would have outstayed his welcome by now."

Dad started the van, and it sputtered to life. "Any ideas, boys? It's kind of a needle-in-a-haystack situation here. There're no bad ideas for places to look."

"What about McDonald's?" Mason said, a hopeful glint in his eye.

Dad sighed. "OK, maybe *that's* a bad idea."

*

We spent the morning driving slowly up and down empty streets. Whenever we saw someone – a dog walker, a person out for a stroll – we pulled over and Mum showed them a picture of Grandad on her phone.

Nobody recognized him.

Plenty of people recognized us though, including a lady with a baby in a sling.

"Oh my days," she said. "Aren't you that family? *Meet the* … whatever it is? The ones who split up but tried to keep it all a secret?"

"Oh—" Mum shook her head. "No, you must be thinking of somebody else."

"No, no. You're definitely them!" the lady said. "I've seen all your videos. They keep me company when this one's up all night teething." She turned round so we could see her baby's squished face. "Do you want to have a hold? I could take a picture of you holding him!"

Mum leaned back from the car window. "Oh. No, thanks—"

The woman reached for her phone. "Or a quick selfie? Go on, it'll only take a second. The girls in the group chat are going to *die* when they see it. Are you two back together, then?"

"*Geoff—*" Mum's voice was stern.

Dad turned the key, but the van wheezed asthmatically.

"*Geoff.*"

Dad tried the key again and the van sprang to life. He didn't hold off on the accelerator, and I watched through the back window at the woman shouting after us. No doubt the whole interaction would be posted on Viral Buzz before dinner time.

"Thanks." Mum looked shaken. "I really wasn't in the mood for a selfie."

Dad's temples pulsed. "People just don't know the time or place, do they?"

We were silent for a while as the van chugged down new streets, some I'd never seen before. Cottages, terraced houses, blocks of flats. Our town was bigger than I thought. I felt lost. And if I felt lost, how would Grandad feel?

"What about the bowls club?" Dad said after a beat. "He used to go there, didn't he?"

"Yes, a million years ago, mind." Mum said. "Still, *anywhere* is worth a shot."

That same logic took us all around town. Anywhere Grandad had ever mentioned, we checked: the cinema, the Salvation Army, Ye Olde English Tea

Room, even the cafe inside Lumpy's Soft Play Centre. No Grandad though.

I grew tired. My eyes kept closing and my head would lurch forward like a bowling ball on a pipe cleaner.

"Ethan," Mason whispered. "You're supposed to be keeping an eye out."

"Sorry."

"What about your old house, Mum?" Mason said. Evening was crawling closer now. The clouds were thick and dark, and spitting rain. "The one where you grew up?"

Mum looked at Dad and they shrugged.

"Chestnut Avenue? It's a bit far away," she said. "I doubt he could have made it that far."

"Like you said though – it's worth a shot, right?" Dad said. "We've still got a quarter of a tank."

"Fine," Mum said. "We'll go to Chestnut Avenue. Just to be sure."

45

Chestnut Avenue was exactly how I'd imagined. Tall red-brick houses from the olden days with wonky chimneys and big front gardens The road was lined by trees with leaves in yellow, orange and brown.

Dad brought the van to a grinding halt and we clambered out. The ground was covered in conkers. All the trees were conker trees. Horse chestnut, I think they're actually called. I guessed that was why this place was called Chestnut Avenue.

Gripping Colin's lead, I picked up a conker with my free hand and prised it from its casing. It was cold and smooth, hefty in my palm. Perfect for battling.

"There it is," Mum said, nodding to a house on the left. "Number forty-seven. My childhood home."

It was more like the shell of a house than a proper

home. Most of the windows were boarded up. The ones that weren't boarded had vines snaking in and out of them. Somebody had sprayed "DO NOT ENTER" in red on the door.

"Why does it look like that?" Mason asked.

"Check the sign," Dad said. "They're converting it into luxury apartments, ready for viewing in summer 2027, apparently."

"I haven't been back here in..." Mum fell silent. "Twenty years, almost. See that room on the top floor, on the left? That was my bedroom."

I looked up at the room. I tried to imagine Mum in there, messing around, playing with her friends, but I couldn't. I could only picture her in our house in Endsleigh Gardens – filming, editing, cleaning, tidying, cooking, looking at her phone. That's what Mum *did*.

"I used to smoke out of that window all the time," Mum said, a smile playing on her lips. "I threw the butts on to the porch, thinking Dad would never know. Then one day I came home to an old plant pot in my room, full of damp, mouldy cigarette butts he'd picked out of the drain."

"Annabel!" Dad chuckled. "Don't encourage them. Smoking is a bad habit, guys."

Mum turned to him. "It was a different time. They know not to start smoking, Geoff. Are you honestly saying you never did anything rebellious growing up?"

Dad shook his head, then winked. "Not that I remember."

A conker fell on to the roof of the van, making us all jump.

Mum laughed. "Liar."

It was weird, seeing them smiling. Did this mean they were getting back together? *No.* I squashed the thought down like dirty clothes in the laundry basket. We were looking for Grandad, not having a family reunion.

"I'm trying not to corrupt our innocent little boys, Annabel," said Dad.

"*Little boys?*" Mason said. "I'm hench, mate. Look at this!" He flexed a muscle that wasn't worth bragging about.

"Yeah, and they're not so innocent either," Mum muttered. "After all they've done recently."

Dad shrugged, which was Dad language for *fair enough*.

"The developers have gutted the place," Mum said. "Grandad would be heartbroken if he knew."

"Best not to tell him." Dad said. "This house was his pride and joy."

"I'm going in," Mum said. "Just to look around the garden."

We all crossed the road, and Mum forced the wooden gate open. The path was made of jagged stones placed at angles across the lawn. A carpet of fallen leaves covered our feet.

Mum knocked on the door, even though it was clear the building was empty.

"I'm half expecting my mum to answer." She smiled, kind of sadly, not like a proper smile. "Silly, really. But it would be something, wouldn't it?"

Dad put his hand on Mum's shoulder. "It certainly would."

We stood there, staring at the door while nothing happened on the other side of it. Colin began to whine.

"Well." Mum turned round. "I guess we'd better go. So long, childhood home. Enjoy becoming luxury apartments."

Colin whined again. He pulled on his lead towards the side of the house, almost cutting off circulation to my fingers.

"What is it, Colin?" Dad said. "Have you spotted a starling? You like chasing starlings."

Colin jumped and strained at his lead. His ears darted forward, and his pink tongue hung out as if ready to lick the most appetizing dog treat ever.

"Keep hold of him, Ethan," Dad said. "It's not safe for him here. It's like a building site."

Colin cried even more – high-pitched, desperate squeaks like a rusty gate opening.

"Wow," Mason said. "Whatever he's seen, he really wants to meet it."

"Or eat it," Dad added. "Come on, Colin. Calm down, boy!"

"As if that's ever worked," I said. "He needs a toy or something." I pulled Colin's lead. "We have treats at home. You hear that, Colin? *Treats!*"

Dad, Mum and Mason left the garden and started crossing the road. Meanwhile, Colin did not want to leave. He tugged harder, dragging me further in the opposite direction.

"Is that my old mate, Colin?" a raspy voice said from the corner of the garden.

A chill trickled to my feet, as if an egg had been cracked on my head.

Colin dragged me right off the path and on to the overgrown lawn. My trainers and socks soaked up the rain.

"Well, would you look at that waggly tail!" said the voice.

Walking closer, I spotted a shadow perched on a bench at the edge of the garden, behind a thick tree trunk. Close up, I saw the wet cotton of his button-up shirt, clinging tight to his skin. Cream-coloured trousers that had soaked up every puddle and splash. Patterned leather shoes caked with mud and covered in fallen leaves. A cardigan with elbow patches, with leaves and twigs caught in the fibres.

"Grandad?"

Relief like I'd never felt before washed over me.

I dropped Colin's lead and he sprinted to Grandad. Reaching him, Colin bounced and licked and squealed with total delight. Then he treated Grandad to a big wet lick on the lips. When Colin calmed down, Grandad looked up at me.

"Well, hello, old chum," he said. "Fancy meeting you here. It's Ellis, isn't it? Evan? Oh, drat. I always mix up the names."

"It doesn't matter, Grandad," I said, before turning round and shouting, "Mum! Dad! Mason! It's Grandad! He's over here!"

Colin rolled on to his back so Grandad could scratch his tummy.

"Dad?" Mum ran to Grandad and took his hands in hers. "What are you doing here? Everyone's been looking for you!"

Grandad chuckled. "Oh, Annabel. I went for a walk, and this was the only direction I remembered. Forty-Seven Chestnut Avenue. I suppose that's one thing I haven't forgotten."

"Everyone was worrying at Sycamore Village," said Dad. "They've had search parties out! We've barely slept!"

"That's it!" Grandad pointed to his head. "*Sycamore Village*. I knew it was called *something* like that, but I couldn't quite grasp the name. But this house here, I could never forget the way."

"Geoff," Mum said. "We need to phone everyone *now*. Sylvia, the police, everyone. Tell them he's fine."

"On it, love." Dad walked a few paces away and began making calls.

Love, again.

"Oh, Dad." Mum's voice was shaking. It sounded as though she was trying not to cry *and* trying not to get angry. "We could have brought you here to see the house if that's what you wanted!"

"No need." Grandad stroked Mum's face. "It looks like Marie isn't here, after all."

"Oh, you—" Mum closed her eyes. "No, she isn't, Dad." She took Grandad's knobbly hand. "You're freezing cold!"

"Here you go, Grandad. Put this on." Mason unzipped his *Zombie Freakout 4* hoodie and wrapped it around Grandad, fitting the hood carefully over Grandad's sopping grey hair so the zombie eyes were right on top of his head. Then Mason sat next to him and started rubbing his back.

"How long have you been sitting here?" Mum asked.

"I'm not precisely sure." Grandad shivered, as if mentioning the cold had made him feel it. "Once I sat down and started thinking, it was hard to know when to stop. Memories. I suppose I wanted to spend a little time with each of them."

"Really?" Mum said, kneading Grandad's hand. "What kind of things have you remembered?"

Grandad shifted on the bench and looked up at the boarded-up house. "So many things. I remember bringing you home from the hospital, so tiny. We called you Raisin for ages, because that's how you were, all raisiny and shrivelled up. Marie nearly baked you into a fruitcake you were that raisiny."

Mum laughed. "Still am, sometimes. After a bad night's sleep."

Grandad frowned. "I remember Marie standing at the end of the path, leaning on that gate. She'd wave me off as I left for work. Every day, she'd wave – rain or shine. Never a day I left without a damn good send-off. And I'd wave back, my arm hanging out of the car window, shirt sleeve soaked with rain sometimes, until she was only a speck in the rear-view mirror."

Mum smiled. "She always did that, didn't she? Waving people off." She used to wait in my bedroom window for me to go past on the upper deck of the school bus. She'd always wave, every single time, even if the bus was running late. I used to think it was embarrassing and duck down in my seat. But I still waved back, sneakily."

"I remember her doing that," Dad said, now off the phone. "Even when we were in sixth form, she waved you off. I thought it was sweet."

I looked up towards Mum's old bedroom. A part of me was hoping to see Granny standing there, waving just like they were describing. But the window was empty and dark.

Grandad cleared his throat. "I remember this tree, this one right here. It started as just a conker in a cup with some mud. You were only a baby, Annabel. Your mum planted a few, but only one sprouted. So she put it in the ground, and here it is today, big as a house nearly." Grandad looked up at the orange leaves. "Dropping conkers of its own. Funny, isn't it? How time passes."

"Oh, Dad." Mum's eyes shone like glass. "I know."

46

We settled Grandad into the back of the van, wrapping him tight in Colin's hairy blanket. Dad cranked the heating up high. We waited while the steam retreated from the windscreen.

Mason took off Grandad's shoes and socks, which squelched when he dropped them on to the floor of the van. Then he took off his own socks and rolled them over Grandad's veiny feet. It wasn't long ago that Mason couldn't stand Grandad, calling him boring and whining about the bad Wi-Fi at Sycamore Village. Now he was standing barefoot in a puddle, giving him his socks.

"Give me your hands," I said, and Grandad placed his hands in mine. His bony knuckles felt like a cold bag of pebbles. I rubbed them, feeling the metal of the wedding ring on his finger.

"That's nice," he said, smiling weakly. "They're coming back to life a bit."

Mum was leaning on the garden wall outside 47 Chestnut Avenue, making more phone calls. Huge puffs of steam kept rising up each time she sighed in relief, telling someone that he had been found safe and well, if a little damp.

"What do you say you spend the night with us?" Dad said. "Colin can keep you company. We've got the spare room and plenty of dry clothes. We won't make you wear that zombie hoodie all night."

"He likes it!" Mason cried. "Don't you, Grandad? That's pretty dank merch, you know. Limited edition."

"It's a perfectly comfortable cardigan," said Grandad, nodding underneath the oversized black hood.

"It's called a hoodie—" Mason began. "But no biggie. I can show you how to play the game if you like, Grandad," he went on. "The controls are fine once you get the hang of it. I'll put it on easy mode too, so the zombies are basically chill and don't even fight back. There's this attack you can do with a modified crowbar—"

"Mason," Dad said. "Why don't we let Grandad warm up a bit before we start slaying zombies? You probably want a nice cup of tea and a sit-down, don't you?"

"Tea would be nice." Grandad shivered. "Biscuits even better. It will be lovely to visit your new home. Whereabouts is it again? I hope you don't mind I'm arriving empty-handed."

A look passed between me, Mason and Dad in the rear-view mirror.

"It's not far, Grandad," I said. "I think you'll really like it."

47

The next couple of days were kind of hectic. It wasn't just Grandad that we had to find room for, it was everything he owned. Mum asked if Grandad wanted to go back to Sycamore Village, and he said no. So it was settled: he was coming to live with us.

But that meant we had to find a place for photos (with labels, of course), ornaments, teapots and cardigans. Mum said he'd always been "a bit of a hoarder".

Mum told us that Grandad moving in was permanent. Plus, we would have extra space when Dad moved out. That settled that, then. It was good and bad at the same time.

Speaking of Sycamore Village, they felt awful about everything that had happened. They sent a doctor over to make sure Grandad was OK. The doctor took his temperature and washed a small cut on his finger. Sylvia visited too, which Grandad liked a lot. And yes, she still called me superstar.

It took a while to turn the spare bedroom into the perfect Grandad habitat. We painted the walls peachy beige, then hung his labelled photographs on them. Mason and Dad built a flatpack table for his jigsaws while I watched, worried about splinters. We ordered a bed with a nice firm mattress and plugged in his tea-making alarm clock.

Seeing as the van had proven roadworthy, Dad decided it was time to take it for a proper spin and go camping. I was sad when he left and I cried for nine minutes. But then Mason reminded me that Dad agreed to camp within half an hour of the house, and then he showed me an ultimate fail where a toddler spilled three litres of milk on a dog. It made me laugh, and laughter helped me remember that maybe Mum and Dad needed a bit of breathing room from each other.

I fed two secrets to Fidget that morning:

I'm glad Dad's gone for a bit.

I wish Dad would stay.

There was a cosy atmosphere in the house, like when a guest comes to stay and everything feels special. Once he'd been unpacked, Grandad treated the house as though it was new, walking from room to room with wide-open eyes, as if he was seeing it for the very first time.

"This is lovely," he said, shuffling into the kitchen on Sunday morning. "Such light, such wonderful natural light. You've made a *fantastic* choice."

"Thanks, Dad," Mum said. "I'm glad you like it."

"How could I not?" Grandad grinned, his eyes only showing a glimmer of doubt. "It just feels great to know that I'll be staying."

"And we're happy to have you," Mum said, squeezing a teabag against the edge of the sink with a spoon.

Mason walked into the kitchen, earbuds stuffed deep into his ears. Tinny music leaked out.

"WHAT ARE WE DOING TODAY?" he roared at Mum.

Grandad veered to the side in shock. I took his elbow to steady him. He grinned and ruffled my hair.

"TAKE YOUR EARPHONES OUT!" Mum roared back. "THERE'S NO NEED TO SHOUT!"

Mason pulled them out with a pop. "Sorry," he said sheepishly. "I didn't realize."

Mum laughed. "Must be hard to hear your own voice over that racket."

"So, what are we doing today?" said Mason. "I need to go into town. My trainers are falling apart."

"I was thinking we could meet up with Oonagh and Luna," Mum said. "Take Colin for a couple of laps around the park."

A stone dropped in my stomach. Mason's face suggested he'd had the same feeling. With all the fuss about Grandad, I'd forgotten that Oonagh was prime suspect as the Viral Buzz leaker.

Mum eyed us suspiciously. "Why do you both look like you've seen a ghost?"

Mason's mouth flapped without producing any words.

"I haven't seen a ghost," I said. "Have *you* seen a ghost, Mason?"

"*No!*" he said, wheezing. "I don't think anyone's seen a ghost!"

"I had a paranormal experience once," Grandad said. "It was way back in… Oh, when was it again?"

Sometimes lucky things happen, and Colin being sick on the floor was one of those lucky things. Before Mum could press us further, Colin coughed three times, then produced a beige-brown gloop of dog food mixed with grass.

I recoiled and Fidget took a massive squeezing in my pocket. I'd have to avoid that part of the floor for a while. Even after it got cleaned, there would still be vomit particles. There were *always* particles.

"Oh, Colin!" Mum sprang into action, grabbing the kitchen spray and paper towel. "Always keeping me on my toes."

Grandad watched Mum as she cleaned up the mess, his thin lips curling with queasiness.

"Can one of you grab the mop?" Mum said.

"I'm going upstairs," I said, swallowing the urge to retch.

"Sorry," said Mason. "We've got something important to discuss."

Together, we headed for the kitchen door.

Mum sighed. "Nothing like dog sick to bond two warring brothers, eh?"

"We need to tell Mum about MumPoweredByLaughter," Mason said, leaning against my bed frame. His jaw was grinding. "We have to."

"Maybe it wasn't Oonagh," I suggested, now doubting myself. "It could be a coincidence!"

"No – it's too specific! You told her about Grandad going missing. About Dad's fake Swedish girlfriend.

Then it was on Viral Buzz, almost word for word!"

I didn't want to tell Mum that I suspected her best friend was the person spilling her secrets online. The thought made me dizzy. After so long wishing I knew more, now I wished I knew less. Much less.

"Boys!" Mum called upstairs. "Are you ready? You need to get your shoes on! We don't want to be late for Oonagh and Luna!"

"Coming!" we both called out, although my voice sounded wobbly.

Mason left my room, shouting, "Where's my *Zombie Freakout* hoodie?"

I gave Fidget a hard squeeze, then stuffed him into my trouser pocket.

"You need to be on duty at all times today, Fidget," I muttered.

"At your service, big man," he replied. "Your old pal Fidget's always here to help."

As I headed downstairs, all I could think was, *What if I've got this wrong?*

48

Sideways rain. Terrible weather for a dog walk, hence why Grandad stayed home in the warm. Terrible weather to break earth-shattering news to your own mum too. We sat in the car waiting for the hammering rain to stop. A text message popped up on the dashboard. Apart from Colin's panting, we fell silent.

> Oonagh: Nightmare traffic hun – be there in about fifteen! X

"Fifteen minutes?" Mum relaxed into her seat. "What shall we do? I spy? I spy with my little eye, something beginning with 'B'."

Betrayal, I thought. I let out a shaky breath that fogged the windows.

"*Bird*, if you were wondering." Mum turned round. "Everything OK, Ethan? You're not still thinking about Colin's puke, are you? I told you I used anti-bac."

"I wasn't," I said. "I am now though."

"You're being awfully quiet too, Mason," said Mum.

"Bro, I'm fine," he muttered, staring out of the window. "I don't even know what you're talking about."

"When did it become cool to call your mum 'bro'?" Mum asked.

Mason shrugged. Silence filled the car once more. Mum's eyes flicked from Mason to me, then back again.

"Something's wrong," she persisted. "Is it about Grandad? I know it's a big adjustment—"

"NO!" we said together.

"We love living with Grandad," I said.

"Good," she said, but then she went on, "Is it about me and your dad? Because we've been thinking some family counselling could—"

"*NO!*" we said again.

"I am *not* doing counselling," Mason said. "I'm *way* too deep for that. They won't know how to handle me."

Mum rolled her eyes. "What is it, then? You can't

be that put out about a dog walk. I know it's raining, but you'll survive."

The silence stretched like the water slime I'd opened for one of our unboxing videos. On and on and on. I rated it ten out of ten, even though I found slime gross.

"I'm not letting this drop, boys," Mum said stubbornly.

"It's about Viral Buzz, Mum," Mason said at last. I braced myself.

"WHAT HAVE I TOLD YOU ABOUT GOING ON THAT SITE?" Mum erupted.

I slid down in my seat.

"There's NOTHING on there that you should be reading!" Mum continued. "It's nothing but a toxic wasteland of trolls who sit behind their keyboards and criticize others when really they should be looking at their *own* lives!"

"I know." Mason held his hands up. "I do know that, *obviously*."

"Your father and I specifically told you NEVER to go on there. Once you've read all that stuff, you can't unread it!"

"I know," said Mason, "but—"

"I swear to God, we will *ban* the internet if you—"

"LISTEN TO HIM!" I shocked myself with how loud it came out.

Mum's eyes met mine in the rear-view mirror. They were wide, more white than pupil.

"It's about…" Mason took a couple of deep breaths. "I don't really know how to say this, but—"

"Spit it out, Mason," Mum snapped.

"It's about MumPoweredByLaughter…"

Mum shook her head. "Don't even say that username around me. It makes my blood boil."

"We know who it is," I said.

"What do you mean?" Mum glared at my brother. "Mason, it wasn't *you*, was it? One of your pranks?"

"No, obviously not!" Mason's voice was high and tense. He looked at me, eyes glistening, cheeks flushed red, and I nodded. "It's—"

"It's Oonagh," I said.

I clamped my eyes shut and braced for impact. I counted *one … two … three*.

Mum started laughing. "Oh, boys. You really had me going! There's no way my best friend of ten years could—"

"It is her, Mum," Mason said. "We proved it. Ethan told her stuff and five minutes later it was on Viral Buzz."

"What things?"

"About Grandad being missing—"

"*Everyone* knew about that. We called everyone we knew so we had a better chance of finding him."

"We made things up. *Specific* things," Mason said.

"Like Dad having a new Swedish girlfriend," I said, wincing.

Mum's jaw went stiff and her nostrils widened. "Yes, I did see that post on the forum," she said quietly. "Started racking my brain about who I knew with a Swedish accent. You told Oonagh that?"

Mason nodded. "And we said you were eating nothing but chocolate biscuits and cheese triangles in bed because you were so sad."

"It was a trap," I said. "You know that sticker on Oonagh's car? *Powered by Family and Laughter*. It reminded me of that username, so we thought…"

Colour drained from Mum's face like water from the bath.

The sound of gravel crunching under tyres interrupted us. Oonagh pulled up in the next parking space, waving. Luna was in the back.

"Maybe we should go home," I said.

Mum stared into the middle distance. Eyes wide, shoulders hunching and falling. Then she suddenly unclipped her seat belt.

"No, no." Mum moved to open her car door. "I think we're going to sort this out right now."

"Mum, no!" Mason tried to grab her arm, but it was too late. He sighed and climbed out too.

I didn't move. I couldn't. I took Fidget out of my pocket and looked into his button eyes. *Say something. SAY something.* But nothing came.

49

"Lovely day for it!" Oonagh pulled up her hood and squinted into the pelting rain. "Come on, Luna – off your phone!'

Still sitting in the car, Luna mouthed something, then returned to her screen.

Oonagh raised her arms to hug Mum, but Mum stormed past her to the back of the red convertible.

"*Powered by Family and Laughter.*" She nodded at the pink bumper sticker. "Interesting."

Oonagh laughed. "Oh, just a silly little thing. Luna got it for me for Mother's Day. Kind of ruins the aesthetic of the car a bit, but what could I do?"

Mum turned to face her. "Is it true?"

I stepped out of the car, into the rain, Fidget in hand. "Mum, please don't."

"Come on, Mum. Let's just head back." Mason linked his arm in Mum's and tried to pull her to our car.

She shook him off and stood firm. "I said, Oonagh, is it *true*?"

Oonagh's eyes widened. "Is what true? Am I powered by family and laughter? Well, I do like my family and having a laugh, if that's what you mean?"

Mum glared at Oonagh.

"You seem frazzled, Annabel," said Oonagh. "You're kind of freaking me out."

Mum's blonde hair was turning dark in the rain. "MumPoweredByLaughter on Viral Buzz. Is it you, Oonagh?"

"What? I really don't know what's going on here. Do you want to just sack off the dog walk and get a smoothie? I know you've had a rough week." Oonagh stepped forward with both arms outreached.

"Don't touch me," Mum said coldly. "And, no, I don't want a flipping smoothie." She stepped back. "I'm only going to ask you once more, Oonagh. Are you MumPoweredByLaughter on Viral Buzz?"

Oonagh laughed shrilly. "No! I deplore that horrible website. The amount of rubbish people put up about me on there, why would I want to see that?"

"Do you swear on our friendship?"

"Of course!" Oonagh was flushing red, not meeting anyone's eye. "You sound paranoid, Annabel. Why would you ever think that?"

Mum squared up to her. "I'll tell you why. Do you remember Ethan phoned you a few days back, when we couldn't find Dad?"

"Yes, of course." Oonagh smiled at me. "Excellent telephone manner, I must say. Very mature."

"Mason and Ethan told you something and it ended up on Viral Buzz five minutes later."

Oonagh blinked fast. "The world is a *very* gossipy place, Annabel. That doesn't mean I'm running off to some creepy forum to write about you. Anyone could have written those things."

"What if I said that *you*, Oonagh, were the *only* person they told? Swedish girlfriend – does that ring any bells? Me living on a diet of nothing but chocolate biscuits and cheese triangles?"

Oonagh breathed deeply, her face blank, then she turned to me. "Why would you do that, Ethan? Somebody's obviously hacked my phone line and now I'm getting the blame."

Mum laughed bitterly. "Oh, give it a rest. Phone hacking? You're not Prince Harry."

"We're influencers, Annabel. We're high-profile individuals. We're probably being hacked right now!" said Oonagh. When Mum didn't respond, she added, "It's either that or your boys are lying about calling me. Ethan, is this something to do with Luna? I've heard you and your little gang always leave her out at school."

I scowled at her. "I'm not lying. Sure, Luna's a massive telltale, but so are you by the looks of things."

Oonagh's mouth fell open. "How *dare* you!"

"No, how dare *you*!" Mum stormed up to Oonagh, her finger an inch from her face. "It's always been you, all along. The divorce, my dad, commenting on my *boys*." Mum cracked into tears. "Everything that's ended up on that forum has been you. It's you. It's you. It's *you*, Oonagh."

"What's going on, Mum?" Luna had opened her car door. "Are we going for this walk or not?"

"No," she snapped. "We're going home. I'm done."

"You don't get to say you're done, Oonagh," Mum hissed. "I'm done. I'm *beyond* done."

Oonagh let out a huff of air, then she turned on her heel, stomped back to her car and climbed in, slamming the door behind her. The tyres crunched on the gravel as she reversed, then accelerated out of the car park.

We watched the 00NAGH number plate speed through the gate, and they were gone.

"I'm sorry, Mum," I said.

"I'm sorry too," Mason said, rubbing her shoulder.

"Don't be." Mum sniffed. Her fists were clenched so the knuckles were white. "You both did me a favour. You did us all a favour."

50

By the time we got home, all traces of MumPoweredByLaughter had disappeared. We scoured Viral Buzz, but the posts had been deleted, and so had the account. Each of Oonagh's posts had been replaced by a simple message:

> @MumPoweredByLaughter. This content is no longer available. This post may have been removed, or the user may have deleted their account.

The days that followed were weird.

Mum spent most of her time muttering to herself and sitting in the dark. She only spoke in short sentences like "Yep" and "Whatever". Grandad kept asking her what was wrong, but Mum wouldn't tell him.

That week was half term, so Mason and I didn't have to face school. It was for the best, what with everything going on. I missed Omar and Arlo loads, but I was also relieved not to have to see Luna.

We weren't allowed outside in case we got recognized. Mum drew the curtains shut, so the house became our world. She even turned her phone off, which was really something.

"I've lost a friend," Mum kept saying. "I've lost my husband and my best friend."

I felt guilty. Maybe if I'd kept my mouth shut… Maybe if my brain hadn't put two and two together… Maybe if I'd never remembered that stupid bumper sticker … then maybe Mum wouldn't be so sad. She said Mason and I had done her a favour, but it didn't feel that way at all.

Fidget got a bumper feeding that week. It was like a banquet from a medieval film that stretched all the way down a long table.

It's all my fault.

I've ruined everything.

What will happen at school?

What if I got it all wrong?

I feel a bit bad for Oonagh.

Will Mum be OK?

I think I broke Mum's heart.

I should have kept it to myself.

Mum's been in bed all day.

Grandad doesn't understand.

Dad's not here.

I'm still avoiding the spot where
Colin puked in the kitchen.

Dad came back from his trip in the van, but he didn't move back into the house. He slept outside in the van, but used the downstairs toilet and kitchen like normal.

He said it was about "maintaining boundaries", whatever that meant.

He wasn't best pleased about Oonagh. Furious would be a better word. His head practically started inflating when I explained everything, and the veins in his forehead went massive.

He tried to make me feel better. He said I'd "done the right thing" and told me it wasn't my fault. But it didn't feel like I had done the right thing because everyone was angry. And it *did* feel like it was all my fault. Every time I did anything, everyone got upset.

Mason and I took cups of tea to Mum in her bedroom, even though she wasn't drinking them. We just swapped out each cold milky brew for another, while she stared at her phone or into space.

After days, Mum finally emerged, all crumpled and not really awake. Her hair stuck out in different directions, and I wasn't certain she had brushed her teeth.

The next day, Dad went in to talk to Mum. He was in there a long time and then, when they finally emerged, they called me and Mason into the living room.

Mum said, "Guys. We've booked us all to see a

counsellor called Deborah, We thought we could do with a bit of help to process what's gone on in the last few weeks."

Mason rolled his eyes. "I already said I don't *need* counselling."

Dad gave him a stern look. "We'll let Deborah be the judge of that. We thought you might want to get things off your chest. You could talk about school. About that boy who was bullying—"

"He wasn't bullying me," Mason said. "It was a misunderstanding, that's all."

"Well, whatever you want to call it," said Mum, "I've booked an appointment to see your head of year to discuss it."

"*Mum!*" Mason's voice went up a few pitches. "Please, *please* don't do that!"

"It's either that or I go in and speak to the boy myself," Dad said. "And I don't think anyone wants that to happen, do they?"

Mason huffed and punched the sofa before storming upstairs.

"Ethan, you can talk about your gloopy thoughts," Dad said.

"*Sticky* thoughts," I said. "But that's what Fidget's here for, thanks." I gave Fidget a squeeze for solidarity.

"Fidget's all well and good," Mum said, hesitating. "But he's a toy—"

"He is *not* a toy! He's an Anxiety Monster!"

Dad sighed. "We just think some of the things you're dealing with…" He lost his words, but Mum picked up the thread.

"Some of the things you're telling Fidget might be best dealt with by a professional. Someone who knows what they're doing."

"I don't *need* a professional!" It was my turn to get huffy.

"You've got some pretty unique stuff going on right now," said Dad. "More than most kids your age. Maybe it's time to think about moving on from Fidget."

I clutched Fidget to my chest and blinked hard. They couldn't take him away from me. Mum and Dad gave him to me in the first place. Anyway, in his care leaflet it said he was mine for ever, so there.

"The thing with Fidget," Mum began, "is that you're stuffing your feelings down – literally. But it's not good to stuff feelings down."

"He eats them!" I said. Then I felt sort of babyish.

"But he can't advise, can he?" Mum said gently. "He can't really help."

"He can! He does it all the time!"

I caught Mum and Dad exchanging a look. They didn't get it. I stormed out, exactly like Mason had done, stamping so hard on the stairs that my feet throbbed afterwards.

Tears bubbled as I scratched in my notebook.

I don't want to get rid of you, Fidget.

They can't take you away from me.

I am NEVER going to talk to stupid Deborah. No matter WHAT!!!

By Saturday morning, I was talking to Deborah.

It was my "Assessment Session". Apparently, even though it was called an assessment, I couldn't pass or fail. Mum, Dad and Mason were waiting outside the room. They'd already had their turns. Everyone came out with a different expression. Mason looked red and embarrassed. Dad's forehead had a sheen. Mum's eye make-up was all smeared.

Deborah wasn't mean like I'd imagined. She seemed kind of nice. She had dyed red hair and red oval glasses. Nobody evil wears bright red oval glasses, right? Her notebook was covered in fluffy red fur and she even had a red pen with a red feather on the end.

Maybe *Deborah* needed counselling to get over her obsession with red stuff.

The room was covered in posters of diagrams called "Mental Health and Me" and "The Cognitive Triangle", whatever that meant. The words "THOUGHTS", "FEELINGS" and "ACTIONS" were laid out at the corners of a triangle, with arrows in between like a flow chart.

I didn't expect to talk much, but Deborah kept tricking me into answering her questions in detail. She didn't ask Yes/No questions like, "Do you like pizza?" It was more like, "Tell me your feelings about pizza." Come to think of it, that wasn't a question at all. It was a command.

So I told her my feelings about Mum and Dad's divorce (confused). Told her my feelings about school (mostly good). Told her my feelings about *Meet the Laceys* (bad). Told her my feelings about Mason (bad, but working on it). Her feather pen bobbed and scratched on her notepad while I poured it all out.

"I understand you have a little companion," she said, smiling.

"You mean Fidget?" I took him out of my pocket and propped him on my knee.

"Do you play together?" she asked.

I went red. "Did Mum and Dad tell you to ask about him?"

"That doesn't matter, Ethan." She smiled. "Tell me about your relationship with Fidget." Another trick not-question.

"He's an Anxiety Monster," I began. "He has a squeezy stress-ball filling surrounded by plush. You can open the zip here and stuff your worries inside his mouth. Then he eats them up."

"Anxiety Monster, I see. He's quite sweet. Interesting-looking." Deborah wrote something down. "What kinds of anxieties do you feed to Fidget?"

"Mainly sticky thoughts, but sometimes secrets too."

Deborah nodded. "What is a sticky thought to you, Ethan?"

"It's like a thought that replays and won't go away until it drives you sort of…" My throat went dry. "Crazy."

"Can you give me an example?" Deborah put her notebook down on her lap. "It's OK. This is a safe and confidential space, Ethan."

I shifted in my seat. I didn't want to tell Deborah

my sticky thoughts. She would think I was weird. She would tell Mum and Dad. She might tell Mason, and he would tell the entire universe.

"Why don't you empty Fidget's tummy?" Deborah said. "We can have a look at what you've written down, if you like."

I zipped Fidget's mouth a little tighter. I didn't want to, because the last secret I'd fed him was: *I am NEVER going to talk to stupid Deborah. No matter WHAT!!!*

"It's OK," I said. "I'd rather leave them in his tummy."

"You might find it helps. Maybe we'll find a way to help you deal with the thoughts a bit better. Wouldn't that be useful?"

I picked at the wooden arms of my chair. Without thinking, I moved my finger underneath the arm. There it settled on a warm, gooey glob of chewing gum. I whipped my hand back. Strings of warm minty gum webbed between my fingers. It was the snotnado at H2O water park all over again. Germs, diseases, strangers' spit. My body went tense.

"I need to wash my hands," I said, holding my fingers apart so they didn't touch. "Is there soap in here?"

"Over there," said Deborah, pointing to a sink in the corner.

I washed my hands in silence, scrubbing soap between each finger, careful not to miss one. Then I washed them again, scrubbing under each nail. I felt Deborah's eyes boring into me.

"Ethan," she said gently when I sat back down. "What would have happened if you hadn't washed your hands just now?"

"I could have died," I said.

"Do you seriously think that, Ethan?"

"No. But I'd think about it for ever," I admitted. "That's what sticky thoughts are. I'd think about the germs. I'd think about how the gum could be stuck under my nails. I'd think about getting ill from the germs and making everyone else get ill too and ending civilization."

Deborah nodded. She looked at me kindly, not like I was weird.

"Is that the type of thing you feed to Fidget?"

"Yep." I coughed, squeezing him in my hand. "That's why I don't want to get rid of him."

Deborah smiled. "You don't have to get rid of him – don't worry about that."

Relief flooded my body.

"But I'd like to keep working with you," Deborah continued. "Fidget, although he's clearly useful, could probably do with some assistance. I'd like to get to the point where you only need Fidget occasionally. Perhaps you'll start to find your sticky thoughts a little less worrying."

I nodded, unsure what to say.

"So how *would* you feel," Deborah ventured, "about showing me what's inside him?"

"Fine. But there's one in there about you. So, sorry if you find it."

"Me?" Deborah clutched her feather pen to her chest.

"I wrote: 'I am *never* going to talk to stupid Deborah. No matter *what*.'" I couldn't meet her eye. "Sorry."

The moment lingered. Then Deborah burst out laughing. I started to laugh too, nervously.

"Bless you, Ethan. I'm not offended. After fifteen years in this job, that's *nothing*."

I let out a breath I'd been holding. "OK. That's good."

I opened Fidget's zip, tipped him upside down and watched my secrets fall from his mouth like confetti. They landed on the table, there for anyone to see.

51

Mason and I stood in the car park outside Deborah's office while Mum and Dad booked our next appointment at the reception desk. There would be a mixture of family appointments to talk about our "evolving dynamic" and individual sessions to work on our "therapeutic needs". It was sunny outside but cold. A clear blue autumn morning.

Mason was kicking a damp pile of leaves down a drain cover. He had a red flush in his cheeks. I bounced Fidget from bollard to bollard. We were both happy knowing he could stay with me for ever.

"Well, that was weird," said Mason.

"I know. Did you clock the whole red thing?" I asked.

Mason smirked. "I know, right. Three guesses what Deborah's favourite colour might be."

I smirked too. "She likes red so much she made *you* go red."

"Shut up!" Mason kicked the leaves so they slopped on to my trainers. I kicked them back, and Mason dodged.

"She seems all right though," he went on. "I think it might be ... OK. You know, seeing her."

"Yeah," I said. "Me too. She said she's going to help with my sticky thoughts and stuff."

"Praise the Lord!" Mason said, raising his hands to the air. He winked at me mischievously. "Nah, in all seriousness. That's good. She's going to help me out with some school stuff too. Y'know. Bullying and stuff…"

"Cool." I nodded. "That's good."

We both sighed. I felt the fresh air on my face and enjoyed it. It cooled the hotness of the tangled feelings inside.

Mum and Dad came out of the reception doors. There were two cars in front of us, parked in neighbouring spaces. Mum's car with the nice cream leather. Dad's spluttering camper van, almost renovated at last.

"I'll put the dates in the joint calendar," Mum said.

"Perfect," said Dad. "Looking forward to it."

"Where's home tonight then?" Mum asked.

Dad shrugged. "I'm not sure. There's this app with free overnight parking spots. I'm thinking I'll find one with a nice view. All within twenty miles, of course. In case anyone needs anything."

"Rather you than me," Mum said. "But enjoy the van while I enjoy the king-size bed all to myself!"

"I will." Dad winked.

They hugged, then Mason and I hugged Dad. We waited while the van heaved itself to life, then we waved as it rolled away. Dad beeped the horn as he turned off and it was hilarious. It sounded like a squeaky clown nose.

On the way home, we listened to the radio in Mum's car. She sang along to all the songs. It had been ages since we'd heard Mum sing.

"Oonagh and Luna are leaving town," Mum said out of nowhere. "Moving to Dublin. That's what the other mums have told me, anyway."

"Dublin?" said Mason.

"Yeah." Mum nodded in the mirror. "That's where Oonagh's from. They thought it would be a good time to relocate."

"So Luna's changing schools?" I asked.

"Yep," Mum said. "Already been deregistered.

Convenient timing, if I do say so myself." Mum's eyes took on a mischievous glint in the rear-view mirror.

I didn't know how to feel. I didn't hate Luna, but I didn't like how she always made mean comments about me. Arlo and Omar would be delighted.

"What do you think about a Just the Two of Us Day this weekend, Ethan?" asked Mum.

"Really?" I said.

Mum nodded. "Yeah, why not? Mason, you're not getting out of it either. You're next."

Mason rolled his eyes, but he was also smiling.

"Would you like to see Arlo and Omar today, Ethan?" Mum asked.

"Seriously?" I sat up straight. "Yes!"

Mum smiled. "Good, because they'll be at ours when we get back. I spoke to their parents. They're walking over now."

I punched the air. I hadn't realized how much I'd missed the Blue Pencil Case Crew. With everything going on, it was like I'd forgotten I'd had friends. Family stuff had overshadowed everything like a total eclipse.

"They've got conkers, apparently," Mum said. "They've even prepped some for you. So you can have that battle you were planning."

"Sweet," I said, grinning.

I played with Fidget while Mum drove. He danced in my lap, nodding his head to the music. I could have sworn his zippy mouth was smiling.

"Didn't I tell you, big man?" he said. "Everything's going to be A-OK."

"Thanks, Fidget," I whispered. "Thanks for everything."

Mason was silent. He just looked out of the window. His eyes were sort of glassy. Not wet, but like when you're about to start crying but really don't want to.

"What are you doing today, Mason?" I asked.

He shrugged. "There's this demo out for *Zombie Freakout Five: Never-ending Plague* that seems pretty gnarly."

"Do you want to hang out with me, Arlo and Omar and smash conkers?"

Mason smirked. But then he seemed to catch himself, as if listening to another voice in his head.

"You're not filming it or anything, are you, Mum?" Mason said.

Mum laughed. "Absolutely not. Dad and I have been thinking maybe it's time to put *Meet the Laceys* to bed."

"Are you serious?" Mason said.

Mum met our eyes in the rear-view mirror. "It's

not bringing anyone joy any more, is it? Look at all this mess it's caused. Correction: all this mess *we've* caused." She paused, then added, "We should never have got you involved. You're kids. You should be out having fun, not filming the whole time."

Mason and I gawped at each other in disbelief.

"And we should never have asked you to lie," Mum continued. "That was wrong, and we're sorry. There was just so much *pressure*. We hope we can make it up to you."

"It's OK," I said. My heart was pounding.

"What will you do?" Mason said. "For work?"

"I've got an interview for a marketing job next week," Mum said. "Dad will keep doing *Dad on the Rocks*, but focusing more on the rocks bit than the dad bit. Turns out there's a big audience for reviews of hiking boots and camper-van conversions."

"So … we don't have to film any more?" I said. "Ever?"

"*Ever.*" Mum nodded sharply. "And I mean it."

A silence filled the car. A warm silence. Not the kind where nobody knew what to say. A silence where nobody needed to say anything. No more Meal-Prep Mondays. No more cameras in my face. No more repeating things until we got it just right.

"Well, in that case," Mason said, "I *will* play conkers with you guys. Just to show you how it's done."

"Sweet," I said. "It's better with four. We can do a tournament."

Mason leaned in for a fist bump. "You're still a Snot Monster though."

GOODBYE FROM THE LACEYS

MeetTheLaceys ✓
@MeetTheLaceys
1.1M subscribers
602 views, posted 7 minutes ago

To everyone who has ever supported us…

By now you will have noticed that the content on the *Meet the Laceys* channel has gone. This announcement will be up for a short time, before being deleted too. This decision has not been taken lightly. Rather, a period of reflection has led us to consider our future online and as a family.

This is a message from Annabel, Geoff, Mason, Ethan and, of course, Colin. We have truly enjoyed making and sharing memories with you – especially the arrival of our two boys and our little puppy, Colin. We made a family before your eyes and hoped to include you in it. We tried to show you each memory as they happened, a glimpse behind the scenes of an ordinary family. It was a pleasure to have each and every follower along for the ride. Arguably, a family of over a million people might be a bit too big for anyone to manage.

However, with followers came success, and with success comes pressure. Pressure to keep making memories, to make those memories seem perfect. But no family is perfect, let alone us Laceys. We argue, we cry, we throw up on roller coasters, we fall in and out of love, we do mean-spirited things, we forget about what's important.

Forgetting has been the worst mistake we have made. We forgot to enjoy the everyday. We forgot to enjoy the small moments, the messy breakfasts, the car rides, the Sunday dog walks, the school run, the grocery shop.

We put a price on laughter, on smiling, on mucking around, on getting muddy, on living life. We thought that these moments were worthless unless they were filmed and edited into a bitesize product. We thought the cameras could forever capture the magic of family.

But those same cameras ended up stealing the magic away. That magic cannot be reclaimed, and it was never ours to keep. *Nobody* gets to keep the magic; we only get to have it for a moment.

Moving forward, we will not be filming as a family any more. We will return to a life mostly offline, without cameras and brand deals. We won't be unboxing anything other than Grandad's possessions as they are relocated to our house. We have no doubt they will fill our home with as many memories as he does.

To those who have watched us for years, thank you. As we have always said, you were just like family to us. But now it's time for us to focus on our real family while we can.

With love,
Annabel, Geoff, Mason, Ethan, Colin and Grandad
The Laceys

Life is so much better this way.

ACKNOWLEDGEMENTS

Much like Ethan, my mind is often of the sticky variety. In fact, during the writing of *Boy Vs Reality*, I often wished I had a Fidget of my own, so I could feed him this juicy little morsel:

I don't think I can finish this book!!!

But, thankfully, we finished it. And I say "we" for a reason. Writing books is a team sport, and I am lucky to have many excellent teammates who collectively helped me reach The End, and who will no doubt shepherd *Boy Vs Reality* as it goes into the world.

Huge thanks go to my editor, Lauren Fortune, for providing everything I've needed during this process – be it space, motivation, advice or just a good laugh.

Equally, huge thanks to Wendy and Genevieve, whose edits and ideas are always incisive and transformative.

To my agent, Chloe Seager, a brilliant cheerleader and support – thank you. Thanks to everyone at the Madeleine Milburn Literary Agency for all you have done for me, *The Boy in the Suit* and now *Boy Vs Reality*.

Credit to the brilliant people at Scholastic who work tirelessly to get stories out into the world. I'd like to thank everyone in sales, export, distribution, editorial, clubs and fairs, production, marketing, design, publicity and beyond. Particular thanks to Tina for being a wonderful publicist, manifester and sidekick at bookish events. Thanks to Sarah Baldwin for the awesome cover design.

Thank you to illustrators Tika and Tata Bobokhidze for once again bringing the characters to life so vividly through your work.

To my family, thank you for being you. I know you'll find our collective humour and turns of phrase throughout the book as always. To my cool generation-alpha nephews Henry, Alastair and Francis – whom I badger at semi-regular intervals to request slang and terminology – thank you for your service.

Thanks to the Morrisons and the Browns for being

all-round good eggs. Shout-out to Dr Chris for kindly talking me through a couple of medical questions related to the book.

To all my friends, you know who you are. What can I say? You're genuinely special. Thank you for your support and for making me laugh. You're all brilliant and beyond talented in your individual ways.

Special thanks to Tom Morrison for your constant support, and for the sacrifices you have made to enable me to write – be it small sacrifices like cooking dinner more often than you should, or big ones like me not having time to watch thirty-six episodes of *Married at First Sight* any more. They don't go unnoticed. You're the best.

To Marge and Peanut (yes, they are cats), thank you for sitting on my lap during all those late-night writing sessions.

I will conclude by thanking you, the reader. In today's world of glittering distractions, it's seriously admirable that you've made the time to spend with a book. Thank you for choosing my book this time – I don't take that for granted one bit. I hope you enjoyed meeting the Laceys, even when things weren't going so well for them.

Don't forget to smash
that like button, you guys!
(Joking.)